The X-Files: Ground Zero

Kevin Anderson is the author of the highly successful STAR WARS novels, along with YOUNG JEDI KNIGHTS and other illustrated STAR WARS titles. He has also written several fantasy novels.

Other X-Files Novels

Goblins (Charles Grant)
Whirlwind (Charles Grant)

Non-Fiction

The Truth is Out There (Brian Lowry)

Voyager

THE
X-FILES

GROUND ZERO

KEVIN J ANDERSON

Based on the characters created by
Chris Carter

HarperCollins*Publishers*

Voyager
an Imprint of HarperCollins*Publishers*
77–85 Fulham Palace Road,
Hammersmith, London W6 8JB

Special overseas edition 1995
3 5 7 9 8 6 4

First published in the USA by HarperPaperbacks,
a division of HarperCollins*Publishers* 1995

ISBN 0 00 648206 6

Set in Palatino

Printed in Australia by
Griffin Paperbacks, Adelaide, South Australia

To Katie Tyree

whose constant insistence and enthusiasm convinced me to watch *The X-Files* in the first place—at which point, of course, I was hooked. Without her encouragement, I never would have been able to do this book.

ACKNOWLEDGMENTS

My sincere thanks go to the team of dedicated people at Fox Television—Mary Astadourian, Jennifer Sebree, Frank Spotnitz, Alexandra Mack, Cindy Irwin, and (most of all) Chris Carter—thanks for the vote of confidence! Chris Fusco provided a great deal of background information on the episodes and characters, which proved invaluable in writing this book. The exhaustive videotape library of Skip and Cheryl Shayotovich helped me to fill in the gaps of episodes I had missed.

A round of applause for Christopher Schelling, Caitlin Deinard Blasdell, and John Silbersack at HarperPrism, and my agent Richard Curtis, without whom this project would never have come into being; Lisa Clancy, Betsy Mitchell, Greg Bear, and Erwin Bush, who provided excellent background information and inspiration; Lil Mitchell for many hours of transcribing my tapes; Mark Budz and Marina Fitch for their helpful suggestions; and Rebecca Moesta for her regular dose of love and support.

ONE

 Even through the thick windows of his laboratory building, the old man could hear the antinuke protesters outside. Chanting, singing, shouting—always fighting against the future, trying to stall progress. It baffled him more than it angered him. The slogans hadn't changed from decade to decade. He didn't think the radicals would ever learn.

He fingered the laminated badge dangling from his lab coat. The five-year-old picture, showing him with an awkward expression, was worse than a driver's license photo. The Badge Office didn't like to retake snapshots—but then, ID photos never really looked like the subject in question, anyway. At least not in the past five decades. Not since his days as a minor technician for the Manhattan Project. In half a century his face had grown more gaunt, more seamed, especially over

1

the past few years. His steel-gray hair had turned an unhealthy yellowish-white, where it hadn't fallen out in patches. But his eyes remained bright and inquisitive, fascinated by the mysteries hidden in dim corners of the universe.

The badge identified him as Emil Gregory. He wasn't like many of his younger colleagues who insisted on proper titles: *Dr.* Emil Gregory, or Emil Gregory, *Ph.D.*, or even Emil Gregory, *Project Director*. He had spent too much time in laid-back New Mexico and California to worry about such formalities. Only scientists whose jobs were in question concerned themselves with trivialities like that. Dr. Gregory was at the end of a long and highly successful career. His colleagues knew his name.

Since much of his work had been classified, he was not assured of a place in the history books. But he had certainly made his place in history, whether or not anybody had heard about it.

His former assistant and prize student, Miriel Bremen, knew about his research—but she had turned her back on him. In fact, she was probably standing outside right now, waving her signs and chanting slogans with the other protesters. She had organized them all. Miriel had always been good at organizing unruly groups of people.

Outside, three more Protective Services cars drove up for an uneasy showdown with the protesters who paced back and forth in front of the gate, blocking traffic. Uniformed security guards emerged from the squad cars, slamming doors. They stood with shoulders squared and tried to look intimidating. But they couldn't really take action, since the protesters had carefully remained within the law. In the back of one of the white official cars, a trained German shepherd barked through the screen mesh of the window; it was a drug- and explosive-sniffing dog, not an attack animal, but its loud growls no doubt made the protesters nervous.

Dr. Gregory finally decided to ignore the distractions outside the lab building. Moving slowly and painfully in his seventy-two-year-old body—whose warranty had recently run out, he liked to say—he went back to his computer simulations. The protesters and guards could keep up their antics for the rest of the afternoon and into the night, for all he cared. He turned up his radio to cover the noise from outside so he could concentrate, though he didn't have to worry about his calculations. The supercomputers actually did most of the work.

The portable boom box tucked among books and technical papers on his shelf had never succeeded in picking up more than one station through the thick concrete walls, despite the jury-rigged antenna of chained paper clips he had hooked to the metal window frame. The lone AM station, thank goodness, played primarily Oldies, songs he associated with happier days. Right now, Simon and Garfunkel were singing about Mrs. Robinson, and Dr. Gregory sang along with them.

The color monitors on his four supercomputer work-stations displayed the progress of his simultaneous hydro-code simulations. The computers chugged through numerous virtual experiments in their integrated-circuit imaginations, sorting through billions of iterations without requiring him to throw a single switch or hook up a single generator.

But Dr. Gregory still insisted on wearing his lab coat; he didn't feel like a real scientist without it. If he wore comfortable street clothes and simply pounded on computer keyboards all day long, he might as well be an accountant instead of a well-respected weapons researcher at one of the largest nuclear-design laboratories in the country.

Off in a separate building on the fenced-in lab site, powerful Cray-III supercomputers crunched data for complex simulations of a major upcoming nuclear test. They were studying intricate nuclear hydrodynamic models—imaginary atomic explosions—of the radical new warhead concept to which he had devoted the last four years of his career.

Bright Anvil.

Because of cost limitations and the on-again/off-again political treaties regarding nuclear testing, these hydrodynamic simulations were now the only way to study certain secondary effects, to analyze shock-front formations and fallout patterns. Above-ground atomic detonations had been banned by international treaty since 1963 . . . but Dr. Gregory and his superiors believed they could succeed with the Bright Anvil Project—if all conditions turned out right.

The Department of Energy was eager to see that all conditions turned out right.

He moved to the next simulation screen, watching the dance of contours, pressure waves, temperature graphs on a nanosecond-by-nanosecond scale. Already he could see that it would be a lovely explosion.

Classified reports and memos littered his desk, buried under sheafs of printouts spewed from the laser printer he shared with the rest of his Bright Anvil team members down the hall. His deputy project head, "Bear" Dooley, posted regular weather reports and satellite photos, circling the interesting areas with a red felt-tip marker. The most recent picture showed a large circular depression gathered over the central Pacific, like spoiled milk swirling down a drain—eliciting a great deal of excitement from Dooley.

"Storm brewing!" the deputy had scrawled on a

GROUND ZERO

Post-it note stuck to the satellite photo. "Our best candidate so far!"

Dr. Gregory had to agree with the assessment. But they couldn't proceed to the next step until he finished the final round of simulations. Though the Bright Anvil device had already been assembled except for its fissile core, Gregory eschewed lazy shortcuts. With such incredible power at one's fingertips, caution was the watchword.

He whistled along to "Georgie Girl" as his computers simulated waves of mass destruction.

Somebody honked a car horn outside, either in support of the protesters, or just annoyed and trying to get past them. Since he planned to stay late, those demonstrators—weary and self-satisfied—would be long gone by the time Gregory headed for his own car.

It didn't matter to him how many extra hours he remained in the lab, since research was the only thing left of his real life. Even if he went home, he would probably work anyway, in his too-quiet and too-empty house, surrounded by photos of the old 1950s hydrogen bomb shots out in the islands or atomic blasts at the Nevada Test Site. He had access to better computers in his lab, though, so he might as well work through dinner. He had a sandwich in the refrigerator down the hall, but his appetite had been unpredictable for the past few months.

At one time, Miriel Bremen would have stayed working with him. She was a sharp and imaginative young physicist who looked up to the older scientist with something like awe. Miriel had a great deal of talent, a genuine feel for the calculations and secondary effects. Her dedication and ambition made her the perfect research partner. Unfortunately, she also had too much conscience, and doubts had festered inside her.

Miriel Bremen herself was the spearhead behind the formation of the vehement new activist group, Stop Nuclear Madness!, headquartered in Berkeley. She had abandoned her work at the research facility, spooked by certain incomprehensible aspects of the Bright Anvil warhead. Miriel had become a turncoat with a zeal that reminded him of the way some former cigarette smokers turned into the most outspoken antitobacco lobbyists.

He thought of Miriel out there on the other side of the fence. She would be waving a sign, taunting the security guards to arrest her, making her point loud and clear, regardless of whether anyone wanted to hear it.

Dr. Gregory forced himself to remain seated behind the computer workstation. He refused to go back to the window to look for her. He didn't feel spite toward Miriel, just . . . disappointment. He wondered how he had failed her, how he could have misjudged his deputy so thoroughly.

At least he didn't have to worry about her replacement, Bear Dooley. Dooley was a bulldozer of a man, with a dearth of tact and patience, but a singular dedication to purpose. He, at least, had his head on straight.

A knock came at the half-closed door to his lab office. Patty, his secretary—he still hadn't gotten used to thinking of her as an "administrative assistant," the current politically correct term—poked her head in.

"Afternoon mail, Dr. Gregory. There's a package I thought you might like to see. Special delivery." She waggled a small padded envelope. He started to push his aching body up from his computer chair, but she waved him back down. "Here. Don't get up."

"Thanks, Patty." He took the envelope, pulling

his reading glasses from his pocket and settling them on his nose so he could see the postmark. *Honolulu, Hawaii.* No return address.

Patty remained in the doorway, shuffling her feet. She cleared her throat. "It's after four o'clock, Dr. Gregory. Would you mind if I left a little early today?" Her voice picked up speed, as if she were making excuses. "I know I've got those memos to type up tomorrow morning, but I'll keep one step ahead of you."

"You always do, Patty. Doctor's appointment?" he said, still looking down at the mysterious envelope and turning it over in his hands.

"No, but I don't really want to hassle with the protesters. They'll probably try to block the gate at quitting time just to cause trouble. I'd rather be long gone." She looked down at her pink-polished fingernails. Her face had a fallen-in, anxious expression.

Dr. Gregory laughed at her nervousness. "Go ahead. I'll be staying late for the same reason."

She thanked him and popped back out the door, pulling it shut behind her so he could work in peace.

The computer calculations continued. The core of the simulated explosion had expanded, sending shockwaves all the way to the edge of the monitor screen, with secondary and tertiary effects propagating in less-defined directions through the plasma left behind from the initial detonation.

Dr. Gregory peeled open the padded envelope, working one finger under the heavily glued flap. He dumped the contents onto his desk and blinked, perplexed. He blew out a curious breath.

The single scrap of paper wasn't exactly a letter—no stationery, no signature—just carefully inked words in fine black lettering.

"FOR YOUR PART IN THE PAST—AND THE FUTURE."

A small glassine packet fell out beside the note. It

was a translucent envelope only a few inches long, filled with some sort of black powder. He shook the padded envelope, but it contained nothing else.

He picked up the glassine packet, squinting as he squeezed the contents with his fingers. The substance was lightweight, faintly greasy, like ash. He sniffed it, caught a faint, sour charcoal smell mostly faded by time.

For your part in the past—and the future.

Dr. Gregory frowned. He scornfully wondered if this could be some stunt by the protesters outside. In earlier actions, protesters had poured jars of animal blood on the ground in front of the facility's security gates and planted flowers alongside the entry roads.

Black ash must be somebody's newest idea— maybe even Miriel's. He rolled his eyes and let out an "Oh brother!" sigh.

"You can't change the world by poking your heads in the sand," Dr. Gregory muttered, turning his gaze toward the window.

On the workstations, the redundant simulations neared completion after eating up hours of super-computer time, projecting a step-by-step analysis of one second in time, the transient moment where a man-made device unleashed energies equivalent to the core of a sun.

So far, the computers agreed with his wildest expectations.

Though he himself was the project head, Dr. Gregory found parts of Bright Anvil inexplicable, based on baffling theoretical assumptions and producing aftereffects that went against all his training and experience in physics. But the simulations *worked*, and he knew enough not to ask questions of the sponsors who had presented him with the foundations of this new concept to implement.

After a fifty-one-year-long career, Dr. Gregory

found it refreshing to find an entire portion of his chosen discipline that he could not explain. It opened up the wonder of science for him all over again.

He tossed the black ash aside and went back to work.

Suddenly the overhead fluorescent lights flickered. There was an intense humming sound, as if a swarm of bees were trapped in the thin glass tubes. He heard the snapping shriek of an electrical discharge, and the lights popped and died.

The radio on his desk gave out a brief squelch of static, right in the middle of "Hang on, Sloopy." Then it fell silent.

Dr. Gregory's failing muscles sent stabs of pain through his body as he whirled in despair to see his computer workstations also winking out. The computers were crashing.

"Awww, no!" he groaned. The systems should have had infallible backup power supplies to protect them during normal electrical outages. He had just lost literally billions of supercomputer iterations.

He pounded his gnarled fist on the desk, then levered himself to his feet and staggered over to the window, moving more quickly than his unsteady balance and common sense allowed.

Reaching the glass, he glanced outside at the other buildings in the complex. All the interior lights were still shining in the adjacent wing of the research building. Very odd.

It looked as if his office had been specifically targeted for a power disruption.

With a sinking feeling, Dr. Gregory began to wonder about sabotage from the protesters. Could Miriel have gone so far overboard? She would know how to cause such damage. Though her security clearance had been taken away after she quit her job and formed Stop Nuclear Madness!, perhaps she had managed to bluff her way inside, to interfere with the simulations only she could have known her old mentor would be running.

He didn't want to think her capable of such action . . . but he knew she would consider it, without qualms.

Dr. Gregory swatted at the insistent hissing, buzzing noise that hovered about his ears, finally noticing it for the first time. With all the power suddenly smothered and machine sounds damped to nothingness, silence should have descended upon his office.

But the whispers came instead.

With a growing sense of uneasiness that he forced himself to ignore, Dr. Gregory went to the door, intending to shout down the hall for Bear Dooley or any of the other physicists. For some reason, the company of others seemed highly desirable right now.

But he found the doorknob unbearably hot. *Unnaturally* hot.

With a hiss, he yanked his hand away. He backed off, staring down in shock more than pain at the bright blisters forming in the center of his palm.

Smoke began to curl around the solid security-locked doorknob, oozing out of the keyslot.

"Hey, what is this? Hello!" He flapped his burned hand to cool it. "Patty? Are you still out there?"

Contained within the concrete walls of his office, the wind picked up, crackling with electrical static. Papers blew, curled up by a foul breath of heat. The glassine envelope of black powder spilled open, spraying dark ash into the air.

Untucking his shirt and using the tail to protect his hand against the heat, he hurried back to the door again and reached for the knob. By now, though, it glowed red-hot, a throbbing scarlet that hurt his eyes.

"Patty, I need your help. Bear! Somebody!" His voice cracked, growing high-pitched with fear.

Like an elapsed-time simulation of sunrise, the light in the room grew brighter and *brighter*, seeming to emanate from the walls, a searing harsh glare.

Dr. Gregory backed toward the concrete blocks, holding up his hands to shield his face from yet another aspect of physics he did not understand. The whispering voices increased in volume, rising to a crescendo of screams and accusations climbing through the air itself.

Reaching a critical point.

An avalanche of heat and fire struck him, so intense that it knocked him into the wall. A billion, billion X rays brought every cell in his body to a boil. Then came a *burst* of absolute light, like the core of an atomic explosion.

And Dr. Gregory found himself standing alone at Ground Zero.

TWO

Teller Nuclear Research Facility
Tuesday, 10:13 A.M.

 The security guard stepped out of a small prefab shack just outside the chain-link perimeter of the large research facility. He glanced at Fox Mulder's papers and FBI identification, then motioned for him to drive his rental car over to the Badge Office just outside the gate.

In the passenger seat Dana Scully sat up straighter. She willed the cells of her body to supply more energy and bring her to full alertness. She hated catching red-eye flights, especially from the East Coast. Already today she had spent hours on the plane and now another hour in the car with her partner driving from the San Francisco Airport. She had rested fitfully on the large plane, managing only a brief nap instead of genuine sleep.

"Sometimes I wish that more of our cases would happen closer to home," she said, not really meaning it.

Mulder looked over at her, flashed a brief commiserating smile. "Look on the bright side, Scully—I know plenty of deskbound agents who envy us our exciting jet-setting lifestyle. We get to see the world. They get to see their offices."

"I suppose the grass is always greener . . ." Scully said. "Still, if I ever do take a vacation, I think I'll just stay home on the sofa and read a book."

Scully had grown up as a Navy brat. She and her two brothers and her sister had been forced to pull up their roots every few years while they were young, whenever the Navy assigned her father to a different base or a different ship. She'd never complained, always respecting her father's duty enough to do her part. But she had never dreamed that when it came to her own career, she would end up choosing something that required her to travel around so often.

Mulder guided the car to the front of a small white office isolated from the large cluster of buildings inside the fence. The Badge Office appeared relatively new, with the type of clean yet flimsy architecture that reminded Scully of a child's step-by-step model kit.

Mulder parked the car and reached behind him to pull out his lightweight briefcase. Scully flicked down the mirror on the passenger side sun visor. She gave a quick glance at the lipstick on her full lips, checked the makeup on her large blue eyes, smoothed her light auburn hair. Despite her tiredness, everything seemed in place, professional.

Mulder stepped out of the car and straightened his suit jacket, adjusted his maroon tie.

FBI agents, after all, had to appear suitable for the part.

"I need another cup of coffee," Scully said,

following him out of the car. "I want to be absolutely certain I can devote my full attention to the
details of any case unusual enough to drag us three
thousand miles across the country."

Mulder held open the glass door for her to enter
the Badge Office. "You mean that 'gourmet' brew on
the airplane wasn't up to your exacting standards?"

She favored him with raised eyebrows. "Let's
put it this way, Mulder—I haven't heard of many
flight attendants retiring to start their own espresso
franchises."

Mulder ran a hand quickly through his fluffy
dark hair, ensuring that at least most of the strands
fell into place. Then he trailed after her into the
heavily air-conditioned building. The interior consisted primarily of a large, open area, a long counter
that served as a barricade to a few back offices, and
some small carrels that held televisions and videotape players.

A row of blue padded chairs sat in front of a
wall of windows that had been tinted to filter out the
bright California sun, though patches of the modern
brown-and-rust tweed carpet already looked faded.
Several construction workers clad in overalls stood
in line at the counter with hardhats tucked under
their arms and folded pink forms in their hands.
One at a time the workers handed their papers to the
counter personnel, who checked IDs and exchanged
the pink forms for temporary work permits.

A sign on the wall clearly listed all of the items
that were not permitted inside the Teller Nuclear
Research Facility: cameras, firearms, drugs, alcohol,
personal recording devices, telescopes. Scully scanned
the list. The items were familiar from her own experience at FBI Headquarters.

"I'll check us in," she said and flipped open a
small notebook from the pocket of her forest-green

suit. She took a place in line behind several large men in paint-spattered overalls. She felt extremely over-dressed. Another clerk opened a station at the end of the speckled counter and gestured Scully over.

"I suppose I must look out of place here," Scully said and displayed her badge. "I'm Special Agent Dana Scully. My partner is Fox Mulder. We're here to meet with—" she glanced down at her notebook, "a Department of Energy representative, a Ms. Rosabeth Carrera. She's expecting us."

The clerk straightened her gold-rimmed glasses and shuffled through some papers. She punched in Scully's name on her computer terminal. "Yes, here you are, 'Special Clearance Expedited.' You'll still need to be escorted everywhere until official approval comes through, but we can issue you badges to allow you access to certain areas in the meantime."

Scully raised her eyebrows, keeping her best professional Meet-the-Public composure. "Is that really necessary? Agent Mulder and I already have full clearances with the FBI. You can—"

"Your FBI clearances don't mean anything here, Ms. Scully," the woman said. "This is a Department of Energy facility. We don't even recognize Department of Defense clearances. Everybody's got their own investigative procedures, and none of us talks to the other."

"Government efficiency?" Scully said.

"Your tax dollars at work. Just be glad you don't work for the Postal Service," the woman said. "Who knows what sort of background check they'd do."

Mulder came up beside Scully. He handed her a Styrofoam cup full of oily, bitter-smelling coffee he had taken from a pot on an end table piled high with flashy Teller Nuclear Research Facility technical reports and brochures about all the wonderful work the R&D lab was doing for humanity.

"I paid ten cents for this," he said, indicating the contributions cup, "and I'll bet it's worth every penny. Creamer, no sugar."

Scully took a sip. "Tastes like it's been on that warmer since the Manhattan Project," she said, but grudgingly took another sip to show Mulder that she appreciated his gesture.

"Think of it as fine wine, Scully: perfectly aged."

The clerk returned to the counter and handed Mulder and Scully each a laminated visitor's badge. "Wear these at all times. Make sure they're visible and above the waist," she said. "And these." She passed them each a blue plastic rectangle containing what looked like a strip of film and a computer chip. "Your radiation dosimeters. Clip them to your badges. Always keep them on your person."

"Radiation dosimeters?" Scully asked, maintaining a calm tone, devoid of any obvious worry. "Is there some cause for concern here?"

"Just a precaution, Agent Scully. We are a *nuclear* research facility, you understand. Our orientation videotape should answer all your questions. Follow me, please."

She set Scully and Mulder at one of the small carrels in front of a miniature television. She inserted the videotape and pushed PLAY, then went back to the counter to call Rosabeth Carrera. Mulder leaned over, watching the static on the leader before the tape began. "What do you think they'll have, a cartoon or previews?" he said.

"Do you believe a cartoon designed by the government would be funny?" she asked.

Mulder shrugged. "Some people think Jerry Lewis is funny."

The videotape ran for only four minutes. It was a sanitized description of the Teller Nuclear Research Facility, with a perky narrator explaining briefly what radiation is and what it can do *for* you, as well as *to* you. The program emphasized the medical uses and research applications of exotic isotopes, gave constant reassurances about the safeguards used by the facility, and made comparisons to background levels of radiation that one might receive taking a single cross-country flight or living a year in a high-altitude city such as Denver. After a final, brightly colored graph, the cheery voice told them both to have a nice, safe visit at the Teller Nuclear Research Facility.

Mulder rewound the tape. "My heart's just going all pitter-pat," he said.

Together they made their way back to the badge counter. Most of the construction workers had already gone inside the chain-link fence to their work site.

Mulder and Scully didn't have long to wait before a petite Hispanic woman bustled in through the glass doors. She spotted the two FBI agents half a second later and came over, looking full of energy, eager to meet them. Scully immediately sized her up as she had been trained to do at Quantico, visually gathering facts to form an estimation of a person upon first glance. The woman held out her hand and quickly shook with the two FBI agents.

"I'm Rosabeth Carrera," she said, "one of the DOE representatives here. I'm very pleased you could come out on such short notice. It is something of an emergency."

Carrera wore a knee-length skirt and scarlet silk blouse that set off her dusky skin. Her lips were generous, embellished with a conservative lipstick. Her full head of rich brown hair, the color of dark chocolate, was pulled back on her head, held by several gold barrettes, and cascaded down her back in a glorious tumble of locks. She was built like a gymnast, filled with enthusiasm, not at all the type of dry bureaucrat Scully had expected.

Scully caught the look on Mulder's face as he stared into the woman's very dark eyes. Carrera laughed. "I could spot you two right away. This is California, you know. East Coasters and a few high management types are the only ones around here who wear monkey suits."

Scully blinked. "Monkey suits?"

"Formal dress. The Teller Facility is pretty casual. Most of our researchers are Californians or transplants from Los Alamos, New Mexico. A suit and tie is a rarity here."

"I always knew I was somebody special," Mulder said. "I should have thought to wear my surfing tie."

"If you'll follow me," Carrera said, "I'll take you into the site and the scene of the . . . accident. We've left everything the way it was for the past eighteen hours. It's so unusual, we wanted to give you a chance to look at it fresh. We'll take my car."

Scully and Mulder followed her out to a pale blue Ford Fairmont with government plates. Mulder caught his partner's eye and scratched the side of his head in a chimpanzee imitation. Monkey suits.

"We keep the doors unlocked around here," Carrera said, indicating the car doors as she slipped inside. "We figure nobody'd want to steal a government car." Mulder climbed in back, while Scully took the seat next to the DOE representative.

"Can you give us any more details about this case, Ms. Carrera?" Scully asked. "We were pulled out of bed early and sent here with virtually no background. The only information we've been given is that an important nuclear researcher here died in some sort of freak accident in his lab."

Carrera drove toward the guard gate. She

flashed her badge and handed over the paperwork that would allow Scully and Mulder to enter the facility beyond the fence. Receiving the counter-signed papers, she drove on, biting her lip as if mulling over the details. "That's the story we've released to the press, though it won't hold up long. There are too many questions yet—but I didn't want to prejudice you before you saw the scene yourself."

"You certainly know how to build suspense," Mulder said from the back seat.

Rosabeth Carrera kept her eyes on the road while they drove past office trailers, temporary buildings, a cluster of old dilapidated buildings with wooden siding that looked like something from an old military installation, and finally to the newer buildings that had been constructed during the large defense budgets of the Reagan administration.

"We called the FBI as a matter of course," Carrera continued. "This is possibly a crime—a death, maybe murder—on federal property, so the FBI has automatic jurisdiction."

"You could have worked through your local field office," Scully pointed out.

"We called them," Carrera said. "One of the local agents, a Craig Kreident, came out for a first glance last night. Do you know him?"

Mulder touched his lips, as he searched his excellent memory. "Agent Kreident," he said. "I believe he specializes in high-tech crimes out here."

"That's him," Carrera said. "But Kreident took one look and said this one was out of his league. He said it looked more like an 'X-File' ... those were his words ... and that it was probably a job for you, Agent Mulder. I don't understand what an X-File is."

"Amazing what a reputation can do for you," Mulder murmured.

Scully answered the question. "'X-Files' is a catchall term for investigations involving strange and unexplained phenomena. The Bureau has numerous records of unsolved cases dating as far back as the early days of J. Edgar Hoover. The two of us have had numerous . . . experiences looking into those unusual cases."

Carrera parked in front of the large laboratory buildings and got out of the car. "Then I think you'll find this one to be right up your alley."

Carrera led them at a brisk pace through the building, up to the second floor. The dim echoing halls, lit by banks of fluorescent lights, reminded Scully of a high school. One of the tubes overhead was gray and flickering. Scully wondered how long it had needed to be replaced.

Cork bulletin boards lined the open spaces of cement-block walls, posted with colorful safety notices and signs for regular technical meetings. Handwritten index cards announced rental properties and time-share condos in Hawaii, cars for sale; one card offered "slightly used rock-climbing equipment." The ubiquitous security awareness posters seemed to be left over from World War II, though Scully found none that said "Loose Lips Sink Ships."

Up ahead an entire corridor had been blocked off with yellow barrier tape. Since the Teller Nuclear Research Facility couldn't be expected to have CRIME SCENE barricades, they had settled for CONSTRUCTION AREA tape. Two lab security guards stood posted on either side of the corridor, looking uncomfortable with their assignment.

Carrera didn't need to say a word to them. One guard stepped aside to let her pass. "Don't worry," she said to the man, "you're on a short shift. Replacements are coming in a few minutes." Then she gestured for Mulder and Scully to follow her as she ducked under the flimsy yellow tape.

Scully wondered why the guards should be so concerned. Was it the simple superstition of being too close to a possible murder scene? These guards probably had very little outright crime to investigate, especially not violent crime like murder. She supposed the body hadn't been removed yet, which would be very unusual.

Down the hall beyond the yellow tape, all other offices stood empty, though their still-running computers and full bookshelves showed that the room had been occupied until recently. Coworkers of Dr. Emil Gregory's? If so, they would have to be interviewed. No doubt all of the workers had been relocated, pending investigation of the accident.

One office door, though, was tightly shut and sealed with more of the barrier tape. Rosabeth Carrera stood beside it and pulled off her laminated picture badge from which dangled a dosimeter and several keys. She searched for the key with the appropriate ID number and slipped it into the intimidating-looking lock in the doorknob.

"Take a quick look," she said, pushing the door open and simultaneously turning her face away. "This is just first glance. You've got two minutes."

Scully and Mulder stood beside each other at the threshold and peered inside.

It looked as if an incendiary bomb had gone off in Dr. Gregory's lab office.

Every surface had been singed with a burst of heat so intense, yet so brief, it had curled and crisped the papers attached to Gregory's bulletin board—*but had not ignited them.* His four computer terminals had melted at the edges and slumped in on themselves, the heavy glass cathode-ray tubes of the screens tilting cockeyed like the gaze of a dead man. Even the metal desks bowed and sagged from the brief molten weakness.

An erasable white board had turned black, its enamel finish dark and blistered, though the colored trails of scrawled equations and notes left identifiable paths in the soot.

Scully spotted Gregory's body against the far wall. All that remained of the old weapons researcher was a horribly crisped scarecrow of a man. His arms and legs were drawn up from the contraction of muscles in intense heat, like some sort of insect sprayed with poison and curled up to die. His skin and the twisted rictus on his face made him look as if he had been doused with napalm.

Mulder stared at the destruction in the room, while Scully focused on the corpse, her mouth partially open, her mind already set in that curious mixture of human horror and detached analysis she slipped into when inspecting a crime scene. The only way she could stave off her revulsion was to look for answers. She stepped forward.

Before she could enter the room, though, Carrera placed a firm hand on her shoulder. "No, not yet," she said. "You can't go in there."

Mulder gave Carrera a sharp look, as if she had just pulled on his leash. "How are we supposed to investigate a crime scene if we can't go inside?"

Scully could tell that her partner's interest had already been piqued. From what she could see at first glance she was going to have a hard time coming up with a simple, rational explanation for what had happened here in the sealed lab.

"Too much residual radiation," Carrera said. "You'll need full contamination gear before you go inside."

Scully reflexively touched her dosimeter as she and Mulder both backed away from the door. "But according to your video briefing none of the labs supposed to contain dangerously high levels of radiation. Was that just government propaganda?"

Carrera pulled the door shut again and favored Scully with a tolerant smile. "No, it's true—under normal circumstances. But as you can see, things aren't normal in Dr. Gregory's lab. Nothing any of us can understand . . . not yet, anyway. There should not have been any radioactive material here; yet we found high levels of residual radiation in the walls, in the equipment.

"But don't worry, those thick concrete blocks shield us out here in the hall. Nothing to worry about—if you stay away from it. But you'll need a much closer look. We'll let you continue your investigation. Come on."

She turned, and they followed her down the corridor. "Let's get you both suited up."

THREE

The thick outfit made Mulder look like an astronaut. He found it difficult to move, but his eagerness to investigate the mysterious death of Dr. Emil Gregory convinced him to put up with the difficulties.

Health-and-safety technicians adjusted the seams of his anticontamination suit, pulling the hood down over his head, fastening the zipper in back, then sealing it with another flap Velcroed over the top to keep chemical or radioactive residue from seeping through the seams.

A transparent plastic faceplate allowed him to see, but condensation formed on the inside, and he tried to control his breathing. Canisters of compressed air on his back connected to a hood respirator that echoed in his ears and made it difficult to exhale. The joints in his knees and elbows ballooned as he tried to walk.

24

Mulder felt detached from his surroundings, armored against the invisible threat of radiation. "I thought lead underwear went out of style with bell-bottoms."

Standing next to him, still clad in her stunning blouse and skirt, the dark beauty Rosabeth Carrera stood with her hands at her sides, looking uncertain as to what she should do. She had declined to suit up in anticontamination gear and accompany them onto the scene.

"You're free to go in and look around as much as you'd like," Carrera said. "Meanwhile, I've arranged for the paperwork to allow you free access to the site—you'll have a 'need-to-know' clearance for this case only. The Department of Energy and Teller Labs are eager to find out what caused Dr. Gregory's death."

"What if they don't like the answer?" Mulder said.

Swathed in her own billowing hood in the anti-contamination suit, Scully flashed him a warning look, one of the usual glances she gave him when he followed his penchant for blundering down a dangerous road.

"Any answer's better than nothing," Carrera said. "Right now all we have are a bunch of disturbing questions." She gestured up and down the hall where the offices of Gregory's coresearchers had been sealed off. "The background radiation in the rest of this building is perfectly normal, except in Gregory's office. We need you to find out what happened."

Scully asked, "I know this is a weapons research laboratory. Was Dr. Gregory working on anything dangerous? Anything that could have backfired on him? A prototype for a new weapons system perhaps?"

Carrera crossed her arms over her small breasts and stood confident. "Dr. Gregory was working on computer simulations. He had no fissile material whatsoever in his lab, nothing that even remotely approached the destructive potential that we see here. Nothing at all deadly. The equipment was no more dangerous than a videogame."

"Ah, videogames," Mulder said. "Could be the heart of our conspiracy."

Rosabeth Carrera gave them each a handheld radiation detector. The gadgets looked just like the kind Mulder had seen in dozens of 1950s B-movies of uncontrolled nuclear tests that accidently created mutations whose bizarreness was limited only by Hollywood's meager special effects budgets of the era.

One of the health-and-safety technicians gave them a quick briefing on how to use the radiation detector. The tech swept the sensor end up and down the hall, taking a sample of normal background readings. "Seems to be functioning properly," he said. "I checked the calibration just a few hours ago."

"Let's go inside, Mulder," Scully said, standing at the door, obviously impatient to get to work.

Carrera used the key on her badge again, pushing the lab door open. Mulder and Scully entered Dr. Gregory's laboratory—and the radiation detectors went wild.

Mulder watched the needle dance high up on the gauge, though he didn't hear the frying-bacon crackle of Geiger counters used so often in films. The silent needle's signal was ominous enough.

Within its concrete-block walls, this office had somehow been the site of an intense burst of radiation that had blistered the paint, seared the concrete, and melted the furniture. The flash had left residual and secondary radioactivity that still simmered, only fading gradually.

Behind them Rosabeth Carrera closed the door.

Mulder's breathing resonated in his ears in the self-contained suit. It sounded as if someone were breathing down his neck, a long-fanged monster riding on his shoulder . . . but it was only echoes inside his hood. Claustrophobia hammered around him as he stepped deeper into the burned laboratory. Looking at the melted and flash-burned artifacts sent a shudder down his spine, tapping into his long-standing revulsion of fire.

Scully went straight to the body, while Mulder stopped to inspect the heat-slumped computer terminals, the melted desks, the flash-burned papers on the bulletin board and on the work tables. "No indication of where the burst might have originated," he said, poking around the debris.

The walls were adorned with images of Pacific islands, aerial photos as well as computer printouts of weather maps of the ocean wind patterns, storm projections, and blistered black-and-white prints of weather satellite images—everything centered on the Western Pacific, just past the International Date Line.

"Not the sort of stuff I'd expect a nuclear weapons researcher to collect on his office walls," Mulder said.

Scully bent over the scarecrowish burned body of Dr. Gregory. "If we can determine what he was working on, get some details of the weapons systems and any tests he was planning to run, we might come up with a more clear-cut explanation."

"Clear-cut, Scully?" Mulder said. "You surprise me."

"Think about it, Mulder. Despite what Ms. Carrera said, Dr. Gregory was a weapons researcher—

what if he was working on some new high-energy burst weapon? It's possible he had a prototype in here and he accidentally set it off. It could have flash-fried everything you see here, killed him . . . if it was just a small test model, its effect would be limited. It might not destroy the entire building."

"Good for us," he said. "But look around—I don't see the remains of any weapon, do you? Even if it exploded, there should be some evidence."

"We should still look into it," Scully answered. "I need to take this body in for an autopsy. I'll request that Ms. Carrera find us a local medical facility where I can work."

Mulder, preoccupied by Gregory's bulletin board, reached out with a gloved hand to touch one of the curled papers still fastened by a slagged push pin to the crisped cork board. When he brushed the paper with his fingertips, it crumbled into ash, rippling away into the air. Nothing remained but a powdery residue.

Mulder looked around for thick stacks of paper, hoping that something might have been left intact, like the photos on the walls. He searched Dr. Gregory's desk for piles of technical reports or journal articles, but found nothing. Then he noticed the unburned rectangular marks on the charred desktop.

"Hey, Scully, look at this," he said. When she came over, he pointed to the pale rectangular patches. "I think there must have been documents here, reports left on top of his desk—but somebody's removed the evidence."

"Why would anyone do that?" Scully said. "The reports themselves probably still have significant residual radioactivity—"

Mulder met her gaze through the thin faceplates on their hoods. "I think somebody's trying to do us a favor. They've 'sanitized' the murder scene to protect us from classified information that maybe we shouldn't be seeing. For our own good, of course."

"Mulder, how can we possibly expect to solve this if the crime scene has been tampered with? We don't have the complete picture here."

"My feeling exactly," he said.

He knelt to look at Dr. Gregory's two-shelved metal credenza. It was filled with physics textbooks, computer-code user's manuals, a copy of *Lagrangian-Eulerian Hydrocode Dynamics*, and straightforward geography and physics texts. The bindings were burned and blackened, but the rest of the books remained intact.

He looked at the burn marks on the shelves themselves. As he had expected, several books had been removed as well. "Somebody wants a quick answer to this, Scully," he said. "A simple answer. One that doesn't require us to have all the information."

He looked toward the closed lab door. "I think we should inspect each of these other offices down the corridor, too. If they're the offices of Dr. Gregory's project team, somebody might have forgotten to yank out the information that was carefully deleted from this scene."

He went back to the bulletin board and touched another piece of the crumbling paper. The ash flaked off, but he was able to distinguish two words before it disintegrated.

Bright Anvil.

FOUR

Veteran's Memorial Hospital,
Oakland, California
Tuesday, 3:27 P.M.

The safety technicians and radiation specialists at the Teller Nuclear Research Facility had assured Scully that any residual radiation in Dr. Emil Gregory's corpse remained low enough to pose no significant safety hazards. Scully found it faintly amusing that none of the other doctors in the hospital wanted to be with her in the special autopsy room they had prepared.

She was a medical doctor and had performed many autopsies, but she preferred working alone—especially in a case as disturbing as this one.

She had dissected corpses in front of her students at the Quantico FBI Training Facility many times, but the condition of Dr. Gregory's body, the specter of a radioactive disaster, bothered her enough on a gut level that she was glad she could think her own thoughts and not be distracted by questions or perhaps even rude jokes from the new students.

Rather than providing general autopsy facilities, the Veterans Memorial Hospital had placed her in a little-used room especially reserved for severely virulent diseases, such as strange tropical plagues or unexpected mutations of the flu. But the room had what she needed. Scully stood in front of Gregory's body. She tried to swallow, but her throat was dry. She should get to work.

She had performed more autopsies than she could remember, on bodies in far worse condition than this burned husk of an old man. But the thought of how Dr. Gregory had died brought back the nightmares she had suffered while in her first year of college at Berkeley: grim and depressing imaginings of the world's dark nuclear future. She had awakened to thoughts of these horrors in the middle of the night in her dorm room. By day she had read the propaganda slogans, the overblown antinuclear brochures designed to foster fear of the atom.

Before this autopsy, she had reviewed medical texts, concise and analytical treatments that avoided the imflammatory descriptions of radiation burns. She was ready.

Scully drew a long, deep breath through the respirator mask. The dual air-filtering cartridges hung heavily from her face, like insectoid mandibles. She wore goggles as well, to keep any of the cadaver's fluids from spraying into her eyes. She had been assured that this simple protective clothing would be sufficient against the low radiation levels in Dr. Gregory's body, but she thought she could feel invisible contamination like gnats on her skin. She wanted to hurry and get this over with, but she was having a hard time getting started.

Scully inspected the surgical implements on the tray next to her autopsy table, but it was merely a stalling tactic. She chided herself for avoiding the corpse. After all, she thought, the sooner she got to it, the sooner she could be finished and out of there.

At the moment, though, she would much rather have been with Mulder interviewing some of Dr. Gregory's fellow scientists—but this was her job, her specialty.

She switched on the tape recorder, wondering if the radiation seeping out of the body might affect the magnetic tape. She hoped not.

"Subject: Emil Gregory. Male Caucasian, seventy-two years of age," she dictated. Curved mirrors reflected the harsh white fluorescents overhead down onto the table. These, along with the surgical lamps, washed away all shadows, allowing no secrets to be hidden.

Gregory's skin was blackened and peeling, his face shriveled to a burned mask over his skull. White teeth poked through the split and charred lips. His arms and legs had been drawn up, folded together as his muscles contracted with the heat. She touched him with one heavily gloved finger. Flakes of burnt flesh fell off. She swallowed.

"Apparent cause of death is sudden exposure to extreme heat. However, other than the several external layers of complete charring . . . " she nudged the burnt layers that peeled away, revealing red, wet tissues underneath ". . . the musculature and internal organs appear relatively intact.

"There are some indications of the damage normally seen when a victim dies in a fire, but other indicators are missing. In a normal fire, body temperature rises throughout, causing extreme damage to internal organs, massive trauma to the entire bodily structure, rupture of soft tissues. However, in this case it appears that the heat was so intense and so brief that it incinerated the subject's exterior, but dissipated before it had time to penetrate more deeply into his body structure."

After finishing with her preliminary summary, Scully inspected the tray and took a large scalpel, holding it clumsily in her gloved hands. When she cut into Dr. Gregory's body cavity, the sensation was like sawing through a well-done steak.

In the background the Geiger counters clicked with stray bursts of background radiation, sounding like sharp fingernails tapping on a window pane. Scully froze, waiting until the counts died down.

She adjusted the lamp overhead and went back to work, probing in detail for any clues the old man's body had left for her to find. She dictated copious notes, removing the intact organs, weighing each one, giving her impression of their condition—but as she proceeded, it became clear to her that something was terribly wrong.

Finally, still wearing her gloves, she went over to the intercom mounted on the wall, glancing back over her shoulder at the remains of Gregory's body. She punched in the extension for the Oncology Department.

"This is Special Agent Dana Scully," she said, "in Autopsy Room . . . " she glanced up at the door, "2112. I need an oncology expert to suit up and come down here briefly for a second opinion. I've found something I'd like to have verified." Though Scully had requested consultation with a specialist, she was already virtually certain as to what they would find.

The voice on the other end of the line reluctantly acknowledged. Scully wondered how many of the specialists would suddenly disappear for lunch breaks or rush off to long-forgotten games of golf, leaving the remaining few to draw straws to see who would have to come in to the room with her and study the burned corpse.

She went back to the body on the polished metal table and looked down, still keeping her distance. Her inhalations through the respirator packs at her mouth hissed like the steaming breath of a dragon.

Long before Dr. Emil Gregory had died from his fatal flash burn, his entire bodily system had been ravaged from within. Tumors upon tumors permeated his system, disrupting his functions.

Even without this bizarre and extreme death, Dr. Emil Gregory would have succumbed to terminal cancer within a month.

FIVE

 A boring routine in a buried trash can that somebody considered an office. Some assignment.

Captain Franklin Mesta had once thought being a missileer would be exciting, protected in an underground fortress with the controls of nuclear Armageddon at his fingertips. Dial in the coordinates, turn the keys—and the fate of the world rested in your hands, just waiting for a launch order.

In reality, it was more like solitary confinement . . . only without the privacy of solitude.

Mesta was stuck down here in a little cell, his only company a randomly assigned partner with whom he had little in common. Forty-eight straight hours without seeing the light of day, without hearing the wind or the ocean, without stretching his muscles, or getting a good workout.

What was the point of being stationed on the

spectacular central coast of California if he had to pull duty down here under a rock? He might as well have been in Minot, North Dakota. One underground control bunker looked like any other underground control bunker. They all had the same interior decorator—no doubt a low-bid government contract.

Maybe he should have asked for EOD duty instead. At least Explosives Ordnance Disposal offered the *chance* that something unexpected and exciting would happen.

From his chair he turned to look at his partner, Captain Greg Louis, who sat out of arm's reach in an identical scuffed red Naugahyde chair. The chairs were mounted to steel rails on the floor that kept the two missileers permanently at right angles to each other. Regulations required that each man remain buckled in his seat at all times.

A circular mirror mounted in the corner between them let the two men look into each other's eyes, but prevented them from being able to touch physically. Captain Mesta supposed there had been instances at the end of a long shift where stir-crazy missileers had tried to strangle each other.

"What do you suppose the weather's like topside?" Mesta asked.

Captain Louis worked intently on a pad of paper, scribbling calculations. Distracted, he looked up, blinking at Mesta in the round observation mirror. Though Louis's flat face, wide set eyes, and full lips gave him a perpetually stupid expression, Mesta knew his partner was a whiz at math.

"Do you want me to call up?" Louis asked. "They can fax us a full report."

Mesta shook his head and looked aimlessly around the old metal control banks. Everything was painted battleship gray or, even worse, sea-foam green, with clunky black plastic dials and analog numerical readouts—technology straight from early Cold War days.

"No, just wondering," he said with a sigh. Louis could be so literal. "What are you figuring out now?"

Louis set down his pencil. "Taking the projected area of our chamber here, and our depth beneath the surface, I can estimate the volume of material in a cylinder above us. Then I'm going to use the average density of rock to calculate the mass. When I'm done, we'll know exactly how much stone is hanging over our heads."

Mesta groaned. "You've got to be kidding, man! You're psycho."

"Just occupying my mind. Aren't you curious?"

"Not about that."

Mesta slid his chair along the rail bolted to the floor, allowing him to check another station, one he had inspected only five minutes earlier. All conditions remained the same.

He looked at the heavy black phone at his station. "I think I'm going to call up and get permission to use the head," he said. He didn't really have to go, but it was something to do. Besides, by the time the decision came down from the watchdogs, his bladder might well be full.

"Go ahead," Louis answered, intent on his calculations again.

A single cot sat behind a heavy red curtain that provided minimal privacy—and minimal stretching space—but each man was allowed to use it only once during a shift, and Mesta figured he could stay awake a while longer.

Then the red phone rang.

Both men instantly transformed into crack professionals, alert and aware, snapping into the programming that had been hammered into them. They knew the drill, and they took each alarm seriously.

Mesta picked up the phone. "Captain Franklin Mesta here. Prepare for code verification." Grabbing the black three-ring binder, he flipped through the laminated pages, searching for the proper date and authorization phrase.

The voice on the phone—flat, high-pitched, and oddly genderless—rattled off numbers in a crisp, precise drone. "Tango Zulu Ten Thirteen Alpha X-ray."

Mesta followed the digits with his finger, repeating them into the phone. "Tango Zulu One Zero One Three Alpha X-ray. Verified. Second, do you concur?"

At an identical phone, Captain Louis studied his own three-ring binder. "Concur," he said. "Ready to receive targeting information."

Mesta spoke into the handset. "We are prepared to input coordinates."

Mesta felt his heart pounding, the adrenaline running through his veins, though he knew this had to be just an exercise. It was the military's strategy to keep the men from going insane with boredom—putting the teams regularly through routine drills, constant practice in aiming their missile, their personal Big Stick, housed in a silo elsewhere at Vandenberg.

In addition to providing simple practice and relief from the tedium, Mesta knew, the constant and unforgiving drills were designed to program the missileers into following instructions without thinking. Buried under however many tons of rock Louis had calculated, the two partners were so isolated they could never know whether they were preparing for a real launch, or just going through the paces. That was exactly the way their superiors wanted it.

But as soon as the coordinates came in, and both captains dialed them in using analog numerical wheels, Mesta knew the launch could never be real. "That's out in the Western Pacific . . . somewhere in the Marshall chain," he said. He glanced at the world map taped up on the metal wall, its edges curling from age. "Are we nuking Gilligan's Island, or what?"

Captain Louis answered in a terse, no-nonsense tone. "Probably in keeping with the government's new nonthreatening posture. The Russians don't like us even pretending to aim the birds at them."

Mesta punched in the TARGET LOCK VERIFIED sequence, shaking his head. "Sounds like somebody just wants a few radioactive coconuts."

Still, he thought, the very possibility of an actual launch, a no-turning-back instigation of nuclear war, was enough to bring out a cold sweat—drill or no drill.

"Ready for key insertion," Louis prompted.

Mesta hustled, ripping open his own envelope to pull out the metal key on its dangling plastic chain. "Ready for key insertion," he repeated. "On my mark—three, two, *one*. Keys in."

Both men jammed their metal keys in the slots, then simultaneously let out a relieved sigh. "Exciting, isn't it?" Mesta said, breaking through his professional demeanor. Louis blinked and looked strangely at him.

Now it would all depend on the command station, where someone else in some other uniform would arm the missile, de-safe the warheads, the small conical cluster of atomic bombs. Each component of the MIRV, the multiple independently-targeted reentry vehicles, packed hundreds of times the wallop of the Hiroshima or Nagasaki bombs.

The voice on the telephone spoke. "Proceed with key rotation."

Mesta gripped the round end of his key in the slot, feeling perspiration slick his fingertips. He glanced up at the round observation mirror to see that Captain Louis had done the same, waiting for him to give the order. Mesta began his short, careful countdown.

At "one" they turned their keys.

The lights went out.

Sparks flew from the old control panels, transistors and capacitors—possibly even obsolete vacuum tubes—overloading.

"Hey!" Mesta shouted. "Is this some kind of joke?"

Despite his bluster, he suddenly felt a primal fear of being trapped in absolute darkness, buried deep underground in a metal cave swarming with tarlike blackness. He thought he could sense every single ounce of the overlying rock Captain Louis had calculated. Mesta was glad his partner could not see the expression on his face.

"Searching for emergency controls," Louis's voice called, eerily disembodied in the blackness. His voice remained pretend-calm, professional, but with a ragged edge that belied his cool demeanor.

"Well where are they?" Mesta said. "Get the power back on."

Images of suffocation and doom swirled in Mesta's mind. Without power, they wouldn't have air, they couldn't call up topside and request an emergency evacuation.

What if the launch had been real? Had the United States just been obliterated in a nuclear fire? Impossible!

"Switch on the damn lights!" Mesta shouted.

"Here they are. No time for a self-diagnostic."

Instead, Louis's voice howled in pain. "Aaaah! The controls are hot! I just fried the palm of my hand."

Mesta could make out the silhouettes of the control banks as the metal racks began to glow a deep brownish red, like a stove burner. A renewed shower of sparks skittered across the electronics. Then another, brighter glow seeped through the wall plates themselves.

"What is going on here?" Mesta said.

"Phone's dead," Louis answered, maddeningly calm again.

Mesta swiveled back and forth in his chair, sweating, hyperventilating. "It's like we're in a giant microwave oven! So hot in here."

The seams in the steel-plate walls split. Rivets shot like bullets from one side of the enclosed chamber to the other, ricocheting and shattering glass instrument panels. Both men screamed. Blazing light poured in.

"But we're underground," Louis gasped. "There should be only rock out there."

Mesta tried to leap to his feet, to run to the emergency ladder, or at least to the secure elevator—but the straps and seatbelts trapped him in the uncomfortable chair. Smoke began to rise from the upholstery.

"What's that noise?" Louis asked. "Do you hear voices out there?"

Light and heat rushed in through the cracks in the walls, like a blinding storm from the core of the sun. The last thing Captain Mesta heard was a raging roar like a whirlwind of vengeful whispers.

Then all the seams split in the walls as the last barrier evaporated. A tidal wave of blazing, radioactive fire flooded over them, engulfing the chamber.

SIX

Teller Nuclear Research Facility
Tuesday, 3:50 P.M.

 With his visitor's badge firmly clipped to his collar, Mulder felt like a door-to-door salesman. He followed his map of the Teller Facility on which Rosabeth Carrera had circled the building number where Dr. Gregory's project team was temporarily stationed. .

He found the building, a dilapidated, ancient barracks, two stories tall, with windowpanes so old that the glass had begun to ripple with age. The doors and window frames were painted a putrid, yellowish tan that reminded him of the Number 2 pencils given out for standardized tests in public schools. The exterior walls were sided with composite shingles, flexible asphalt sheets slapped on in a repetitive overlapping pattern. They looked like the wings of a freakish mutant moth grown to gargantuan size.

"Nice digs," Mulder said to himself.

From a brochure he had picked up in the Badge Office, Mulder knew that the Teller Nuclear Research Facility occupied the site of an old U.S. Navy weapons station. Looking at the barracks, he decided that these must be a few of the original structures that had just barely held on while others were demolished and replaced with prefabricated modular office buildings.

He tried to guess what groups would be relegated to these forlorn places: projects winding down after losing budget battles, new employees awaiting their security clearances, or administrative staff who didn't need the high-tech laboratories of the bread-winning nuclear researchers.

It looked as if Dr. Gregory's project had lost a bit of prestige.

Mulder trudged up the old wooden stairs and yanked at the door, which stuck briefly in its frame before opening. He entered, ready to flash his visitor's badge and his FBI ID card, even though Rosabeth Carrera had assured him this section of the research facility was open to approved visitors. The building was inside the perimeter fence and therefore remained inaccessible to the general public, but no classified work could be performed in any of these offices.

The hall was empty. Mulder saw only a kitchenette with a coffeemaker and a big plastic jug of spring water perched on a cooler. A laser-printed sign on salmon-colored paper was tacked to the wall, and Mulder saw several other copies posted up and down the hall on doors and bulletin boards.

> **WARNING**, Asbestos Area.
> The Hazard Removal Team will be working
> the following dates: _____

Naturally, the dates handwritten on the blank line were precisely the days he and Scully planned to be in the area.

Beneath, in a brush-stroke script, as if someone had gotten cute changing fonts on their word-processing program:

"Please pardon the inconvenience."

Mulder followed the short kitchenette-hall to where it intersected with the main corridor of offices. The ceiling creaked, and he looked up to see water-stained acoustic tiles barely hanging on to a suspended structure around fluorescent lights. Footsteps on the second floor continued; the old support beams groaned with weariness.

He stopped at the end of the hall. The entire area to his left was swathed in plastic wrap, as if some mysterious preservation activity was under-way. Workers wearing overalls and heavy, full-facepiece respirators wielded crowbars behind a translucent plastic curtain, tearing the sheetrock off the walls. Others used high-powered shop vacu-ums to suck away the dust that came out. They made a tremendous racket. Yellow tape blocked the corridor farther on, with another handmade sign dangling from the flimsy X barricade.

> ASBESTOS REMOVAL OPERATIONS IN PROGRESS.
> **DANGER!**
> DO NOT CROSS.

Mulder glanced at the little yellow note of paper on which he had written Bear Dooley's temporary office number. "I hope it's not down there," he said, looking at the asbestos work site. He turned right instead and began checking doorways, most of which were closed—not necessarily because the rooms were empty, but because the people couldn't work with so much noise in the halls.

He followed the room numbers down the hall, listening to the construction workers batter away, excavating the old asbestos-contaminated insulation, which would be replaced with new approved materials. Asbestos insulation had been considered perfectly safe decades earlier. But now, because of new safety regulations, the workers seemed to be creating an even larger hazard. To fix the problem, they gutted the old building, spending huge amounts of the taxpayer's money, and quite probably releasing far more broken asbestos fibers into the air than would ever have been released in the natural lifetime of the building during normal use.

He wondered if, a decade or two down the road, someone would decide that the *new* material was also hazardous, and the entire process would repeat itself.

Mulder remembered a joke from an old *Saturday Night Live* that he had considered enormously funny while sprawled out on his sofa late one Saturday evening. The Weekend Update commentator proudly announced that scientists had at last discovered that cancer was actually caused by . . . (drum roll) *white lab rats!*

Now, though, the joke didn't seem quite as humorous.

He wondered how Scully was doing with her autopsy on Dr. Gregory's body.

He finally reached Bear Dooley's half-closed office door, which was burdened with numerous layers of thick brown paint. Inside the dim room, a burly man wearing a denim jacket and flannel shirt and jeans stacked boxes onto tall black file cabinets, arranging items hastily retrieved from his old office.

Mulder rapped on the door with his knuckles and pushed it farther open. "Excuse me. Dr. Dooley?"

The broad-shouldered man turned to look at him. He had long, reddish brown hair and a shaggy beard that looked like it was made of copper wire, except for a striking shot of white down the left side of his chin, as if he had spilled a dribble of milk there. His mouth and nose were covered with a white filter mask.

"Get a mask on—are you crazy?" he said. Dooley moved like a quarterback to the battered temporary desk, where he popped open the top right-hand drawer and snatched out a filter packet. With his meaty hands he tore off the plastic and tossed the mask to Mulder. "You FBI guys are supposed to be so smart—I'd think you could manage a few simple safety precautions."

Mulder sheepishly fastened the mask around his face with a long elastic band and breathed through the paper-smelling covering. He held his badge in his hand, flipping open his ID to display the photo and badge. "Bear Dooley, I presume? How did you know I was from the FBI?"

The big man let out a loud laugh. "Are you kidding? A suit and a tie means you're either with the DOE or the FBI—and with Dr. Gregory's weird death I assumed you were FBI. We were told to expect you and to cooperate."

"Thanks," Mulder said, coming in and sitting in a chair next to the man's cluttered desk without being invited. "I've got only a few questions for you at the moment. I'll try not to take too long. We're still at the beginning of our investigation."

Dooley continued to unload his possessions from cardboard boxes, shoving folders into file-cabinet drawers and dumping pens and notepads into the long center drawer on his desk.

"First off," Mulder said, "can you tell me about the project you and Dr. Gregory were working on?"

"Nope," Bear Dooley said, turning back to pull out framed photos and some sheaves of what appeared to be weather satellite printouts, technical reports, water temperature maps of the oceans. "Can't tell you about that. It's a classified project."

"I see," Mulder said. "Well, can you think of any *unclassified* way that any part of this project might have backfired and killed Dr. Gregory?"

"Nope again," Dooley said.

Mulder got the impression that Bear Dooley was usually this gruff with newcomers—that he did not suffer fools gladly—but that right now the man was particularly distracted. Perhaps he was more than a little overwhelmed to have the entire project thrust upon him so suddenly. Mulder watched the engineer's movements, listened to his abrupt answers. He tried to piece together a scenario where Dooley, wanting to become the new big shot, would arrange for the death of the real project head, thereby setting himself up to become the obvious successor. . . .

But it didn't ring true. Dooley didn't seem to be enjoying himself.

"Maybe we'd better try a safer area. How long have you worked for Dr. Gregory?" Mulder asked.

Dooley stopped and scratched his head. "Four or five years, I guess. Most of the time as a technician. Thought I was working hard *then*, but now he's left me with a set of big shoes to fill."

"How long have you been his deputy project director?"

Dooley answered that one more quickly. "Eleven months, ever since Miriel flaked out on us."

Outside in the hall a circular saw made a loud racket, followed by a sharp yelp. The clanging sound of metal and dropped pipes, crashed sheetrock and wood prompted a brief outburst of cursing and a scurry of frantic efforts to get the hazardous asbestos under control. It made Mulder think of a dentist drilling deep into a patient's molar, and suddenly whispering "Oops!" under his breath. His stomach knotted.

"What is all this stuff about the South Sea Islands?" he said, gesturing to the photos. "Aerial images and weather patterns."

Dooley shrugged and hesitated a moment as he concocted an explanation. "Maybe I'm planning a vacation—get away from it all, you know. Besides, that's the Western Pacific, not the South Seas."

"Funny. Dr. Gregory had similar photos in his office."

"Could be we had the same travel agent," Dooley answered.

Mulder leaned forward. He found it difficult to conduct a serious interrogation while both of them were wearing these absurd filter masks. His breathing made his cheeks and lips hot. His voice was muffled and subdued. "Tell me about Bright Anvil."

"Never heard of it," Dooley answered crisply.

"Yes you have."

"You don't have a need-to-know," Dooley countered.

"I have a security clearance," Mulder said.

"Your FBI clearances don't mean a damn thing to me, Agent Mulder," Dooley said. "I've signed papers. I've gone to my security briefing. I know the level of classification my work falls under. Unlike certain other assistants of Dr. Gregory, I take my oaths seriously."

Dooley pointed a blunt finger at Mulder. "You might not realize this, Mr. FBI—but you and I are on the same side. I'm fighting for this country, doing what our government deems necessary. If you want a blabbermouth, why don't you go see Miriel Bremen at her Stop Nuclear Madness! headquarters? You can find the address in any one of the thousand or so leaflets they left scattered in the ditches and along the fence yesterday. Go ask her your questions. Then arrest her for divulging national security information.

"In fact, why don't you ask her a *lot* of questions. She was around when Emil Gregory died, and she had plenty of motive to mess up our project."

Mulder looked sharply at him. "Tell me more."

Bear Dooley's color deepened as his long-standing resentment boiled to the surface. "She and her protesters were here the whole time. They threatened to stop at nothing—*nothing*, if you take the clear implications of that word—to sabotage our work. Miriel would know how to do it, since she worked here long enough. Maybe she's the one who planted something in Gregory's office. Maybe she's behind it all."

"We'll check it out," Mulder said.

Dooley set a box full of office supplies down heavily on the desk. Pens and pencils and scissors clattered next to his stapler and tape dispenser.

"Now I've got a lot of work to do, Agent Mulder. I was already up to my nose in responsibilities, and now it's gotten even worse. Add to that the fact that I've been pulled out of my comfortable offices and stuck in this godawful hole trying to make do, working on a project in a barracks building where I can't even pull out any of my classified papers."

Mulder thought of something else as he stepped to the door. "I noticed in Dr. Gregory's office that some of his reports and papers had been taken away from the death scene. Disturbing the evidence at a crime scene is a serious offense. You didn't have anything to do with that, did you?"

Bear Dooley emptied the last items out of a cardboard box, then upended it on the floor and took great pleasure in stomping the cardboard flat. "All of our project reports are controlled documents, Agent Mulder—numbered and assigned to a specific user. Some of Dr. Gregory's reports were one-of-a-kind. Maybe it was something we needed for our work. Our project takes precedence."

"Over a murder investigation? Who told you that?"

"Ask the Department of Energy. They might not tell you much about the project, but they will tell you that much."

"You sound pretty confident," Mulder said.

"As my old girlfriend used to say, self-confidence isn't one of my weak points," Dooley said.

Mulder pressed the issue. "Could I get a list of the documents that you took from Dr. Gregory's office?"

"No," Dooley answered. "The titles are classified."

Mulder kept his cool. He reached into his pocket and removed one of his cards. "This is the main office of the Bureau. You can reach me through the federal telephone system here on your lab phone, or call me on my cellular if you think of anything else you can tell me."

"Sure." Dooley took the card and offhandedly opened up the center desk drawer already cluttered with pens and rulers, push pins, paper clips, and other debris. He tossed the card inside, where he would probably never be able to find it again, even if he wanted to.

Mulder didn't get the impression Bear Dooley would want to.

"Thank you for your time, Dr. Dooley," he said.

"That's *Mister* Dooley," the engineer said, then lowered his voice. "Never finished my Ph.D. Been too busy working to worry about things like that."

GROUND ZERO

"I'll let you get back to your project then," Mulder said, and slipped out into the hall, where the construction workers continued to rip out sheets of asbestos-containing material behind thin curtains of plastic.

SEVEN

 The key fit the lock, but Mulder knocked loudly anyway, pushing the door open a crack before poking his head inside. "Ding, dong—Avon calling," he said.

Emil Gregory's home greeted him with only a shadowy silence.

Beside him, Scully pursed her lips. "There shouldn't be anyone here, Mulder. Dr. Gregory lived alone." She opened the folder that she had been holding against her dark blue jacket. "It says in this report that his wife died six years ago. Leukemia."

Mulder shook his head, frowning. He thought of the terminal cancer Scully had found while doing the autopsy on Gregory's body the previous afternoon. "Doesn't anyone die peacefully in their sleep of old age anymore?"

The two of them hesitated outside the cool, dusty house that sat alone at the end of a cul-de-sac.

The architecture of Gregory's home seemed out of place compared to the neighboring houses, its rounded corners and curving arches reminiscent of a Southwestern adobe mansion. Colorful enameled tiles lined the front doorway, and grapevines coiled around an arbor that shaded the porch area.

After waiting a few extra seconds, Mulder pushed the door all the way open. In the foyer, they walked across large, cool terra-cotta tiles and took two steps down to the main living level.

Though Gregory had died only a day and a half before, the place already had an abandoned feel to it, like a haunted house. "Amazing how fast that oppressive atmosphere can settle in," Mulder commented.

"It's obvious he was a bachelor," Scully said.

Mulder looked around and saw no particular untidiness to the house. In fact, it reminded him of the condition of his own apartment much of the time. He wondered if she was somehow ribbing him.

The main room had all the usual furniture— sofa, love seat, a television, a stereo set—but it didn't look as if it had been used terribly often. On the coffee table in front of the sofa a pile of old magazines lay partially buried under a dozen technical reports bearing the logo of the Teller Nuclear Research Facility and several more from the Los Alamos and Lawrence Livermore National Laboratories.

The pale tan walls had a smooth and buttery appearance, like soft clay. Alcoves molded around a fireplace displayed an assortment of small knick-knacks. Painted Anasazi pots sat on small shelves; bright spirit-catchers decorated the walls. A wreath of dried red chili peppers hung centered over the mantel.

The entire house had the authentic Santa Fe

flavor, but Mulder got the impression these decorations must have been artfully arranged by Dr. Gregory's long-dead wife, and the old scientist had not had the stamina or the incentive to redecorate the main part of the house in his own style.

"After he lost his wife, Dr. Gregory didn't seem to have any interests aside from his work," Scully said, flipping through the dossier again. "According to this record, he took a two-month leave of absence to arrange for the funeral and to get his mind back on things—but apparently he didn't know what to do with himself. Since his return to work at the Teller Nuclear Research Facility, his employee file is stuffed with commendations. It seems he threw himself into his research with complete abandon. It was his entire life."

"Any record there of what he was really working on?" Mulder asked.

"Because his project was highly classified, it doesn't specify."

"Same old story," Mulder said.

In the kitchen Scully found several bottles of prescription pain killers on the countertop. She shook them and studied the labels. Some of the bottles were half empty.

"He was taking some pretty heavy medication . . . analgesics and narcotics," she said. "The pain from his cancer must have been incredible. I haven't gotten his personal medical record unsealed yet, but Dr. Gregory undoubtedly knew he only had a few months to live."

"Yet he still went to work every day," Mulder said. "Now that's dedication."

He wandered around in the empty house, not sure what he was looking for. He crossed the living room and stepped down a side hallway that led to the back bedrooms and study. Along these walls, in the private part of Gregory's home, was a completely different style of decoration.

Framed photos adorned the wall in a haphazard arrangement that implied a man with a hammer and a nail, but without the patience or desire to use a yardstick and level. It looked as if the photos had been mounted as Dr. Gregory collected them over the years, one at a time, and placed wherever he found room.

Each image was different, yet with one striking similarity: the repetitive fury of huge atomic mushroom clouds, nuclear blasts, one after another— some more powerful than others. Mulder spotted a desert backdrop behind some of the blasts, while many others showed the ocean and Navy destroyers. Teams of scientists, identifiable in their cotton shirts and black-rimmed glasses, smiled for the camera beside military officers and other men in uniforms.

"And to think some people collect paintings of Elvis on black velvet," Mulder said, studying the mushroom clouds.

Scully came up beside him. "I recognize some of those pictures," she said. "Classic photos. Those were the Marshall Islands hydrogen bomb detonations of the mid-fifties. These others . . . I think they were aboveground blasts at the Nevada Test Site, a few shots from Project Plowshare." She stared at the photos. Mulder looked at her, surprised by the disturbed expression on her face.

"Something wrong?"

She shook her head, then tucked a strand of light auburn hair behind her ear. "No . . . no, it's not that. I was just remembering that, according to his file, Dr. Gregory had worked on nuclear weapons since the days of the Manhattan Project. He was present at the Trinity Test, then worked at Los Alamos.

He took part in many of the H-bomb detonations in the fifties."

Mulder stared at what appeared to be the largest mushroom cloud, an enormous eruption of water and fire and smoke out in the ocean. It looked as if an entire small island had been vaporized. Handwritten on the bottom border of the glossy were the words "Castle Bravo."

"Must have been quite something to see," he said.

Scully gave him a quick surprised look. "Not something I'd ever want to see," she said.

He quickly ran a hand through his mussed hair. "Rhetorically speaking, I meant." He read the strange names scrawled on each of the photos. They had been written with different pens but obviously by the same hand. Some of them had faded over the years; others had retained their color and darkness better.

"Sawtooth"

"Mike"

"Bikini Baker"

"Greenhouse"

"Ivy"

"Sandstone X-ray"

"What's this, some kind of code?" Mulder said.

Scully shook her head. "No. Those were the names of the test shots, different bomb designs. Each one was given a kind of nonsense name. The tests themselves weren't a particular secret, just the details of the device, time, anticipated yield, and core assembly. One whole series of underground blasts out at Nevada was named after California ghost towns. Another series used the names of various cheeses."

"What a bunch of funny guys."

Mulder left the photo gallery behind and stepped

into the large, disorganized office where Gregory had done his work at home. Despite the clutter of papers, notes, and books scattered in various piles around the room, he suspected that Dr. Gregory could have found any item at a moment's notice. A den or an office in the home was a man's private sanctum, and, despite the random appearance of all the paraphernalia, over the years the old scientist must have gradually arranged it exactly the way he wanted.

Now, seeing unfinished ideas jotted down on yellow legal pads and in bound lab notebooks, Mulder experienced the poignant sense of a life suddenly stopped. It was as if an amateur filmmaker had placed his videocamera on PAUSE while Dr. Emil Gregory did an EXIT STAGE LEFT, leaving all the props in place and untouched.

Mulder carefully looked at the notes, papers, technical reports. He found a stack of colorful travel brochures for various small Pacific islands. Some were flashy and produced professionally while others appeared to be crudely made by people who didn't exactly know what they were doing.

"You don't expect to find anything here, do you?" said Scully. "It's unlikely that Dr. Gregory ever took any classified work home."

"Probably not," Mulder said. "But he was brought up during the Manhattan Project days. Security was a little more lax than it is now, since everyone was working on the same team against the same bad guys."

"And here we are still building bombs to fight against the bad guys—yet we're not at all certain who the bad guys are anymore," Scully said quickly, almost as if by reflex.

Mulder looked sidelong at her, raising his eyebrows. "Was that an editorial comment, Agent Scully?"

She didn't answer. Instead she picked up a framed certificate that had been taken off the wall and set atop one of the low bookshelves. Mulder could still see the naked nail on the wall where it had hung.

"I wonder why he took this one down," she said, tilting it so he could see.

The certificate was a competently made printout from a laser printer with a logo designed with a low-end computer art program—just a joke, but someone had obviously spent a lot of time on it. The symbol in the center of the parchment was a stylized bell with a clapper dangling beneath its shell. Superimposed on top was the slashed circle of the universal "No" symbol. The words underneath read, "This prestigious NO-BELL prize awarded to Dr. Emil Gregory by the Bright Anvil Project staff."

"No-Bell prize," Mulder said with a groan. "The strangest part, though, is that Bear Dooley—Dr. Gregory's number one man—insisted to me vehemently just yesterday that the Bright Anvil Project doesn't exist. Who signed that certificate?"

Scully glanced down. "Miriel Bremen—the woman who used to work for Gregory but then quit to become a protester."

"Ah," Mulder said. "Based on this, and what Bear Dooley told me yesterday, I think it's time we spoke with Miriel Bremen. The offices of the protest group are in Berkeley, aren't they? Not far from here."

Scully nodded, preoccupied. Her answer surprised him. "I'd like to go see her by myself, Mulder."

"Any particular reason why you're giving me the afternoon off?"

She shook her head. "Old stuff, Mulder. Nothing to do with this case."

Mulder nodded slowly. He knew enough not to push her when she didn't want to come out with what was bothering her. He trusted his partner to tell him in her own time.

EIGHT

 Two days of maniacal asbestos-removal construction—*de*struction, actually—had left a disconcerting whitish film all over Bear Dooley's desk, his notebooks, his computer terminal, and his telephone.

Using an industrial-strength paper tissue, he wiped down the exposed surfaces, telling himself that it was probably just flakes of drywall, gypsum from the plasterboard, nothing hazardous. All of the stray asbestos fibers would certainly have been removed with meticulous care. The contractors were, after all, government employees.

That thought sparked uneasiness in him all over again.

Dooley wanted his old office back. He passionately disliked these temporary quarters. He felt as if he were camping in his own workplace. "Roughing it," Mark Twain would have called it.

Such distractions annoyed him. The Bright

Anvil project was too important for him and his coworkers to "make do" while the investigation into Dr. Gregory's death continued. What did that have to do with the progress of the test? Who set the priorities around here, anyway? The project had a very narrow window of time, and conditions had to be exactly right. A murder investigation could continue indefinitely, regardless of the time of year or weather conditions.

Just let Bright Anvil go off without a hitch, he thought, and the FBI agents could have all the time they wanted.

He glanced at his watch. The new satellite images were ten minutes overdue. Dooley reached for the phone, then heaved a sigh of disgust. It wasn't his own phone in his own office with numbers preprogrammed on the dialing pad. Instead he had to ransack the desk drawers for a facility phone book and flip through the pages until he found Victor Ogilvy's extension. He punched it in, rubbing his fingers together and looking at the fine white dust he had picked up. Scowling in disgust, Dooley wiped his hand on his jeans.

The phone rang twice before a thin voice answered.

"Victor, where's that weather report?" he said without wasting time on greetings or cordialities. His young assistant could certainly recognize his booming voice by now.

"We've got it, Bear," came the researcher's nasal reply. "I was just double-checking and triple-checking the meteorological projections. Uh, I think you'll like them this time around."

"Well, get 'em over here," Dooley said, "so I can check them a fourth time. Things have to be exactly right."

"On my way!" Victor hung up the phone.

Dooley sat back in the creaking old chair, trying to get comfortable. The air-conditioning was turned up too high in the old barracks building, so he had not taken off the denim jacket that covered his red flannel shirt. With his long hair and bushy beard he looked like a mountain man.

His demeanor intimidated many of the people around him, particularly those who didn't work for him. Bear Dooley didn't think he was all that difficult a taskmaster, so long as everyone did what they were expected to do. If they weren't willing to do their jobs, then they shouldn't have bothered to apply in the first place. Victor and the other engineers who had been on Dooley's team for several years understood that he was perfectly easy to get along with, that he trusted them and their abilities—but his team members also knew they'd better run for cover if they ever let him down.

Out in the halls, the construction workers continued their hammering and pounding, tearing down the walls. Plastic sheeting lay draped over everything as the laborers ransacked another wing of the building.

The barracks' outside door opened, and red-headed Victor Ogilvy bounded up the wooden stairs, then down the linoleum hallway to Dooley's temporary office. He burst in, his face florid, grinning with the eagerness of Jimmy Olsen hot on a news story. His wire-rimmed glasses slipped down his nose.

"Here's the satellite printouts," he said. "And here's the overlays." He spread the projections on Dooley's cleared desk, weighting the curling edges with a stapler and a pair of scissors.

"See the storm clouds here, Bear? Ninety-five percent probability that this depression will follow the path I've marked with red dashes." He traced a big-knuckled finger along a contour in the Western Pacific, just past the International Date Line in the Marshall Islands. "I've looked for projected landfalls, and there seems to be an absolutely perfect target— right here." Victor's finger completely obscured a minuscule dot that looked like a printer's error in the middle of the ocean. "Bingo!"

Dooley looked down. "Enika Atoll."

"It's in the ephemeris," Victor said, then jerked his head over to Dooley's bookshelf.

Dooley leaned back in his chair to grab the thick book, blowing the white gypsum dust from its spine. He riffled the pages, studying the nautical coordinates and finding the brief listing for Enika.

"Oooh, exciting," he said, reading the brief description. "A big flat rock out in the middle of nowhere. No recent photos, but it sounds tailor-made for our purposes. No existing settlements, not even any history."

"Nobody will ever notice anything there," Victor agreed.

"Let me see those weather charts again." Dooley reached forward, snapping his fingers to make Victor hurry. The younger man spread out the charts again, showing the angry-looking knot of cloud swirling across the ocean like a clenched fist.

"Hurricane warnings have gone out to all the adjacent islands. There's not much in the vicinity, only a few sparsely populated islands such as Kwajalein and Truk. It's even in U.S. protectorate waters."

"And you're sure the storm is going to hit land there?" Dooley asked. He was already convinced, but he wanted someone else to say it.

Victor gave an exasperated sigh. "Look at the size of that storm system, Bear! How could it miss? We've got a week until projected landfall—that's an eternity as far as weather projections go, but not much time to set up our preparations . . . if we decide to go, that is." The whip-thin redhead stepped back, shuffling his feet as if he had to go to the bathroom badly.

Dooley fixed Victor with his best don't-give-me-any-bullshit glare. "What do you mean, *if* we decide to go? Is there anything to recommend against it? Be straight."

Victor shrugged. "Nothing that I can see—but it's still your call, Bear. Without Dr. Gregory, you're the one pulling all the strings."

Dooley nodded, knowing full well when he could trust his people—and this was one such time. "All right, let's start making phone calls. As of right now I am activating Bright Anvil. We're on our way. Let's get the Corps of Engineers flown out to Enika, get our destroyer on standby down at Coronado Naval Base ready to move out as soon as we arrive."

Victor nodded quickly. "We've already done the paperwork with the Department of Transportation for the SST. The Bright Anvil equipment, diagnostics, and the device itself will be shipped down to San Diego posthaste. The Coronado Base is waiting to receive it."

Dooley nodded. Sending the SST, or Safe Secure Transport, was no minor task, requiring clearances from numerous counties, the federal highway system, as well as city commissions.

"Pull everybody's travel papers. We need to get a move on," he said. "I'll be with the first crew going out to Enika. Support Team B—that's you, Victor—will be ready to take a transport plane out to the islands once everything's set up."

Victor scrawled copious notes in handwriting that Bear Dooley had once foolishly tried to decipher, but never again. Breathless, Victor looked as if he might suffer from a stroke in his excitement.

"Let's go. No time to waste," Dooley said.

The young assistant scuttled toward the door, but Dooley called after him. "Oh, and Victor?" The other man turned, blinking owlishly behind his glasses, his mouth partly open. "Don't forget to pack your swim trunks."

Victor laughed and disappeared down the hall.

Dooley stared down at the maps and weather charts again, letting a smile creep across his face. Finally, after all this time, they were moving on to the next step. There could be no turning back once the wheels started moving.

Besides, he had to admit he wasn't terribly sorry to get away from those nosy FBI investigators. He had work to do.

NINE

Stop Nuclear Madness! Headquarters,
Berkeley, California
Wednesday, 12:36 P.M.

 Scully took the rental car and drove alone into Berkeley, following once-familiar highways. Now, though, she sensed she had become an intruder in a place where she had previously felt at home.

Heading down Telegraph Avenue toward the campus, Scully saw that the university remained basically unchanged. It stood like an island of ferociously independent culture—the People's Republic of Berkeley—while the rest of the world went on its way. The unbroken string of pizza joints, student art galleries, falafel stands, and recycled clothing shops made her feel warm with nostalgia. She had spent her first year of college here, getting her first taste of independence, making her own choices on a day-to-day basis.

Scully watched the usual smattering of students, some on old bicycles wearing white helmets, some jogging, some even Rollerblading. Young men and women wore clothes that were somehow one step sideways from fashion; they moved as if their every action was a Statement. Behind the steering wheel of the new car—itself out of place—Scully surprised herself by looking down at her conservative business jacket and slacks, her professional briefcase, with some measure of embarrassment.

As an undergrad at Berkeley, Dana Scully and her friends had laughed at people very much like what she herself had become.

Scully parked in a public ramp and walked out into the sunshine, pushing sunglasses up on her nose and scanning the streets to get her bearings. She walked along, glancing at kiosks that announced student film festivals, rallies, and fund-raising events.

A black dog lay panting beside a tree to which it had been leashed. A long-haired woman sat on a blanket in front of a strewn display of handmade jewelry for sale, though she seemed more interested in strumming her guitar than in pressuring potential buyers. Outside the door to an old apartment complex, a cardboard box stuffed with ragged paperbacks begged for customers; a sign taped to the box announced that the books were "50 cents each!" A coffee can sat next to the box, awaiting contributions.

Tracking addresses by the numbers on the sidewalk, Scully finally found the Stop Nuclear Madness! Headquarters in a tall old building that looked as if it could have been the set for a courthouse in an old black-and-white movie. A diner and coffee shop shared the street level of the building with a large new-and-used bookstore that catered to students buying and selling their used textbooks as well as grabbing a quick read between exams.

A short flight of concrete steps led down from

the sidewalk to below street level. An easel propped beside the stairs held a posterboard with stenciled letters announcing the protest group and something called the "Museum of Nuclear Horrors."

Scully went down the stairs, her heels clicking on the cement. The place was typical of temporary headquarters on any university campus, she thought. The owners of these old buildings specialized in low-rent, short-term-lease offices, utilizing their extra space as quick-setup bases for political campaigns, activist groups, and even tax-preparation businesses around April.

On the building's outside wall she noticed a faded Civil Defense symbol, the three-bladed radiation sign surrounded by deep yellow, identifying the lower levels of the building as a bomb shelter in the event of a nuclear emergency. Scully stared at the symbol for a minute, thinking of the irony . . . and experiencing a sense of familiarity as well. She had been in places like this many times during her own student days.

She pushed open the basement door and entered the Stop Nuclear Madness! Headquarters. She felt transported back in time. She remembered when she had been younger, filled with enthusiasm to change the world.

Even in her first year she had been a good student, dedicated to her physics classes and to learning. She knew how much money her parents were spending on tuition, a good portion of her father's Navy salary, just to give her the chance to go to a big university.

But swept up in the alienness, the excitement of a culture so different from her military upbringing, Scully had flirted with activism. She read the pamphlets, listened to her fellow students talk far into the night, and grew more and more upset at what she heard. Believing everything she read and discussed, she had spent long sleepless nights in her dorm room, imagining what she could do to Make a Difference. She had even contemplated joining one of the protests scheduled out at the Teller Nuclear Research Facility—but ultimately she had been too practical to follow through on the idea.

Still, her involvement had been enough to let her engage in spirited discussions—no, she decided to be truthful with herself: they had been outright *arguments*—with her father, a conservative and dignified Navy captain stationed at the nearby Alameda Naval Air Station. It had been one of the first subjects on which she and her father had truly disagreed. That was before she had decided to join the FBI, which had also brought her parents' disapproval.

Scully loved her father greatly. She had been profoundly affected by his recent death just after the Christmas holidays. He used to call her Starbuck, she called him Ahab . . . but that was all in the past. She would never see him again.

Scully had spent only a year at Berkeley before the Navy had transferred her father, and she herself had gone to the University of Maryland to study. Most of their wounds had been bandaged a long time before, and no doubt her father had simply considered her brush with the protesters to be an example of the brashness of youth.

Now that she stood on the threshold of the Stop Nuclear Madness! Headquarters, those sore spots grew tender again. But Scully had not come here to join in the protest movement this time. She had a death to investigate. And some of the clues had led her here.

As she entered the small offices, the woman behind the desk turned to give her an automatic smile—but froze with instant suspicion upon seeing her professional garb. Scully felt a sinking in her stomach.

The young receptionist was in her early twenties, with skin the color of light milk chocolate and bushy hair knotted into a medusa swirl of dangling dreadlocks. Her necklace consisted of enormous rectangles of enameled metal; the voluminous wrap covering her body was a dizzying geometric pattern—some sort of Swahili tribal dress, Scully decided.

She glanced down at the fancy engraved nameplate—probably a minor concession of importance for the volunteer workers—on the table that served as a makeshift front desk. "Becka Thorne." Beside the nameplate, the table held a telephone book, telephone, an old typewriter, and some preprinted leaflets.

Scully pulled out her ID. "I'm Special Agent Dana Scully from the FBI. I'm here to speak with a Ms. Miriel Bremen."

Becka Thorne's eyebrows went up. "I . . . I'll see if she's here," she said. Her voice was cold and uninviting, her guard up. Again Scully felt a pang of disappointment.

Becka Thorne seemed to be pondering whether or not to lie. Finally she got up and glided to the back of the offices, her colorful wrap swishing as she moved. Somewhere out of sight behind movable fabric partitions Scully could hear an overworked photocopy machine churning out leaflets.

While she waited, Scully studied the posters and photo enlargements mounted on the wall, presumably the Museum of Nuclear Horrors promised on the sign outside.

A computer-printed banner had been tacked up at ceiling level, proclaiming in large dot-matrix letters: "WE'VE ALREADY HAD ONE NUCLEAR WAR—WE MUST

PREVENT THE NEXT ONE!" Grainy black-and-white enlargements of awesome mushroom clouds adorned the painted cinderblock walls. They reminded her of the hallway in Dr. Gregory's home. There, though, the photographs had been trophies occupying honored positions. Here they were accusations.

One poster listed known international atomic bomb tests and the amount of radiation each aboveground blast had showered into the air. She saw a chart with rising bars that showed the increase of cancer in the United States attributed to such residual radiation, particularly strontium 90 contamination in grass consumed by dairy cows, which was then carried into their milk and ingested by children who poured it over their artificially sweetened breakfast cereals. As the bars rose from year to year, the numbers appeared staggering.

Another display listed the islands that had been destroyed in the Pacific Ocean, with pathos-filled photographs of natives from Bikini Island and Eniwetok Atoll as the U.S. military evacuated them from their island paradises to make way for atomic bomb tests.

At the time, the evacuation efforts had been undertaken at enormous cost. For years the Bikini Islanders had petitioned the United States and the United Nations to be allowed to return to their homeland, but only after the United States footed the atrocious bill to remove the residual radioactivity from their coral reefs, their beaches, their jungles.

Thinking of the island photographs on Dr. Gregory's walls, as well as the satellite images and weather projections in his lab office, Scully inspected the exhibit with greater interest.

In 1971 the Bikini Atoll had been declared safe, and the islanders were allowed to return. But tests in 1977 showed that the atoll still seethed with dangerous levels of radiation, and the inhabitants were forced to evacuate again. Residents of Eniwetok Atoll, which also was used for a prolonged series of hydrogen bomb tests, returned to their homes in 1976, only to learn that a nuclear waste dump on the islands would remain contaminated for thousands of years. In the early 1980s it was found that residents of islands even one hundred and twenty kilometers away from the original tests had developed an unusually high incidence of thyroid tumors.

Shaking her head, Scully moved on to the worst part of all, the centerpiece of the museum—a gallery of gut-wrenching photos showing the blasted remains of Hiroshima and Nagasaki, burned corpses left in the wake of the fireball that had blazed across Japanese skies a half-century before. Some of the bodies had been incinerated so completely that nothing remained but greasy shadows of black ash splashed against the walls of surviving buildings. Worse even than the corpses were the blistered and suppurating survivors.

As Scully looked at the photos she noticed an unsettling familiarity between those bodies and the corpse of Dr. Emil Gregory in his own radiation-washed laboratory.

"Yes, Agent Scully?" a woman's terse voice said.

Scully turned to see Miriel Bremen, a tall woman with short, wavy mouse-brown hair cut in an unflattering squarish style. Her chin was long, her nose pointed, and her gray eyes seemed weary. She was not an attractive woman, but her bearing and her voice bespoke a no-nonsense quality of intelligence.

"So now what did we do?" Miriel said impatiently, not allowing Scully to speak. "I'm getting tired of all this harassment. We've filed the appropriate papers, given the required notices, obtained the correct permits. What on earth has my group done to attract the attention of the FBI?"

"I'm not investigating your group, Ms. Bremen," Scully said. "I'm looking into the death of Dr. Emil Gregory two days ago at the Teller Nuclear Research Facility."

Miriel Bremen's cool mask cracked, and her whole body sagged. "Oh," she said. "Emil . . . that's different."

She paused, gripping the receptionist's table with one hand and took a deep breath. Becka Thorne watched to see if she could help, then surreptitiously disappeared to attend to the photocopy machine. Miriel glanced around as if for reassurance at the posters of Nagasaki victims, at the forlorn Bikini Islanders.

"Sure, let's talk, Agent Scully—but not here."

TEN

Triple Rock Brewery and Cafe,
Berkeley, California
Wednesday, 1:06 P.M.

 Miriel Bremen led the way to a small microbrewery and restaurant only a few blocks' walk from the heart of the university. Scully followed Miriel through the wood-framed glass doors into a room full of booth tables layered with a thick armor of glossy varnish, and a bar lined with empty stools. The droning background noise of pedestrians on the sidewalk and constant traffic on the main streets faded as they stepped inside.

Metal signs advertising long-out-of-business beer manufacturers from the 1940s and 1950s covered the walls. Above the brass-railed bar, a chalkboard listed the four handmade brews on tap. On the back wall, next to a dartboard and pool table, a large green slateboard suggested deli sandwiches, hot dogs, nachos, or salads from the food-prep window.

"You order food over there," Miriel indicated a smaller counter. "Vegetarian chili is their specialty, but the soup's pretty good, too . . . and of course a sandwich is a sandwich is a sandwich. People come here for the beer. Best you'll find anywhere."

She left Scully to prop her briefcase in one of the booths far from the door and gestured with her shoulder at the list of house beers on tap. "What are you having?" Miriel said. "The stout is to die for."

"I'll just have an iced tea," Scully said. "I'm on duty."

Miriel frowned at her. "Listen, Agent Scully—the whole point of going to a microbrewery is to taste some decent beer. This isn't Budweiser Lite, you know. They'd probably throw us out on our ears if we ordered iced tea in here."

Scully didn't think the manager would do any such thing, but the place did remind her of her student days enough that she felt a pang inside. She wasn't much of a beer drinker, but Scully couldn't afford to scorn an overture of friendship, if she wanted Miriel to open up and answer probing questions.

"All right, let me try one of the stouts, then. But just a small one—and only one."

Miriel forced a faint smile onto her hard face. "That'll be up to you to decide." She went to the bar while Scully perused the list of sandwiches. "Get me a hot dog and a cup of chili," Miriel called back. "I take it Uncle Sam is paying?"

"I am," Scully said, noting the prices and realizing that they both could get by on less than ten dollars for lunch.

When they returned to their table, Scully sat down, reaching across the table to pick up her pint of dark malty stout. "Looks thick enough to hold up a spoon," she said.

She took a sip and swallowed, surprised at the *density* of the drink. The taste was overpowering, almost chocolaty. A true liqueur of a beer, not the light, sour-tasting stuff she occasionally drank very cold out of a can at picnics or birthday parties. Scully raised her eyebrows and nodded in approval at the woman in the seat across from her.

She tried to think of where to begin, but Miriel pre-empted her. The protester seemed to have no problems with self-expression, bypassing time-consuming pleasantries and the dance of conversational give-and-take before Scully could get around to the real questions.

"So, let me tell you why I think you're here," Miriel Bremen said. "It's one of two possibilities. Either you think I, or someone from my protest group, has in some way caused the death of Emil Gregory—or you've been stymied by your escorts at the Teller Facility, your lack of appropriate security clearances, and your inability to access classified documents. Nobody'll tell you anything, and you've come to me thinking I have some answers."

Scully spoke slowly. "A little of both, Ms. Bremen. I've completed the autopsy on Dr. Gregory. There's little doubt as to the primary injuries that resulted in his death, but I haven't yet been able to determine how they came about. What could Dr. Gregory have stumbled into that caused his death?

"I'll have to admit that your protest group does have a credible motive for wanting Dr. Gregory out of the picture, so I have to look into it. I also know that Dr. Gregory—a man you worked with—was involved in some sort of classified weapons project, something called Bright Anvil. But nobody will tell us what that is. And here you are, Ms. Bremen, at the intersection of both of my lines of investigation."

"Well then, let me tell you something," Miriel Bremen said, folding her hands around her pint of dark beer and taking a long swallow. "It sounds clichéd to say that I have nothing to hide—but in this instance I truly don't. It works to my benefit to tell more and more people about what's really going on at the Teller Nuclear Research Facility. I've been trying to blow the whistle on them for the past year. Here, I brought along some of our group's brochures." She reached into her pocket and handed over two of the hand-folded, photocopied pamphlets that some volunteer had no doubt designed on a personal computer.

"Back when I worked at the Teller Facility, I was quite a devoted assistant to Emil Gregory," she said, settling her long chin into her hand. "For many years he was my mentor. He helped me through the politics and the paperwork and the progress reports so I could do some real work.

"Your imagination is probably going to blow this out of proportion, thinking we were lovers or something—but that's just plain wrong. Emil was old enough to be my grandfather, and he took an interest in me because he saw that I had the talent and the enthusiasm to make a good partner. He coached me, and we worked well together."

"But you had some sort of falling out?" Scully said.

"In a sense . . . but not exactly the way you might be thinking," Miriel said, then sidestepped the question. "You want to know what Bright Anvil is? It's an unorthodox type of nuclear explosive. These days, despite the end of the Cold War and the supposed downscaling of nuclear weapons development, we're still designing new ones. Bright Anvil is a very special type of warhead using a technology that . . . " She paused, then stared at the walls, her eyes unfocused, as if she was thinking of anything but the decorative metal signs.

"A technology that . . . ?" Scully encouraged.

Miriel sighed and met Scully's gaze. "It's a technology that seems to operate beyond the laws of physics, as I know them—and I do know physics, Agent Scully. I'm not aware of how much physics they taught you in your training as an FBI agent, but—"

Scully interrupted her. "My undergraduate degree was in physics. I spent one year here at Berkeley before I transferred to the University of Maryland. I wrote my thesis on Einstein's Twin Paradox."

Miriel's eyes widened. "I think I might have read that." She contemplated. "*Dana* Scully, right?"

Scully nodded, surprised. Miriel sat up and looked at her with greater respect. "That was interesting stuff. Okay, now I know I don't have to put it in kindergarten terms—but I wish I could, because I don't understand it myself.

"The whole Bright Anvil Project was funded by non-traditional means, invisible on the ledger sheets, money skimmed from other projects, to pay for new tests, cutting-edge research, unorthodox concepts. Bright Anvil was never listed on any budget submitted to Congress, and you won't be able to track it down.

"Emil had worked in the nuclear weapons industry for decades. He was even at the Trinity Test, back in 1945." She smiled wanly. "He used to tell us stories. . . . " Her lips trembled for just a moment, but she covered it by eating some of her vegetarian chili. "But by now he was at the end of his career. He thought he was hiding it from all of us, but I don't think he was in very good health."

"No, he wasn't," Scully said.

Miriel nodded, but asked no further questions. "Emil wanted to do something important to end his career on a high note. He wanted to leave a legacy behind. But all the work he'd been doing in the past decade or so was just 'fine tuning a paper bag,' as we physicists call it.

"Then Bright Anvil fell in his lap. Someone else had done the preliminary physics. We got designs for exotic, high-energy, pulsed-power sources. It was a done deal. The components worked. I couldn't figure out *how* or *why*—but Emil didn't worry about that. He got all excited. He saw how such technology could be used to create a fundamentally new kind of warhead. Emil took it and ran with it.

"Even from the start, I had my doubts—but I kidded myself. I followed along because Emil had done so much for me. This was our new project. I helped him run simulations, scenarios that had little likelihood of ever coming about for real. But the more I worked with it, the creepier it became. Bright Anvil was just too weird. It didn't seem to come from any physics I was ever taught in school. No technology I know can do what it does. Some of the components of the device were fabricated elsewhere. We never knew where or how—we just *received* them from the program offices in Washington."

Miriel finished off her beer. She glanced over at the bar as if she wanted to order another one, but instead settled back to look across the table where Scully sat in rapt attention. Miriel leaned over, placing her elbows on the polished tabletop.

"I'm a scientist by training. But for me to understand, my science has to have some foundation. And Bright Anvil has no scientific basis that I can grasp. It's something so exotic I couldn't conceive of it with my wildest imagination. So I backed off, I raised too many objections, and in the process made a lot of enemies.

"Then, in one of those serendipitous occurrences, I went to a conference in Japan. Just out of curiosity I took a side trip to Hiroshima and Nagasaki—you know, a weapons researcher's pilgrimage. Both cities have been rebuilt, but it's like putting makeup over a scar. I began to check into things. I read the literature that I'd studiously avoided before, not wanting to look too closely at my own conscience.

"Do you know what they did to the Marshall Islands with the nuclear tests in the fifties? Do you know the horrible aboveground tests they did out in Nevada, staking out livestock at various distances from Ground Zero just so they could analyze the destructive effects of the blast and flash on living tissue? Do you know how many Pacific Islanders were booted off their homes, their peaceful idyllic island existence destroyed, just so somebody could blow up a big bomb?"

"Yes," Scully said. "I know."

Miriel Bremen shoved her plate away, having finished most of her lunch. She brushed off the front of her shirt. "I apologize. I was giving you a sermon." She nudged the Stop Nuclear Madness! brochures across the booth closer to Scully. "Read these if you want more information about it, and about us. I won't take up any more of your time." She slipped out of the seat.

Scully glanced down and saw that she had eaten only half of her own meal. Miriel Bremen had already ducked out the door, leaving Scully alone in the restaurant before she could think of an intelligent follow-up question.

Considering what she had just learned, Scully picked up her sandwich and chewed slowly.

Someone dropped a quarter in the jukebox, which began blasting a classic Bob Seeger single that seemed too rowdy for the lunch hour.

Scully quickly finished her meal and picked up the protest brochures before stepping outside to head back to the parking ramp. Mulder would be interested in the details, the new developments. She stopped on the sidewalk at a wire trash can as a big city bus heaved by, belching oily blue-gray exhaust. A skateboarder rattled past, dodging pedestrians with reckless ease.

Scully stood tapping the homegrown pamphlets against her palm, on the verge of tossing them into the wastebasket. Then she reconsidered. "STOP NUCLEAR MADNESS" the title proclaimed.

Giving herself the excuse that she could consider them evidence, Scully pocketed them instead.

ELEVEN

From the Coronado shipyards the ocean sprawled westward, stretching toward the curve of the earth, deep blue and dazzling with reflected morning sunlight. The downtown skyscrapers rose high and white across the narrow San Diego Bay. Cruise ships waited like colorful behemoths at the public docks; a maze of piers bristled with the masts of sailboats.

The weather struck Bear Dooley as incredibly mild, sunny but cooled by fresh breezes, so that even his flannel shirt and denim jacket were tolerable. While riding in the taxi from the airport, he drank in the colorful and clean city, surprisingly pleasant for such a large urban area. But here, on the thin peninsula, the naval base looked like a naval base, and the ships at the restricted docks demonstrated quite clearly why the color had been named battleship gray.

GROUND ZERO

A young officer in white dress uniform met Bear Dooley at the docks. Dooley didn't know the regulations of when sailors were supposed to wear certain uniforms, but he got the impression that this blond-haired, clean-cut Navy man might be someone of more-than-average importance.

The sailor—Dooley corrected himself: they probably wanted to be called "seamen"—gave him a smart salute, though Dooley didn't believe he warranted one, according to military protocol. He clumsily returned the salute without knowing whether that was correct either.

"Mr. Dooley, sir," the man said, "I'm Commander Lee Klantze, executive officer of the USS *Dallas*, here to escort you on board our ship. If you'll follow me, sir, Captain Ives is ready to see you. We've recalled the entire crew and kept them busy provisioning the ship and preparing to shove off. We'll be ready to get under way as soon as you're situated."

Dooley's jeans and flannel shirt were a marked contrast to the razor-folded and bleached-white uniform of the Navy destroyer's exec officer. But Dooley wore his own personality like a shield. He never let his attire bother him. He had been hired for his abilities, not for his appearance.

Dooley had trimmed his beard and shaved his cheeks and neck that morning before rushing off to the San Francisco Airport for a quick shuttle flight down the coast. He had spent the last two hours in the air and then being taxied through the sparkling city of San Diego over to the spit of land that held the Coronado Naval Base.

He had then wasted another half hour bulldozing his way through paperwork and clearances and approvals, even though everything had already supposedly been taken care of. Dooley hated to think of what hassles he would have encountered if everything *hadn't* been in order. The military did have its way of doing things, and little short of an all-out war could get them to streamline their operations.

"How was your trip?" Klantze asked. "No complications other than the military inefficiency getting on the base?"

"Yeah, the flight was fine, but nobody will give me a straight answer," Dooley said. "Did the SST arrive okay, all equipment safe and on board?"

"I believe so, sir," Klantze answered. "Sometime late last night. Sorry for all the added security." He pushed his wire-rimmed glasses up on his nose. Their Photogray lenses had turned dark, so Dooley could not see the man's eyes directly.

The disguised and armored semi truck, the Safe Secure Transport, had left at sunset the previous day and driven south through the night on the California freeways to reach San Diego. The drivers were escorted front and back by armed, nondescript vans, whose drivers and passengers had orders to shoot to kill, no questions asked, should anything threaten the nuclear device. No part of the caravan was allowed to stop for so much as a bathroom break.

Dooley was glad he didn't have to bother with those difficulties. He would have preferred to have the entire expedition depart from the Alameda Naval Air Station, a short hop away from the Teller Nuclear Research Facility. But the Navy destroyer assigned to take them out to the Marshall Islands was docked in San Diego. It was easier—and less conspicuous—to move the Bright Anvil device and all its equipment than it was to move an entire destroyer.

Klantze turned about, ready to march off, then glanced over his shoulder in sudden embarrassment. "Oh, excuse me, sir—may I take your duffel, or your case?"

"Sure." Dooley handed over the soft-sided satchel that contained a week's worth of clothes crammed into its various pockets. "I'll carry the briefcase though," he said—not that it was handcuffed to his wrist as in a spy thriller, but it contained classified documents crucial to the Bright Anvil Project. It was securely locked, and Dooley planned to hold on to it.

"As you wish, sir."

The two of them strode along the dock, past several other chain-link fences and gates guarded by armed military police. Dark, creosote-covered planks formed the edge of the dock, while a narrow paved road ran along the center. Klantze walked down the middle of the road, keeping an eye out for government vehicles and puttering Cushman carts that traveled up and down the dock on military business.

Finally, Dooley saw the large Navy destroyer that had been assigned to his project. The enormous, sleek ship looked like a skyscraper in the water, with weapons mounts and control towers, radar antennas, satellite uplink dishes, meteorologic instruments, and various superstructures Dooley could not identify. Navy stuff, he figured.

Along the deck ran barricades of rope mesh, painted to look remarkably like a chain-link fence. Everything was the same shade of gray—the rails and pipes and rigging and steps and ladders. Even the long cannons. Only the bright orange life preservers mounted every fifty feet along the hull provided a few spots of color. The U.S. flag and Navy flags flew from all four corners of the ship.

Dooley stopped and looked along the length of the gigantic cruiser. Despite his usual gruff demeanor, he was impressed with the vessel.

"There she is, Mr. Dooley," Klantze said. He snapped to attention and began to rattle off the ship's statistics. They seemed to be a matter of pride with him, rather than a memorized speech.

"The *Dallas*, Spruance Class, built in 1971. Five hundred sixty-three feet overall length, powered by four sets of GE gas turbines. She's got a small captain's gig for quick trips ashore, plus an entire surface-to-air missile battery, antisubmarine weapons, and torpedo tubes. This class of destroyer was designed primarily for antisubmarine warfare, but she's lightly armed and carries a minimal crew. The *Dallas* is the finest vessel in her class, if you ask me, sir. She'll get us out to the islands, no matter what the weather."

Dooley looked sharply at the exec. "You already know the details of our mission, then?" He had thought that very few of the crew members would have been briefed on the assignment out to Enika Atoll.

"Captain Ives has explained it to me, sir," Klantze said, then smiled faintly. "I am the executive officer, if you'll recall. If my information is correct, and if your device is successful, nobody on board is going to be unaware of the test."

Dooley agreed. "I suppose it's tough to keep a secret on board a ship."

"It's also difficult not to notice a giant mushroom cloud, Mr. Dooley."

The exec led him up a wide gangplank the size of a freeway entrance ramp and marched him across the deck and up several flights of hard metal steps to the bridge tower, where he introduced Dooley to the captain of the *Dallas*.

"Captain Ives, sir, this is Mr. Dooley," Klantze said after he had exchanged salutes with the captain. The executive officer nodded to Dooley. "I'll take your duffel to your stateroom, sir. I'm sure Captain Ives wishes to speak with you privately in greater detail."

"Yes I do," the captain answered. Klantze spun about sharply, like a mechanical marionette on a glockenspiel, and marched off.

"Pleased to meet you, Captain Ives. Thanks for your help." Dooley extended his hand, and the captain took it with a firm shake. The captain's arms, contained within his captain's uniform, had muscles like steel wires. Dooley got the impression that he could crack walnuts in his fist.

Ives was a lean man in his late fifties, as tall as Dooley but less burly. His stomach remained washboard flat. He moved with a spare grace, as if every exertion counted for something important. His chin was narrow, his eyes slate gray under heavy salt-and-pepper eyebrows. A bristling mustache rode his upper lip, and steel-gray hair lay neatly beneath his white captain's cap. He showed no sign of sweating in the heat. Perhaps he didn't allow it.

"Mr. Dooley, I'm sure your first concern is for your delicate equipment. Let me reassure you that everything arrived safely and intact, as far as we can tell."

"Good," Dooley said, his voice curt. He wanted to make certain at the outset that the captain understood that *Dooley* was in charge and that his instructions were not to be questioned. "If that equipment is damaged, we might as well not even bother to go. When do we set sail?"

"The *Dallas* can leave port at about four o'clock this afternoon." Captain Ives said. "But you may have noticed that this vessel has no sails."

Dooley blinked at him, then understood. "Oh, just a turn of phrase," he said, annoyed. "Do you have any weather charts or updates for me?"

"We received an encrypted signal," the captain said, "a report from a fast flyby of an aircraft out of our Kwajalein tracking station. Enika Atoll checks

out. We'll be heading out for the Marshall Islands at
full throttle, but it'll still take us five days."

"Five days?" Dooley said. "I was afraid of that."

Ives met his look with a steely gaze. "This isn't
an aircraft, Mr. Dooley. It takes a long time to get a
ship this size across that much water."

"All right, all right," Dooley said. "I suppose I
knew that. Do we have weather satellites? Is the
storm system still doing what we expected?"

Ives led him over to a chart table where weather
maps and satellite photos lay spread out. With one
long finger the captain indicated the swirl of clouds
out over the deep, featureless water. "The tropical
depression is worsening, as expected. Within a few
days it should be at full hurricane strength.
According to our projections it is heading straight
toward the atoll."

"Good, good." Dooley leaned over, rubbing his
hands together. Though he was a physicist and an
engineer, he had learned a great deal about meteo-
rology during the preparations for this test.

Captain Ives leaned closer and lowered his voice
so that the other crewmen would not hear him from
their communications or navigation stations. "Let me
be blunt, Mr. Dooley. I have already notified my
superiors of my extreme objections to the entire purpose of this mission. I have grave doubts about the
wisdom of resuming aboveground nuclear tests, no
matter where they occur."

Dooley stiffened, pausing just a moment to
scratch his beard and allow his blood pressure to
drop slightly. "Then maybe you just don't understand the necessity, Captain."

"I understand all right—more than you know,"
Ives replied. "I've been present at several hydrogen
bomb tests already, one of which I doubt even *you*
know about, since all results were highly classified."

Dooley raised his eyebrows. "When?"

"Back in the fifties," Ives said. "I was just a sea-man recruit then, but I was there, out in the islands, Eniwetok, Bikini, even Johnston Atoll near Hawaii. I worked with plenty of eggheads who were com-pletely amazed by their own calculations, absolutely confident in what they had invented. But I can tell you this, Mr. Dooley: every single time, those weapons developers, like yourself—people who were so smug about their own abilities—were liter-ally turned to jelly with awe when they watched their devices go off."

"I look forward to it then," Dooley said crisply. "You have your orders. Let me take care of the test details."

Captain Ives stood straight, backing away from the chart table. He adjusted his white cap. "Yes, I have my orders," he said, "and I will follow them, despite my objections—not the least of which is that it goes against all of my years of seamanship to head deliberately into a brewing hurricane."

Dooley walked around the bridge, puffed up with his own importance, glancing offhandedly at the outdated computer monitors, the various tactical sta-tions. He turned to look back at the reluctant captain.

"The hurricane is the only way we can pull this test off. Let me do my work, Captain Ives. You just keep the ship from sinking."

TWELVE

As if playing a scene from an old John Wayne movie, Oscar McCarron slid out of the saddle and tied his horse, a spry two-year-old palomino mare, to the fence post outside the General Store. He made sure to stomp his worn, pointy-toed cowboy boots on the boardwalk porch. The spurs gave a satisfying jingle as he *ambled*—the English language had no other word for it—to the store entrance.

McCarron's face was as seamed and leathery as his old boots, and his pale blue eyes wore a perpetual squint from a lifetime spent in the pounding desert sun. He eschewed sunglasses—they were only for sissies.

He had shaved this morning for his weekly trip into town, though the grizzled old whiskers could barely punch their way through his tough cheeks anymore. He didn't bother wearing gloves; with the

90

several layers of calluses on his hands (calluses that penetrated to the bones themselves) gloves would have been redundant. His squash-blossom silver-and-turquoise belt buckle was so large it could have been used as a coaster for cold drinks; it was one of his most prized possessions.

McCarron rode into the don't-blink-or-it's-gone town from his outlying ranch no more often than once every seven days to pick up his mail. There were limits to the amount of human companionship one man could stomach.

The door creaked as it always did when he stepped inside the General Store. He moved his left boot over by one floorboard so he wouldn't step on the loose plank.

"Afternoon, Oscar," said Fred, the store owner. His elbows rested on the countertop, but other than shifting his gaze, Fred didn't move a muscle.

"Fred," he replied. It was all the greeting he could manage. A man who was eighty years old couldn't afford to change his public personality this late in life. "Get any mail this week?"

He had no idea what Fred's last name was. He still considered the shopkeeper a newcomer to the area, though Fred had bought the General Store from an old Navajo couple a full fifteen years earlier. The Navajos had run the store for thirty-five years or so, and McCarron had considered them part of the landscape. Fred, on the other hand . . . well, Fred he still wasn't too sure about.

"We've been waiting for you to come in, Oscar. You've got the usual junk mail, but there's a letter here from Hawaii. Postmark says Pearl Harbor. Imagine that! It's a package. Any idea what it is?"

"What it is, is none of your damn business," McCarron said. "Just get me my mail."

Fred levered himself off of his elbows and

disappeared behind the counter to the small post office and storeroom in the back. McCarron brushed his hands down the snaps of his denim shirt and pants, knocking the whitish desert dust away. He knew everyone else called them "blue jeans" these days, but he hadn't gotten used to thinking of them as anything other than dungarees.

Fred returned with a handful of mail, junk newspapers, solicitations, advertising circulars, a few bills, and no letters. Nothing interesting—except for a medium-sized padded manila envelope.

McCarron took the stack and deliberately flipped through the junk mail first, driving back his own curiosity, knowing it would fluster Fred to no end. The junk mail always did a good job of starting his campfire when he slept out under the stars every Thursday night after coming into town. Finally, he held up the padded envelope, squinted at the postmark: *Honolulu, Hawaii*. The package bore no return address.

Fred leaned over the counter, cracking his big knuckles and blinking his brown eyes eagerly. His cheeks sagged on his lantern-jawed face. When he got a little older the shopkeeper would have jowls like a bulldog's. "Well, aren't you going to open it?" Fred asked.

McCarron glared at him. "Not in front of you, I ain't."

He had never forgiven Fred for his blatant indiscretion two years back of opening one of McCarron's packages when he was a day late coming into town. It had happened to be a boxed set of videotapes, the old *Victory at Sea* series, one of McCarron's favorites. He had always been fascinated by World War II.

Fred had been scandalized, not because of the subject matter of the tapes—McCarron suspected the old store owner had a few girlie films hidden back in his own house behind the store—but because Oscar McCarron had ordered the tapes at all, thereby exposing the secret that the old man actually had a television set and a videotape player. That went completely against the rancher's carefully cultivated image of living off the land and scorning all modern conveniences.

Back at his own ranch, McCarron kept an outhouse in plain sight of the main building and had a pump out front for water that came up pure and sweet from the White Sands aquifer. But in truth, he had modern bathroom facilities inside the house, electricity, and not only a TV and VCR but also a large satellite dish hidden back behind the adobe main house. He had purchased all the equipment up in Albuquerque, had it brought down and installed without telling anyone in the small town. McCarron enjoyed keeping up his "old codger" image, but not at the expense of his own comfort.

Fred had indeed kept his mouth shut over the past two years, at least as far as McCarron could tell, but he would never forget the offense.

"Awww, come on Oscar," Fred said. "I've been waitin' all day for you to come in just so's I could see your smiling face."

"Ain't that sweet," McCarron said. "Next thing, you're gonna be asking me to marry you, like one of them California faggots." He slapped the padded envelope unopened on the top of his junk mail and tucked the pile under his armpit. "If the package contains anything that concerns you, I'll be sure to tell you next time I come in." He turned and ambled back toward the door, intentionally stepping on the creaking board this time.

Outside, the still-hot afternoon sun had turned a buttery yellow as the light slanted toward the black lava teeth of the San Andres Mountains.

The palomino whickered when she saw him and stamped her foreleg, impatient to be off and trotting again. Seeing no one else out on the sleepy street, McCarron allowed himself to break into a smile of delight. The young mare was so eager. She seemed to love these pack trips even more than McCarron did.

His curiosity burned within him to see the contents of the mysterious envelope. But his pride wouldn't allow him to show any outward interest, not within sight of the General Store, where Fred was probably even now peering at him through the fly-specked windows.

He untied the horse and mounted up, stuffing the mail into one of the saddlebags before he rode off down the street, and then headed east overland into the sprawling open desert of the White Sands Missile Range.

Through long habit, McCarron found the loose gate in the barbed-wire fence that ran for hundreds of miles along the government-owned wasteland. He slipped the wire loose and led the palomino through the fence, fastening the gate behind him.

He fingered the bent but laminated old pass card that had been issued to him so long ago that every one of the original signers had died years ago. Oscar McCarron's right to go onto the missile site hadn't been questioned for several years now, not even by the hot-rodding young MPs who loved to roll over the dazzling gypsum sands in their all-terrain vehicles, as if they were surfers in dune buggies going to a beach party. But McCarron had a deep respect for authority and for the government itself, after all Uncle Sam had done for him.

Besides, he didn't want to mess with patriotic

young enthusiasts who were willing to defend even such a desolate wasteland against foreign invaders. That kind of mindset was something you didn't play around with.

McCarron rode toward the low craggy foot-hills. The desert was stark and flat, like a huge stretch of Nebraska sprayed with weed killer, then plopped down inside a ring of volcanic mountains. The bleakness somehow had made it an appropri-ate place to have hosted the world's first atomic explosion.

Oscar McCarron's family once had owned all of this land, a worthless swath of New Mexico, not good for ranching or even mining, since it was devoid of desirable minerals and ore. But back in 1944 the Manhattan Engineering District had expressed a passionate interest in the land—and McCarron's father had been only too happy to strike a deal. He had sold the spread for a small price, but still far more than it was worth.

The government paid extra when McCarron's father agreed to allow them to doctor the Land Bureau documents, removing his name from origi-nal ownership, keeping the land transfer secret so that it would show on archival documents that the government had leased it from a fictitious ranch family, the McDonalds.

The government and its Manhattan Project engi-neers had erected farm buildings and a windmill, concocting a story of the McDonalds who had lived at the Trinity Site. Only later, after the Trinity atomic bomb test in July 1945, had McCarron understood the reason for such secrecy. The nuclear detonation had taken place in what would have been the landowners' backyard. But reporters and, much later, protesters never located the mythical McDonalds.

McCarron's father had driven another hard bargain as part of the deal. It was during the bleakest part of World War II, when the Germans seemed to be making great strides toward global conquest and the Japanese Empire was sweeping the Pacific Rim. American soldiers were dying in record numbers. McCarron's father had not wanted to count his young, strong son as one of the casualties. He had exchanged the land in a secret transfer in order to make his son forever exempt from military service.

Also, because he loved the land despite its seared countenance, he and his family were guaranteed permanent access, if they chose to visit. Because that had meant so much to his father, dead these thirty-four years now, Oscar McCarron had made it a tradition to spend at least one night a week out in the open, reveling in the solitude under the vast desert skies on the land they had once owned.

The palomino enjoyed the desolate landscape, and without encouragement from McCarron, broke into a trot that gradually gave way to an all-out gallop as the energetic horse stretched her muscles, leaping over low basalt outcroppings and pounding across the baked hardpan. McCarron had his favorite camping spot, and the palomino knew full well how to get there.

They reached the bowl-shaped depression with daylight to spare. Hardy lichens spattered the black rocks, showing off their vitality with a display of bright colors. Gypsum sand filled the depression, as if a hot blizzard had cascaded across the desert. A sinkhole between the rocks cradled a small, pure pool from a spring that bubbled up, filtered clean through yards of fine sand.

McCarron went first to the spring and took deep gulps of water, which was cool from being in shade all day long. He swallowed the sweet wetness, not wanting to waste the water in his canteens. The palomino nudged his shoulder, urging him to hurry. But McCarron took his time, enjoying the water before the palomino could slobber all over inside the spring. Then he let her drink her fill.

He unsaddled the horse and tied her to a gnarled stump. He went out with his hatchet to chop up some of the dead mesquite brush and haul it back to his makeshift firepit. The fire would burn hot, crackling and popping into the night, filling the still air with a rich aromatic smoke.

Taking his mail out of the saddlebag, he held the mysterious padded envelope for an extra second, then decided to let the curiosity tickle his belly a little more. Oscar McCarron got few surprises in his life these days.

He rolled up the advertising flyers and junk mail and placed them under the chopped mesquite wood, then lit the fire with a single match, as he usually did. The twigs were so dry they practically ignited themselves.

McCarron unrolled his blanket and thin sleeping bag, then got out the cooking utensils. Looking up into the sky, he watched a shower of stars spray across the deepening darkness, the swarms of bright lights twinkling with a diamond richness that city dwellers never saw in their light-polluted skies.

As the resinous flames blazed bright and hot, McCarron finally sat back on his favorite rock, took the padded envelope, and tore it open. He dumped the contents into his callused palm.

"What the hell?" he said, disappointed after his hours of anticipation.

He found only a scrap of paper and a small glassine envelope filled with a powdery residue, some sort of greasy black ash that squished in his fingers as he pressed the envelope. A scrap of paper also fell out, displaying a message inked in precise razor-edged letters.

"FOR YOUR PART IN THE PAST."

No signature, no date, no address.

"What the hell?" he said again. "For my part in the past of what?"

He cussed at the horse, as if the palomino might somehow be able to give him an answer. The only thing of significance Oscar McCarron could think of having done in his entire lifetime had been an accident, a coincidence of fate—having owned the land on which the Trinity Test had taken place.

He did feel deeply proud of that part in his country's history, helping to spark the beginning of a nuclear age that had ended World War II and prevented those bloodthirsty Japanese from conquering half the world. That single successful atomic test had, in effect, begun the Cold War, leading to the development of more powerful superweapons that had kept the Commies in check. Sure, Oscar McCarron had been proud of his part in all that . . . but it wasn't as if he had actually *done* anything.

What else could the mysterious message mean?

"Some crazy nutcase," he muttered. With a rude noise, he tossed the note and the package of ash into the crackling mesquite fire.

He unbuckled his food pack and pulled out a can of chili, which he opened with a handheld can opener. He dumped it into a pot, which he hung from a tripod above the flames. He took out his special treasure, plastic zipper-lock bags of jalapeños and fresh-roasted Hatch green chilis, which he added to the mix to give the bland, commercialized recipe a little more bite.

As the food simmered, he listened to the utter quiet, the absence of birds or bats or insects. Just the desert silence, an opaque stillness that allowed him to hear himself breathe, hear the pulse in his ears, hear his own thoughts without being disturbed by a chatter of background noises. He let his eyes fall closed as he inhaled deeply of the stinging spices in the sizzling chili.

The palomino snorted and whinnied, breaking the silence.

"Awww, shut up," McCarron said, but the mare blew loudly through her nostrils again, stomping from side to side as if afraid of something. She tossed her head, sniffing and snorting.

"What is it?" he asked, slowly rising to his feet on creaking old knees. The horse acted as if she had scented a cougar or a bear, but McCarron knew that was ridiculous. Nothing larger than a few lizards, rattlesnakes, and kangaroo rats could survive out here in the Jornada del Muerto Desert.

Then he heard the voices, whispering, like a wind of words in a foreign language, a chant, drumbeats, building to a scream. The hissing white background noise reminded him of the harsh static he heard when his TV was turned up too loud and the videotape ran out.

"What the hell is it?" he said. "What's out there?"

McCarron stood and went to his saddle to pull out his rifle. The wind picked up, and he felt a hot breeze against his leathery cheeks—much hotter than the desert night. A dust storm? Brush fire?

The palomino thrashed back and forth, straining against the rope. Her eyes rolled, wild and white. The mare reared and then leaped sideways, crashing into the rough lava as if pinned to the walls of the shallow depression.

"Easy, girl! Easy!" McCarron turned to see a smear of blood on the rock from where the horse had scraped her flanks raw. But he didn't take the time to soothe his horse.

He waved the rifle's barrel back and forth into the buzzing, roaring night air. Somebody, or something, had to be out there.

"If you think you're gonna mess with me, you got another think coming!" he shouted. His eyes watered, stinging. He fired a shot into the air, a warning, but the crack of the rifle vanished in the rising, howling noise.

The desert air seared his mouth like a blast from the hottest oven, parching his throat, burning his teeth. He backed away. The horse squealed in terror, a bizarre animal insanity that frightened the old man more than his own confused senses possibly could.

Suddenly the night around McCarron exploded as the angry presence behind those voices, behind the whispers and screams and the sudden heat, surged into the depression, as if someone had dropped a miniature sun right into his lap.

Oscar McCarron's world filled with an intolerable burst of atomic fire.

THIRTEEN

Trinity Site, near Alamogordo, New Mexico
Friday, 11:18 A.M.

 Scully took her shift driving south from
Albuquerque across the flat, dry south-
ern half of New Mexico. The air-conditioning in the rental Ford Taurus began
to complain as she drove up a steep
grade and then began the long descent
into the deeper desert.

Beside her in the passenger seat Mulder folded
and unfolded his copy of the faxed Unusual
Occurrence Report that DOE representative
Rosabeth Carrera had given him early that morning.

"Thought you might find this of interest, Agent
Mulder," the dark-haired woman had said, pointing
to the brief description that had come to her office
on a standard distribution list from the Department
of Energy headquarters. "The DOE requires that certain people be notified of unusual accidents relating
to radiation. I'm one of those people—and this incident certainly qualifies."

Scully had taken the sheet from her partner, scanning the description of yet another mysteriously burned body, presumably washed by a flood of radioactive fire. This one had occurred far from the Teller Nuclear Research Facility, out in the White Sands Missile Range, near a barren memorial that Scully knew of all too well—the Trinity Site, the location of the first test of an atomic explosion back in July 1945.

"But how can this incident be relevant to Dr. Gregory's death?" Scully had asked. "The victim was an old rancher, with no connection to current nuclear weapons research."

Rosabeth Carrera simply shrugged. "Look at the details. How could it *not* be related? These sorts of deaths don't occur every day."

Mulder had eagerly taken back the Unusual Occurrence Report, rereading the summary. "I want to check it out, Scully. This could be the lead we've been looking for. Two clues instead of one."

Scully sighed and agreed. "The very fact that they seem so unrelated could be the break we need . . . once we figure it out."

And so they had raced to the Oakland airport, hopped a Delta flight to Salt Lake City, and then down to Albuquerque, where they had rented a car for the long drive south.

Scully kept the car at ten miles over the speed limit, but the traffic still roared by in the fast lane. She gripped the steering wheel more tightly as a large three-trailered semi truck exploded past.

Scully ran ideas by her partner as she drove. "Mulder, so far our working theory is that a weapons test went wrong in Dr. Gregory's lab, or possibly that a protester engaged in some sabotage that led to his death. I don't see how any of that fits with a dead rancher out on a deserted missile range."

Mulder folded the Unusual Occurrence Report and stuck it in the pocket of his jacket. "Maybe we're not thinking big enough, Scully. Maybe there's a broader connection, an overall relationship to nuclear weapons. Missile range . . . nuclear research lab . . ."

"You may as well include the whole government, Mulder," she said.

"At least it gives us plenty of room to maneuver," he said.

After a brief moment of silence, Mulder narrowed his eyes and looked at Scully. "We'll know more when we get there, I hope. I made a call back to Headquarters while we were at the airport. I'm expecting the people at White Sands to have some information faxed to them, a broader ID check on Oscar McCarron. We'll see just how disconnected he is from Dr. Gregory. It might be something really obvious."

Scully returned her attention to the road unreeling ahead of her. "All right, we'll see."

They decided to table further discussion until they actually arrived at the site where the old rancher's burned body had been found.

Mulder fidgeted, trying to avoid the heat that baked through the windows. "Next time let's find out if the car has black seats before we sign the rental papers," he suggested.

"I agree." As Scully drove, letting the speedometer top seventy-five, then eighty, she recalled that New Mexico with its desert highways had traditionally been the first state in the country to raise its speed limits, to the cheering of the state's residents.

They passed signs on the highway that read, "NOTICE! DO NOT PICK UP HITCHHIKERS. PRISON FACILITIES NEARBY."

"Charming place," said Mulder.

The Ford Taurus reached a small town past Socorro, called San Antonio, where they turned east, heading deeper into the Jornada del Muerto—the aptly named "Journey of Death" desert. At Stallion Gate, the northern entrance to the White Sands Missile Range, they stopped at a guard checkpoint and flashed their papers. A military escort came out to meet them, and then waved them through onto the bleak missile test site.

Scully shaded her eyes and looked at the uninviting landscape—like the corpse of a once fertile land. She had seen the place in photos, but had never made it down to visit.

"These gates are opened once a year," she said, "so that tourists and pilgrims can go out to the actual Trinity Site and see what's left of the McDonald Ranch. That's ten miles deeper into the missile range, if I remember correctly. Not much to see, just a cairn of stones and a commemorative plaque."

"Just what I want to do on my summer vacation," Mulder said. "Go out and stand right on Ground Zero."

Scully kept her silence. She didn't think her partner knew about her peripheral involvement in protest activities in the past, and she preferred to keep that bit of her life private. It made her uncomfortable, though. She had always shared so much with Mulder. This uneasiness felt foreign to her, and she tried to identify her feelings. Embarrassment? she wondered. Or guilt? She drew a deep breath. They had a job to do here.

Two military policemen pulled up in a Jeep. Scully and Mulder reluctantly left the air-conditioning of their Taurus and climbed down to meet the MPs. Neither of them was dressed properly for driving across the dusty gypsum sands, but the MPs didn't seem to notice. They motioned for the two FBI agents to join them. Mulder secured their briefcases under the seat, then helped Scully climb into the back of the vehicle.

The two of them sat on hot seats in the jouncing vehicle, holding on for dear life as the Jeep roared across the rutted flatlands, oblivious to the lack of any road. The MPs tightened their helmets and gritted their teeth against the flying dust.

They arrived at a bowl-shaped depression where a dozen other MPs and Air Force officers stood at a cordoned-off site. Someone wearing anti-contamination clothes and carrying a handheld Geiger counter had stepped deeper into the blockaded area, inspecting the site.

Scully got out, ignoring the pain in her stiff legs. She felt dread build within her. Mulder walked silently beside her as they came to the edge of a depression bordered by dark volcanic rock.

It looked as if the entire hollow had been melted.

She and Mulder introduced themselves. A colonel waiting there had expected them. He handed Mulder a drooping sheet of thermal fax paper. "This came from your Bureau Headquarters, Agent Mulder," he said, "but I could have told you that information. We know all about old Oscar. That's how we found him there."

"So tell me," Mulder said, raising his eyebrows hopefully. "We need every detail you can give us."

"That rancher is an old fart who's come out here practically every week since before the Red Sea parted. He and his father originally owned the ranch land around here that was deeded to the Trinity Site—for the test, you know—but because of some wartime secrecy act, the names were changed on the paperwork so it couldn't be discovered who had originally owned the land. I guess they were afraid of crazy protesters even back then, or maybe Nazi spies." The colonel nodded down toward the blasted bowl. "And maybe they had good cause, considering what's happened."

Scully couldn't tear her eyes from the scene. The gypsum sand had been roasted by such extreme heat that it had become like a pottery glaze, turning into hardened glass with a greenish, jadelike consistency.

"Trinitite," she said.

"What's that?" Mulder asked.

She nodded toward the glassy fusion that lined the sands. "I'll bet we'll find out that glassy sand and rock is Trinitite. Around Ground Zero during the Trinity Test the heat was intense enough to fuse the surrounding sand into a glasslike solid. Very unusual. People even collected the stuff."

"Come on, we can go closer," the colonel said. "You'll want to take a look if you're to get any information from this."

"Thank you for your cooperation, Colonel," Scully said.

The gaunt, sunburned man turned to her. "We sure don't want to have to solve this one, Agent Scully. You're welcome to it."

She followed the colonel past the cordon, and down toward the flash-burned sands. Against one rock wall they could see the sprawling bowl glittering in the sunlight where the gypsum had turned molten.

Fused into the ground by the intense heat were the blackened remains of two burned figures, a nearly disintegrated man, and a horse, flattened and incinerated, pushed into the melted sands. The hardened glass had frozen the corpses into an eerie tableau, like tortured insects in amber.

Mulder shuddered and turned away from the

crisped horror of the victim's face. He grasped Scully's arm briefly for support. "I really hate fire," he muttered.

"I know, Mulder," she said. She didn't tell him how much she herself hated the threat of radiation and fallout. "I don't think we should stay here any longer than we have to."

As she turned away, all she could think of were the hideously burned corpses, the photographs of Nagasaki victims at the Stop Nuclear Madness! museum in Berkeley.

How could it be happening again, here?

FOURTEEN

 Before reaching the interstate on their trip back to Albuquerque, Scully and Mulder decided to stop at the "Historic" Owl Cafe, a rusty-tan adobe building that looked like an abandoned movie set. The large building seemed the only thing of note in the entire city of San Antonio, New Mexico. The gravel parking lot hosted four battered and dirty pickup trucks, two Harley-Davidsons parked side by side, and an old-model Ford station wagon.

"Let's risk it, Scully," Mulder said. "We've got to grab lunch anyway. It's a long drive north."

Scully folded the highway map and climbed out of the car into the sweltering heat. She shaded her eyes. "I wish at least one other city in this state had a major airport," she said. She followed Mulder to a big glass door encrusted with road dust. He held it open for her, and she noted from the sticker on the glass that the restaurant was AAA approved.

Inside, the place was a dim and noisy dive, just the type of place she generally avoided. Mulder adored it. "Come on, Scully," he said. "It's *historic*. Read the sign."

"Wait," she said. "I think I've even heard of this place before. Something to do with the Manhattan Project or the Trinity Test."

"Then we've stopped at the right place," Mulder said. "Our hamburgers will be work-related."

Shadowy figures hunched over the counter: ranchers who had not deigned to take off their wide cowboy hats, a few truckers wearing old baseball caps, and a tourist or two. Someone played pinball in the far corner. Neon signs for various brands of low-end beer flickered over the bar and in the dining area.

"Looks like genuine Naugahyde seats," Mulder said. "This place is great."

"You *would* think so, Mulder."

A big Navajo man with long gray-black hair tied in a ponytail came around the corner to the cash register. He wore jeans, a checked cotton shirt with mother-of-pearl snaps, and a turquoise bolo tie. "Take any seat," he said, gesturing to the array of empty booths like an ambassador welcoming them into his kingdom. He went back to wiping down the Formica counter where others were eating and swapping loud unbelievable stories.

The walls of the Owl Cafe were dotted with posters, framed photographs of White Sands experimental missile launches, along with official-looking certificates of participation in Nuclear Emergency Search Team exercises. Photographic prints of mushroom clouds from desert detonations hung framed on the paneled walls, while smaller reprints were available for sale in the small glass display case near the old cash register . . . as were glassy jade-green rocks—Trinitite.

"I'd like to look around, Mulder," Scully said. "Might be some interesting stuff here."

"Let me just grab us a seat," he said, "and I'll order for us."

"I don't know if I should trust you to do that," she said.

He waved good-naturedly at her. "Have I ever been wrong?" He disappeared deeper into the dim labyrinth of Naugahyde booths before she could give him an honest answer.

She waited by the display case beneath the cash register and picked up a small mimeographed brochure showing a grainy photo of the Owl Cafe. The poorly written text described the restaurant's claims to fame. She scanned the words, refreshing her memory—and it all came back to her from when she had obsessively studied the Cold War and the arms race and the beginnings of the U.S. nuclear program.

In the days before air-conditioned cars, the Owl Cafe had been an unofficial stopping place for Manhattan Project scientists and engineers during their frequent long drives from the northern mountains at Los Alamos down to the Trinity Test Site. They had no interstate highways, only state roads, and the trip must have been gruesome in the heat of summer in 1945.

Technically, the crews were not allowed to stop along the way. They were ordered by the military to drive straight through. But the Owl Cafe, isolated at a desert crossroads out in the middle of nowhere, was ideal for the small automobile convoys to stop at before heading east into even more murderous terrain. The crew couldn't help but want lunch or a cold drink before heading out to the restricted land area the government had set aside for the first atomic bomb blast.

The big Navajo saw Scully standing by the display case and came over, speaking in a rich deep voice. "What can I get for you?"

Startled, Scully looked down and pointed to the selection of small rocks. "I'd like one of those pieces of Trinitite, please."

"That five-dollar one?" Without another word the broad-shouldered man pulled out a little key and opened the rear of the display case, removing one of the smallish rocks. After a pause, he set it back down on the shelf, selecting a larger sample instead. "Here, take this one," he said. "They're all overpriced anyway."

Scully took the glassy lump and squeezed it in the palm of her hand, trying to imagine the hellish fury that had created it—not any geologic process deep in the core of the earth, but a man-made inferno that had lasted only a few seconds. The stone was cool and slick on her palm; any tingle she felt came strictly from her imagination.

Scully paid for the rock and wandered over to the other exhibits.

An old bottle collection covered half of one wall. Brown glass, green glass, clear glass, even a few bright blue bottles, were all on display without identifying tags—except for a single typewritten sheet of paper, yellowed with age, tacked to the wall.

The bottle collection had been there since before World War II, the prized possession of another old Navajo who had originally owned the Owl Cafe. The former owner knew nothing of the secret nuclear project or the impending test, although he couldn't help but notice the official government vehicles, military brass, and the suit-and-tie engineers who could never disguise themselves as local ranchers or reservation Navajos.

In fact, Scully thought, the Manhattan Project

engineers must have looked as out of place as she and Mulder did this afternoon. She continued reading.

Several days before the actual test explosion in July 1945, one of the engineers, a regular—if unofficial—customer at the Owl Cafe, had tipped off the old owner. He gave no classified details, said only that it might be wise to take down the fragile bottles for a few days. The skeptical Navajo owner had complied . . . and thus the bottle collection had been saved when the Trinity blast had rattled walls as far away as Silver City and Gallup, nearly two hundred miles distant. The name of the considerate Manhattan Project engineer was not mentioned, no doubt to keep the man from getting into trouble.

Taking her Trinitite souvenir, Scully wandered back into the dining room in search of Mulder. He was slumped back comfortably on the Naugahyde seat as he reread the fax he had received out at the White Sands testing range. He sipped iced tea from a red plastic cup.

Scully slid into the padded seat across from him and saw that he had ordered her an ice tea as well. She set the lump of glassy rock on the Formica table in front of him. He picked it up, turning it over in his hand with curiosity.

"You once called me a sucker for buying souvenirs at a tourist-trap cafe like this one."

"This is different," she said.

"Of course." He gave her a wry smile.

"It *is*. That's Trinitite," she said, "the stuff I was telling you about."

He studied it under the dim light cast by a flickering Coors sign. "Looks just like the stuff out at the death site."

She nodded.

The waitress interrupted by bringing their meals. She gave each of them a basket of sizzling french fries and an enormous burger so juicy it had to be wrapped in paper to catch the grease.

"You're gonna love this, Scully," he said. "The house specialty, a green chili cheeseburger." Mulder held his up, took a big bite, and spoke around a dripping mouthful. "Delicious! They grind their own meat here, and the green chilis really enhance the flavor. You can't get this stuff in Washington, D.C."

"I'm not sure I'd want to," Scully said, picking up her own huge burger. She inspected it to determine the best method of attack, making sure she had plenty of napkins within easy reach. Despite her skepticism, though, she found the meal absolutely delicious, the bite of green chilis unlike anything she had ever expected.

"So, Scully," he said, finally getting down to business, "let's see what we can come up with. We now have two bodies—three, if you count the horse—killed by a sudden flash of heat like a miniature atomic explosion. One in an isolated weapons lab office, and another out here in the middle of the desert."

Scully held up one finger, saw that some ketchup had run down to her knuckle, and plucked up a napkin to wipe it clean. "The laboratory death site was being used by a nuclear weapons researcher developing a secret and intense new atomic device, and the second death occurred out in the White Sands Missile Range, where the military might be expected to test such a device. Could be a connection."

"Ah," Mulder pointed out, "but Dr. Gregory's office was not an engineering and experimental lab. In fact, it wasn't much more than a room full of computers. You wouldn't find a nuclear warhead stashed in his file cabinet drawer. And, if the military intended to test this Bright Anvil device, why do it out at White Sands? The government already has a perfect nuclear testing site in Nevada. It's official and everything, with all the security they could ask for. Besides, did you get the impression that the colonel at White Sands *expected* this?"

Scully had to admit he was right. "No, he didn't seem at all prepared to deal with the situation."

Mulder wiped his mouth with napkin. "I think we should look for a broader connection—and it might not have anything at all to do with Bright Anvil."

"If not Bright Anvil, then what do you have in mind?"

Mulder finished the last bite of his cheeseburger, then set to work on his remaining fries. "Emil Gregory and Oscar McCarron had a few obscure connections dating all the way back to World War II. Oscar McCarron was an old rancher who had probably never set foot out of New Mexico in his entire life. Dr. Gregory was also from New Mexico. He worked on the Manhattan Project more than fifty years ago, then spent time at Los Alamos before coming to the San Francisco area to work for the Teller Nuclear Research Facility."

"So what are you suggesting, Mulder?"

He shrugged. "It's only a shot in the dark, and I'm not sure I've come up with anything yet. Just thinking that maybe we should use our imaginations a little, consider alternative possibilities. What else could those two men have in common? We know Gregory worked on the Trinity Test, and McCarron's family owned the land where the test took place."

Scully picked up a french fry and ate it quickly. "Mulder, sometimes your imagination is far too active."

He pointed to himself, miming *Moi?* "And how often are my alternative solutions proven to be correct, Scully?"

Scully ate another fry. "That all depends on who you ask."

Mulder sighed. "Scully, you're an impossible skeptic sometimes—but I like you anyway."

She rewarded him with a smile. "Somebody's got to keep you in line."

Wiping his hands on another napkin, Mulder pulled out their map of New Mexico. "I wonder how far Roswell is from here?" he said. "It might be worth a side trip."

"Absolutely not," Scully said. "We've got a plane to catch."

He looked at her with a *Gotcha!* expression to show that he hadn't been serious. "Just thought I'd ask."

FIFTEEN

 Sitting at his impeccably neat and carefully arranged desk in the high-rise office building, four floors of which were devoted to his own imports company, Ryan Kamida carefully addressed a padded envelope.

His calligraphic pen moved in precise strokes, and the letters came out perfectly, the wet black ink like scorched blood.

Expansive windows covered two walls of his corner office, offering a panoramic view of Oahu. But Kamida kept the mini-blinds half-closed most of the time. He dearly loved feeling the gentle warmth of the sun, letting its heat bathe his scarred skin, soothing, caressing his body, as it had in the barely remembered idyllic days on an isolated Pacific island.

But too much bright sunshine felt like fire to him. It reminded him of that other blaze from the

116

sky, the searing flash so intense that it had set the air molecules themselves on fire.

Kamida's snow-white hair lay neatly on his head, thick and perfectly maintained. Because of the almost supernatural good fortune he had experienced during his adult life, Kamida had plenty of money for things like that: clothes, grooming, possessions.

But his money couldn't buy everything. He didn't *want* everything.

His lumpy, wax-textured hands gripped the polished pen as if it were a weapon—and in a sense, it was. The words resounded in his head. He filled out the address in a careful, perfect script, feeling for the right spot on the padded envelope. He could sense the accuracy of his letters.

Satisfied, Kamida rested the pen in the familiar groove on his desk next to the ink reservoir. Then he reached out to hold the special envelope, feeling its edges, the sharp corners. He took it on faith that he had filled out the address correctly. He would never ask anyone else to double-check it, though he could not see it himself.

Ryan Kamida was completely blind.

The list in his mind grew shorter and shorter with each package sent, each target identified. Kamida had the names of those responsible etched clearly in his well-honed memory.

As he sat at his desk with the warm Hawaiian sun suffusing around him through the mini-blinds, letting him feel its kind touch, he felt very alone—though he knew he had asked for this. He had sent all the workers on this floor home for the afternoon. They had objected, pointing out the work they had to do, shipping records, finders' fees, sales commissions. Kamida simply offered them time-and-a-half pay, and they went home satisfied. They were well accustomed to his eccentricities.

He now had the offices to himself to do his important work.

No doubt to assuage its unacknowledged pangs of guilt, the government had assisted Ryan Kamida through the years, sometimes offering veiled handouts, at other times blatantly approving his bids and choosing him over his competitors. He was a handicapped businessman, an ethnic minority—though here in Hawaii being a Pacific Islander was hardly remarkable. Between the Japanese tourists and the Pacific Islanders who made their homes here, middle-class Caucasian families were the true minorities.

Kamida had used every resource at his disposal to help his company succeed. His business specialized in exotic imports from little-known Pacific islands—Elugelab, Truk, Johnston Atoll, the entire Marshall chain—impressing tourists with trinkets that came from faraway places with interesting names.

He needed the money to accomplish his true mission.

Kamida fingered the envelope, stuffed the hand-written note and a small glass vial inside, then sealed it. That simple act of closure brought a shudder of relief to him, but it lasted only a moment.

No matter how many such packages he sent, no matter how many of the guilty he identified, he could never make up for the loss of his people. It had been a completely successful genocide, more thorough than anything Adolf Hitler had accomplished. In a single stroke Ryan Kamida's family, his relatives, his tribe . . . his *island* had vanished in a surge of light and flames. A small boy was the sole survivor.

But Kamida did not consider his survival to be either a miracle or a blessing. He had been given an entire lifetime to endure the memory of those few seconds, while for all the others it had been over in an instant.

Or so he had thought.

The voices in his head had not stopped screaming since that day when he was ten years old.

Setting the envelope aside, Kamida sniffed the stuffy air in his office. He tilted his burned face and blank white eyes toward the ceiling. He couldn't see, but he could feel, could sense the gathering storm.

A seething sea of white-hot luminescence boiled in a suspended pool against the acoustic tiles, like froth in a pot, swirling with spectral screaming faces. Though blind, he *knew* they were there. They wouldn't leave him alone.

The ghosts of his incinerated people grew more and more restless. They would strike out at their own targets if he refused to offer them a victim of his own choosing. The ghosts had waited so long, and Ryan Kamida could no longer keep them under control.

Walking with the grace and confidence of a sighted man through the familiar offices, he picked up the hand-addressed envelope and left his room, taking it to the mail drop, from which the package would be rushed to an airplane and shipped to the United States. He deemed the expense of overnight mail delivery across the Pacific insignificant. The envelope would be delivered to a particular low-profile but very important official at the Department of Energy headquarters near Washington, D.C.

It was probably already too late to stop Bright Anvil, Kamida supposed, but perhaps this would be enough to prevent the nightmare from occurring again.

SIXTEEN

 After an uneventful weekend—for once—Mulder drove back to the Teller Nuclear Research Facility, whistling "California Dreaming." Scully pretended to heave a long-suffering sigh, as if to say that since he was her partner, she would put up with his odd sense of humor. Mulder smiled at her in appreciation of her tolerance.

The condition of the old rancher's body at the Trinity Site had been so unmistakably similar to that of Dr. Emil Gregory that Scully couldn't discount some sort of connection. But they had come back to the San Francisco-area nuclear weapons laboratory with more questions than before.

They stopped at the guard gate, flashing visitor's badges and FBI credentials. They needed to talk to the rest of Dr. Gregory's Bright Anvil team— deputy project head Bear Dooley and the other researchers and engineers. Scully still insisted there must be some technical explanation for the deaths, a test of a small yet powerful nuclear device, something that had backfired on Dr. Gregory, something that had been tested out in New Mexico.

That didn't ring true, though, to Mulder. He thought there must be some reason they hadn't considered yet, though Scully would hold onto her explanations until she found a better, more logical one.

After they passed through the guard gate, Mulder reached over to unfold the map of the Teller Facility. He traced the access roads with his finger to find the main lab building where Dr. Gregory had died and the temporary barracks offices to which Bear Dooley and the other team members had been relocated.

"Now that you've found out some details about Bright Anvil through, uh . . . " Mulder raised his eyebrows, "shall we say, 'unofficial means,' let's see what Mr. Dooley has to say for himself. Solid information is our best weapon."

"I just wish we had the information to solve this case," Scully said.

"If wishes were horses . . . " Mulder began.

Scully shuddered, thinking of the equine corpse at the White Sands Missile Range. "I withdraw the comment."

They arrived at the converted barracks building and left their car in a Government Vehicle Only parking space. This time, Mulder knew to take a paper respirator mask to protect himself from wild asbestos fibers floating in the air. Handing another mask to Scully, he helped her fasten it over her hair. He carefully scrutinized his partner's new appearance.

"It's a fashion statement," he said. "I like it."

"First dosimeters and now breathing masks," Scully said. "This place is a health nut's paradise."

Down the corridor the construction workers had moved the translucent plastic barrier curtains after demolishing another entire section of the wall. A loud generator roared, maintaining negative air pressure in the enclosed work area, supposedly to prevent the lightweight asbestos fibers from drifting past the barricade.

"Down here," Mulder said, turning right and motioning for Scully to follow. "Bear Dooley's new office makes my basement at Bureau Headquarters look like Club Med."

When they reached Dooley's temporary office, the door stood wide open, despite the racket of crowbars and the generator and shouts from the workmen.

"Excuse me—Mr. Dooley?" Mulder called. "I don't know how you can work in this environment."

But when Mulder popped his head inside, the office appeared abandoned. The desk had been cleared, the file drawers taped shut. Framed photos were still stacked in cardboard boxes and various office paraphernalia lay scattered in disarray, as if someone had packed up frantically, leaving unnecessary items behind. Mulder pursed his lips and glanced around.

"Looks like nobody's home," Scully said.

Suddenly a young redheaded man entered the office. With his glasses, plaid shirt, and pocket stuffed full of pens, he looked like a poster boy for the "nerd's dress code." His badge identified him as Victor Ogilvy. Mulder couldn't tell if the young man was smiling or frowning behind his white breathing mask.

"Are you the Department of Defense people?" Ogilvy asked quickly. "We've got the preliminary reports ready, but nothing else I can deliver to you just yet."

"We're looking for Mr. Bear Dooley," Mulder said. "Can you tell us where he is?"

Behind his round eyeglasses, Victor Ogilvy blinked rapidly. "Well, that was in the initial briefing. I'm sure of it. He left for San Diego last Thursday morning. The *Dallas* should arrive at the atoll in another day or two. The rest of us are getting all packed up to be flown out."

"Flown out to where?" Mulder asked.

The question took Ogilvy entirely by surprise. "What do you mean? Are you sure you're from the Department of Defense?"

Scully stepped forward. "We never said we were, Mister Ogilvy." She flipped out her badge and ID. "Federal agents. I'm Special Agent Dana Scully, and this is my partner Agent Mulder. We need to ask you a few questions about Bright Anvil and the death of Dr. Gregory . . . and this test that's taking place out on an atoll in the Pacific," she said.

Mulder was amazed at how quickly and easily she had put together the details into a rapid, professional-sounding string of inquiries.

Ogilvy's eyes bulged out so far that they practically bumped the lenses of his glasses. He stumbled over his words. "I . . . I don't think I should say any more," he said. "It's classified."

Mulder noted how intimidated the young man was and decided to press his advantage. "Didn't you hear what Agent Scully said? We're with the *FBI*." He said the words with dire import. "You have to answer our questions."

"But I could lose my clearance," Ogilvy said.

Mulder shrugged. "One way or the other. Would you like me to start quoting you FBI statutes? How about this one: if you refuse to cooperate with our ongoing investigation, I just might cite you under Statute 43H of the FBI Code."

Scully quickly squeezed his arm. "Mulder!"

He shook his head. "Let me handle this, Scully. Victor here doesn't know what kind of trouble he could get himself into."

"I . . . " Victor Ogilvy said, "I think you should talk to our Department of Energy representative. She's authorized to answer those types of questions. If she gives me the go-ahead, then I can respond. You'll have no cause to cite me. Honest!"

Mulder sighed. He had just lost this round. "Well, get her on the phone so we can talk to her."

Ogilvy rummaged around Bear Dooley's abandoned desk until he found a Teller Nuclear Research Facility phone listing. He nervously paged through it, then punched in the number for Rosabeth Carrera.

Scully leaned over and whispered in his ear. "Statute 43H?"

"Unauthorized Use of the Smoky the Bear Symbol," Mulder mumbled, smiling sheepishly. "But he doesn't know that."

Within moments Rosabeth Carrera was on the phone. Her voice started out rich and sweet, its Hispanic undertones mostly hidden. She sounded polite, helpful. "Good morning, Agent Mulder. I didn't know you had returned from New Mexico."

"Seems like a lot has happened over the weekend," he said. "Most of Dr. Gregory's team has disappeared, and we can't get any answers on what's happened to them. Since they are quite clearly involved in this case, we'll need to interview them further—especially now that we've uncovered a clear connection between Dr. Emil Gregory and the other victim at White Sands."

Scully's eyebrows shot up. Mulder was overstating his case, but Carrera had no way of knowing it.

"Agent Mulder," Carrera said, her voice a bit

crisper now, "Dr. Gregory was working on a very important project for this laboratory and for the United States government. Such projects have milestones and schedules and a great deal of momentum behind them. People in very high political circles have a lot at stake in seeing that the research continues as planned. I'm afraid we can't call our scientists back on a whim."

"This is no whim, Ms. Carrera," Mulder said, growing more formal. "Your main researcher is dead under highly suspicious circumstances, and now another victim has turned up at the White Sands Missile Range, killed by the same means. I think that's ample reason for proceeding with caution and asking a few more questions before moving on to the next stage. I'd like you to postpone this Bright Anvil test."

"Bright Anvil? No such test has been announced," Carrera answered.

"Let's not play games," he said. "It wastes valuable telephone time."

"I'm afraid that's impossible," Carrera said dismissively. "Dr. Gregory's work will go on, as planned."

Mulder took the challenge. "I can make some calls to Bureau Headquarters, and I've got a few connections in the Department of Defense."

Carrera's tone was brisk, almost abrupt. "Make whatever phone calls you feel you have to, Agent Mulder. But Dr. Gregory's test will take place as scheduled. No question about it. The government has many priorities, and I have no doubt that you will find that your murder investigation is rather far down the list compared to the national interests that are at stake."

After he hung up, Scully said, "From the look on your face, I take it Rosabeth Carrera didn't bend over backward to offer you her assistance."

Mulder sighed. "I've had more helpful conversations."

Victor Ogilvy hovered nervously by the door. "Does that mean I don't have to answer your questions?"

Mulder shot him a quick glare. "Depends on how badly you want to be on my Christmas card list."

The young redhead quickly ducked out of sight.

Scully put her hands on her hips and turned to face Mulder. "Well then, I guess it's my turn to ferret out some details," she said. "Time to check my other source of information."

SEVENTEEN

 Scully returned to the headquarters of the Berkeley antinuclear protest group, but when she trudged down the half-flight of stairs to the bomb-shelter basement, she found the temporary offices in the sort of chaos that might be expected at a fly-by-night business suddenly afraid of a bust.

A group of student volunteers busied themselves removing the posters of Nagasaki victims from the walls, the poignant photographs of homeless Bikini Islanders, the long listing of aboveground atomic bomb tests, and the colorful graphs showing cancer statistics.

Scully stepped through the door and stared at all the movement, the confusion, the shouting. Behind the fabric room dividers, the exhausted photocopier still whirred, working overtime.

Standing on a stepstool, the receptionist, Becka

Thorne, yanked push pins from the wall to release the draped, dot-matrix banner that warned against a second nuclear war. The black woman turned, her dress an even more dizzying riot of colors than her previous voluminous wrap had been, her hair still clumped together in its lumpy, tentacular dreadlocks.

"I'm looking for Miriel Bremen again," Scully shouted into the chaos. "Is she here?"

Becka undid a last push pin, and half of the paper banner drooped to the floor like a falling streamer of fireworks. She climbed down off the stepstool and wiped her hands on her colorful dress. "You're that FBI lady, right? Well, Miriel's not here. As you can see we're shutting down the office. No more Stop Nuclear Madness!"

"You're shutting down the office?" Scully asked. "Are you moving to a new location?"

"No. Miriel just up and pulled our lease. We only had a month left in it anyway, but she handed it over to the next group coming in. These office spaces on campus are in great demand, you know."

Scully tried to understand. "Did your organization lose its funding unexpectedly?"

Becka laughed. "Not in the least. We were probably the healthiest group Berkeley has seen in five years, lots of money dumped in from some corporation in Hawaii. But Miriel just pulled the plug and told us to call the next group on the waiting list. Said she had a change of heart, or something. Guess she became 'born again' again, but in another direction this time."

"What's moving in here now?" Scully asked, still taken aback by the protester's sudden disappearance. What could have driven Miriel Bremen to give up the work that had so ignited her passions that she would jettison her career and her security clearance, leaving a blot on her employment record that would haunt her for the rest of her working days.

Becka Thorne gestured to the other volunteer workers. "It's an environmental activist group," she said. "I can show you some of their posters—very disturbing. They're calling attention to increasing levels of environmental pollutants in our groundwater, how toxic chemicals are seeping into every part of our daily lives and causing an avalanche of health problems."

The receptionist flipped through several large foam-core posters, some with tables that listed organic and toxic chemicals discovered in a sample of everyday tap water. Scully recognized many of the organic substances, but others seemed like the ingredients from a chemistry set. Some of the listed concentrations gave Scully cause for concern, and she wondered if their "random" analysis was reproducible.

She flipped to another chart that showed cancer statistics rising year after year—only this time they were blamed on toxic pollutants in the groundwater. The graph looked identical to the one used by Stop Nuclear Madness! that had connected the same increase in cancer to background radiation from nuclear tests in the 1950s.

One of the student workers slid the stepstool to the other side of the wall with a loud rattling sound, then climbed up to pluck the remaining push pins. The entire paper banner fell rustling to the floor.

"So what will you do with yourself now, Ms. Thorne?" Scully asked. "Does your group give you a reference to find a job someplace else?"

Becka Thorne blinked at Scully with her huge brown eyes. "No, I'll just work for the new group. I follow the protesters. Whatever cause they've got is fine with me. They're all interesting. And everybody's got a point, as far as I can see. Can't trust anybody these days, you know—especially not the government. Uh, no offense to you."

Scully smiled. "I think my partner might agree with you."

Becka Thorne gave a quick smile, then wiped the perspiration off her forehead. "Well, send your partner down here then. We always need new recruits for our work."

Scully had to keep herself from laughing. "I think he's too preoccupied for that—on this case, for instance." She finally succeeded in getting back to the point. "We really need to talk to Miriel Bremen. Do you know how we can get in touch with her?"

The receptionist looked at Scully carefully. "She didn't leave a phone number, if that's what you're after—but mostly likely she's gone to the islands, or something. When her conscience gets too bad, she sometimes goes off on these pilgrimages. She even went to Nagasaki once, another time to Pearl Harbor. Who knows where else? She's a pretty private person, our Miriel."

Scully furrowed her brow. "So she's somewhere in 'the islands,' but you have no idea where she might have gone? Jamaica? Tahiti? New Zealand?"

Becka shrugged. "Look, Miss FBI—Miriel was in one hell of a hurry to get out of here. Came in last Friday afternoon and told us we were done—done. Just like that. She was turning over the lease, and the rest of us were on our own.

"Oh, she thanked us for our efforts and told us to use her as a reference if we ever needed it—as if a big company would pay the slightest bit of attention to a reference from someone like Miriel Bremen! She's just lucky most of us have our own connections with the protest groups around here. We're not going to starve."

Scully handed Becka a business card. "If you learn where she is, Ms. Thorne, or if you get in touch with her, have her call me at this number. I think she'll be willing to talk to me."

"If you say so," the receptionist said. "We need to get back to work now. The environmental group wants to hold a rally this Saturday, and they've got flyers to go up on all the kiosks and light posts. We've got about a thousand phone calls to make. No rest around here. I sure wish *I* could go to the islands for a vacation."

Scully thanked her again and then left, climbing the concrete stairs to street level. She was deeply troubled. First Dr. Gregory had been killed in his office, and then Bear Dooley and his team had suddenly pulled up stakes and fled to the Pacific to set up their secret test, and now Miriel Bremen, former member of the Bright Anvil Project and outspoken radical protester against the test itself, had also left abruptly, heading out for "the islands."

Could it be a coincidence? Scully didn't like coincidences.

And how did old Oscar McCarron fit in?

The pieces of the puzzle seemed too widely separated, yet connected by invisible threads. Scully just had to feel around until she found the connections that bound the mystery together. She and Mulder would just have to keep looking.

The truth was out there. Somewhere.

EIGHTEEN

Scheck Residence, Gaithersburg, Maryland
Monday, 6:30 P.M.

Late afternoon in the Washington, D.C., area, hot and humid.

The air hung as thick as a damp rag. Brooding thunderheads in the sky promised only an oppressive increase to the mugginess, rather than a refreshing and cooling rain shower.

On days like this, Nancy Scheck felt that the hassle of maintaining an in-ground swimming pool in her fenced backyard paid off.

She let the front screen door close by itself as she entered her brick-front house with the black shutters. Flowering dogwoods and a thick, well-trimmed hedge surrounded its white colonial pillars. It was just the kind of imposing mansion an important Department of Energy executive was supposed to own, and she relished it.

Since she had been divorced for ten years and her three children were all grown and away at college, the place gave her plenty of room to breathe, space to move about. She enjoyed the freedom, the luxury.

Such a mansion was far more than she needed, but Nancy Scheck didn't like the implications of settling for a more modest dwelling, not now. All her career she had been concerned with moving *up* in the world, clawing her way to the top. Exchanging an impressive big house for a smaller one did not fit in with the plan.

She dumped her briefcase on the small Ethan Allen telephone table in the front hall, then shucked out of her stifling business jacket. Her entire career had been inside the Beltway, and she was used to dressing in conservative formal outfits and uncomfortable pantyhose. At her level, such items were just as much of a required uniform as the quaint outfit a teenager wore behind the counter of a fast-food restaurant.

At the moment, though, Nancy couldn't wait to peel off her clothes, get into her sleek black one-piece swimsuit, and take a long, luxurious dip in the pool.

She snagged the usual pile of mail and dropped it unceremoniously on the kitchen counter. She punched the answering machine to listen to the two recorded messages. The first was an offer from a company eager to come and give her a free, no-obligation quote for aluminum siding.

She snorted. "Aluminum siding on my house? I think not."

The second message was in a rich, familiar voice. The words sounded formal and innocuous, but she could detect the hidden passion behind them that went orders of magnitude beyond a mere business relationship . . . or even good friendship.

In her persona at work and at DOE social functions, she called him "Brigadier General Matthew

THE X-FILES

Bradoukis." During his frequent visits here in her backyard or on the patio, she allowed herself to call him "Matthew"—and while they were in bed, she moaned endearing and never-to-be-repeated names into his ear.

He didn't identify himself on the answering machine, not that he needed to. "It's me. I'm a little late at the office so I won't be over until seven-thirty or so. I'm going to stop by my house and pick up the two Porterhouse steaks I've been marinating in the fridge all day. We'll throw them on the barbecue grill, then we can take a swim and . . . whatever. With so many parts of the project coming to a *head*, reaching their *climax*—"

Nancy giggled, knowing he had picked the turn of phrase intentionally. She found it very erotic.

"—we both need a little release from our tension." The tone beeped, and the tape rewound.

In her bedroom, she shed her clothes and, smiling to herself, she yanked down the satin sheets on her bed before changing into her bathing suit, black and smooth and slick.

She admired herself in the mirror. At forty-five she knew she wasn't as gorgeous or sexy as she might have been at twenty-five, but she had a body that stood out above most other women her age. She kept in shape. She dressed well. She exercised, and she had retained her appetite in sexual pleasures. Her hair was short and neatly trimmed. Luckily, blondes didn't become gray—instead they turned "ash."

Nancy grabbed one of the plush beach towels from the closet and went through the kitchen, pausing to pour herself a gin and tonic. She swished the alcohol and mixer around with the ice, making it good and cold. No sense not getting the buzz started before Matthew got here. He would fix his own drink when he arrived.

134

With the towel slung over her shoulder, Nancy took the mail and her drink out the back patio door to sit by the pool. She pulled a chaise lounge up to her small patio table, then went to turn on the bug lights. The mosquitoes and gnats never relented, especially not near sunset. Finally, she picked up the pool skimmer and swept the net around the surface of the water, removing the drowned bugs and the leaves that had fallen from the neighbors' trees. When the blue water sparkled clean and inviting, she returned to her shaded chair.

Nancy settled back to relax, sipping the strong drink, tasting the tonic and the Tanqueray that burned along the back of her throat and into her sinuses. She imagined the taste of the rich steaks Matthew would soon be cooking. She could imagine the salty sweet flavor of his kisses as their breath mingled.

She squirmed in anticipation on the lounge chair, then ran her hands over the swimsuit.

It was so good to have a man whose security clearance was as high as her own, someone who worked on the same classified project, who knew about the money skimmed off the operating budgets of other programs, leaving no paper trail of funding. No accounting could ever be made for highly sensitive projects such as Bright Anvil.

She didn't have to worry about pillow talk when she needed conversation, since Brigadier General Matthew Bradoukis handled the Department of Defense's operations of the new warhead concept, while she took care of the DOE side. No worries there. He was her perfect match . . . for now.

Nancy slicked baby oil on her bare legs and arms and shoulders, massaging it into her neck . . . imagining Matthew's strong fingers working it there. She had to stop herself from thinking like that, or she wouldn't be able to stand waiting until he arrived.

She tried to distract herself by opening the mail, sifting through the form letters, advertising circulars, and junk mail without interest—until she came upon an express-delivery package with a postmark from Honolulu but no return address.

"Maybe I won a free trip for two," she said, and tore open the envelope. To her disappointment, she discovered only a small glass vial of fine black ash and a scrap of paper. The message was written in neatly printed, razor-edged letters, carefully formed capitals, in a hand that showed elaborate patience.

"FOR YOUR PART IN THE FUTURE."

She frowned at the note. "What's that supposed to mean?" Out of curiosity, she shook the vial of black ash, holding it up to catch the light. "Am I supposed to convince people to stop smoking cigarettes?"

Nancy stood up, disgusted at somebody's lame idea of a joke. Whoever was trying to threaten her, or pull her leg, couldn't succeed unless she understood what the point was. "Next time try adding a few more details," she said, tossing the note on the patio table.

Nancy decided not to worry about it. The sun was dropping lower, though the humidity would hold the heat in the air for a long time to come. She was wasting good swimming time.

By the edge of the pool, the bug light crackled and snapped. She watched it give off blue sparks as it fed upon whatever gnats or mosquitoes had been lured to their doom in its voltage differential.

"Take that," she said with a grin. "Hah!"

Then the other bug lamps began to spark, frying loudly, buzzing, popping. The lights flickered violently. The sparks returned like miniature lightning storms.

"What is this, a June bug invasion?" Nancy said, looking around. Only the large beetles would cause the lights to sizzle so much. She wished Matthew would hurry up and get here—she wanted him to see this craziness.

Finally, one by one, each bug light erupted like a small bomb, with a geyser of blue electrical sparks like a Roman candle into the air. Nancy groaned in disgust. Now they would have to waste valuable weekend time replacing the fixtures.

"What's going on here, dammit?" Stilling holding the weird vial, Nancy slammed her drink down, somehow managing not to shatter the glass and dump ice cubes across the concrete patio. She felt unprotected and defenseless out here wearing nothing but her black bathing suit. Maybe if she could get to a phone . . .

Voices came at her from all sides, speaking in some strange and primal tongue, swirling invisibly around her ears—but she could see nothing.

The air itself sparkled and discharged, as if every object on her patio had become a lightning rod. Blue-white arcs shot from her lounge chair to the patio table. "Help!" she cried.

Nancy turned to run, but slipped and reached out instinctively for support. When she touched the chair, skittering electricity shot up her arms in a burning discharge.

She opened her mouth to scream, and sparks danced from the fillings in her teeth. Her ash-blond hair rose up into the air like serpents, waving from side to side, spreading into a nimbus around her head.

Nancy staggered toward the edge of the pool, desperately seeking sanctuary there. Her skin crawled and burned, alive with static electricity. She dropped the vial of ashes into the water.

A gathering storm of harsh light surrounded her. The screaming voices grew louder.

Critical mass.

A sudden rush of thunder engulfed her.

The intense firestorm crisped her eyes. The force of the blast of heat and radiation slammed her backward into the pool with a surge of light. A cloud of vaporized water swept upward like a fog bank into the sky.

The final afterimage on Nancy Scheck's optic nerve was of an impossible, spectral mushroom cloud.

NINETEEN

X The body looked the same as the others, Mulder thought—severely charred, crackling with residual radiation, twisted in a flash-burned, insectlike pose that reminded him of that famous lithograph by Edvard Munch, "The Scream."

Somehow, though, finding a radiation-blasted corpse in the backyard of an expensive suburban home seemed far more eerie. The mundane surroundings—swimming pool, lounge chairs, and patio furniture—gave the death scene a more frightening aspect than even the blasted bowl of glassy sand out in the New Mexico desert.

A local policeman blocked them from entering the pool area, but Mulder flashed his badge and ID. "Federal agents," he said. "I'm Special Agent Mulder, this is Agent Scully. We've been flown in to look at the site and examine the body."

A homicide detective was studying clues and

139

taking notes around the pool and patio. He looked baffled. He overheard Mulder's introduction, and looked up. "FBI? Now that's calling in the big guns. Why were you brought here?"

"We might have a certain background on this case," Scully answered. "This death may be related to another investigation we're working on. There have been two similar deaths in the past week."

The detective raised his eyebrows, then gave a weary shrug. "Anything you guys can do to help. Takes work off my shoulders. This is a weird one, all right. Never seen anything like it."

"No question: this one goes in *your* special file cabinet," Scully said quietly to Mulder.

Scully began a perimeter inspection of the crime scene, working around the bustling evidence technicians and detectives. She took out a small knife to probe a large charred patch on the redwood fence that bounded the Scheck property.

"The burn doesn't go very deep," she said, flaking away an external film of charcoal. "As if the heat was intense, but very brief."

Mulder inspected the mark she had made with her knife. Then he noticed the shattered bug lights around the pool. "Look, they're all destroyed," he said. "Like some sort of power surge blew them up, every one. Doesn't happen every day."

"We can check electrical company records to see if there were local power fluctuations at the estimated time of death," Scully suggested.

Mulder nodded. He placed his hands on his hips and turned slowly around, hoping that an answer would jump out at him. But nothing did. "Okay, Scully," he said. "This time we're not at a nuclear research lab or a missile testing site—just somebody's patio in Maryland. How are you going to explain this one scientifically?"

Scully sighed. "Mulder, right now I'm not even sure how *you're* going to try to explain it."

"Not necessarily by the book," he said. "First off, I'm going to see if there was any connection between Nancy Scheck and Emil Gregory and Oscar McCarron. Or nuclear weapons testing. Or even the Manhattan Project. It could be anything."

"She wasn't old enough to be involved with the Manhattan Project in World War II," Scully pointed out. "But she did work for the Department of Energy, an important person, according to the dossier. But that's a tenuous link at best. Tens of thousands of people work for the DOE."

"We'll see," Mulder said.

The coroner had already wrapped up the charred body in a black plastic bag. Mulder went cautiously over to the coroner and motioned him to unzip the body bag so he could study again what remained of Nancy Scheck.

"Weirdest thing I ever saw," the coroner said. He sneezed, then sniffled loudly, and muttered something about his allergies. "Never seen a death like it. Isn't just a burn victim. Can't imagine off-hand what could blaze that hot. I'm going to have to dig in my reference books."

"An atomic bomb could have done it," Mulder said.

The coroner gave a nervous chuckle, then sneezed again. "Yeah, good one. Everybody has an A-bomb go off in their backyard. Must have been *some* argument with the neighbors! Unfortunately, no witnesses reported seeing any mushroom cloud."

"I'd agree that it sounds preposterous—" Mulder said, "if this weren't the third identical death we've seen in the last week or so. One in California, one in New Mexico, now here."

"You've encountered this before?" the coroner

perked up, then rubbed his reddened eyes. "What on earth caused it?"

Mulder shook his head and allowed the stocky man to zip the bag shut again. "Right now, sir, I'm as stumped as you are."

A man in a general's uniform stood just outside the glass patio doors speaking with two policemen, who took copious notes in their small notebooks. The general was short, broad shouldered, with close-cropped black hair and a swarthy complexion. He appeared deeply distraught. The scene instantly captured Mulder's curiosity.

"I wonder who that is," Mulder said.

"I heard one of the policemen talking," Scully said. "I think he's the one who discovered the body last night."

Mulder hurried over, eager to pick up on what the general was saying and ask a few questions of his own.

"The concrete was still hot when I got here," the general said, "so it couldn't have been long. The back fence was smoldering. The paint was bubbling, and the smell . . . " He shook his head. "*The smell!*" The general turned to look at Mulder, standing beside them, but didn't seem to register his presence. "Listen to me—I've seen combat before, and I've witnessed some accidents, awful ones . . . even helped recover the bodies from a plane crash once, so I've gotten a glimpse of death and how hideous it can be. But . . . in her own backyard. . . ."

Mulder finally managed to read the general's engraved plastic name tag. "Excuse me, General Bradoukis—did you work with Ms. Scheck?"

The general seemed too much in shock to challenge Mulder's right to ask questions here. "Yes . . . yes, I did."

"And why were you here last night?"

The general stiffened, his eyebrows drawing together. "We were going to have dinner. Steaks on the grill." His wide face flushed somewhat. "Our relationship was not a complete secret, though we were discreet."

Mulder nodded, understanding the general's extra measure of distress. "One thing, General—I understand that Ms. Scheck was a fairly important person in the Department of Energy, but I'm not sure I know which program she ran. Can you tell me?"

Bradoukis averted his black eyes. The two policemen fidgeted, as if uncertain whether they should chase away this new investigator, or let the FBI agent ask their questions for them.

"Our . . . uh, Nancy's work wasn't much talked about."

Mulder felt a quick thrill of excitement, a new trail to follow. "You mean it was one of those black programs, an unofficially funded project?"

The general cut him off. "The media call them 'black programs.' There's no official designation for them. Sometimes it's necessary to get certain things done by nontraditional means."

Mulder leaned forward like a hawk swooping in for the kill. Everything depended on the next question. "And was Ms. Scheck's work connected with a project called *Bright Anvil*?"

The general reared back like a startled cobra. "I'm not at liberty to discuss that project, especially not here in an un-secured area."

Mulder gave him an understanding smile. "That won't be necessary, General." Bradoukis's reaction had been answer enough. The sound Mulder heard in his mind was the clicking of puzzle pieces falling together. Things were still not entirely in place, but at least they were arranged into some semblance of order. He decided his best tactic would be to leave the distraught man alone for now.

"That's all for me, General. Sorry to have bothered you during this time of great distress. I take it you have an office in the Pentagon? I may visit you in person if I have further questions."

Bradoukis nodded without enthusiasm, and Mulder stepped over to the pool, looking down at the blistered, blackened paint that had once been sky blue around the concrete rim. Half of the water had boiled away in the flash of intense heat, leaving the pool warm and murky with brownish scum collecting in the corners.

The fireball must have been utterly intense—yet it had not set Nancy Scheck's home on fire, nor had it spread to the neighbors' yards. Almost as if it had been *directed*, intentionally focused in a specific area. Several people on the block claimed to have seen a brief, bright flash, but had not bothered to investigate. Neighbors kept to themselves in these upscale areas.

Mulder's usually sharp eye glimpsed an object floating near the bottom of the pool, a small glass bottle that drifted about as if only partially waterlogged. He searched until he found a skimmer net and yanked it off its hooks near the patio doors. The flash of heat had twisted the handle, but the net remained surprisingly serviceable.

Mulder took it to the edge of the pool and dipped the skimmer deep, swirling it around until he succeeded in netting the dark object and fishing it out. Water trickled off the edges of the skimmer.

"I found something here," he called. He lifted free a small vial that contained a black substance. Some pool water had leaked into the vial, but just a few drops. The detective and Scully came over to look. Mulder held the vial between his thumb and forefinger, tilting it to the light. The object seemed very odd to him, and by its sheer oddness he decided it must be important to this case.

He offered it to Scully, and she took it, shaking it to disturb the contents. "I can't say what it is," she said. "Some sort of black powder or ash, but how did it get to the bottom of the pool? Do you think it has something to do with her death?"

"Only one way to find out, Scully," Mulder said. He turned to the homicide detective in charge. "We have exceptional analytical facilities at the FBI crime lab. I'd like to take this back with us to run a full analysis. We'll copy you on all reports, of course."

"Sure," the detective said. "One less thing for my people to do." He shook his head. "I've never seen anything like this case, and I think it might be beyond me. Do me a favor and figure this one out." With one hand, the detective brushed his hair back. "Sheesh, give me a stabbing or a drive-by shooting any old day."

TWENTY

 After so much time on the road, Scully found it comforting to be working in her own lab for a change, even on as gruesome a subject as this.

She basked in the solitude and familiar surroundings. She knew where all her equipment was located. She knew whom to call for help or a technical consultation. She knew specialists whose skills she respected in case she needed an unbiased person to verify what she found.

The FBI crime lab was the most sophisticated facility of its type in the world. It was filled with an oddball assortment of experts in the forensic sciences whose unusual interests or skills had proven time and again to be the keys to solving bizarre and subtle cases: a woman genetically predisposed to detect the bitter-almond odor of cyanide that many people could not smell, a man whose interest in

146

tropical fish had led him to identify a mysterious poison as a common aquarium algicide after all other methods of analysis had failed, another man who specialized in identifying the type of photocopying machine that had made a particular copy.

In their numerous X-Files cases, Scully and Mulder had stretched the capabilities and imagination of the FBI crime lab more often than most other field agents.

The labyrinth of labs lay on an interconnecting grid supposedly designed to facilitate cooperation between separate units, each with its own jurisdiction and expertise: Chemistry/Toxicology, DNA Analysis, Firearms and Toolmarks, Hairs and Fibers, Explosives, Special Photography, Video Enhancement, Polygraph, Latent Fingerprints, Materials Analysis, and other more esoteric specialties. After her years with the Bureau, Scully still didn't understand the actual organization of the units. But she did know where to find what she needed.

Scully entered the main lab of Berlina Lu Kwok, in the receiving area for the Biological Analysis Unit, where specimens were given their first cursory inspection before being subjected to other, more specific analysis routines. When she stepped through the door, the stench that assailed Scully's nostrils was far worse than usual, and the heavyset Asian lab director was in a foul mood.

"Agent Scully!" Lu Kwok said, her sharp voice slicing through the air, as if Scully were somehow to blame for the smell. "Is it too much to ask? Don't we have clear-cut and regularly posted procedures for submittal of samples? Isn't it as easy to do it the *right* way as to do it the *wrong* way?"

Scully clutched a packaged sample of the black residue Mulder had retrieved from Nancy Scheck's backyard pool; she shifted it to her side in embarrassment. "I thought I'd fill out the forms in person—"

But the lab director was determined to finish her lecture, sniffing the sour air with disgust. "The FBI has every right to expect that local law-enforcement officials will make some sort of *attempt* to follow simple procedures, isn't that correct? It helps us all out, doesn't it?"

She waved an old memo in her hand, squeezing the edge with fingers powerful enough to snap wooden boards. Without pausing for a response, she began to read from it. "'All submissions should be addressed to the FBI's Evidence Control Center. Bullets should be sent by the United Parcel Service, registered mail, or private courier. Human organs should be *packed in dry ice* and sent in plastic or glass containers via UPS, private express mail, or special delivery.'" Berlina fluttered the memo in the air to fan away the stink.

"Now some podunk town in South Dakota has sent me a victim's liver for toxicology analysis. They stuffed it in a zipper-lock plastic bag labeled with handwriting on masking tape—and they didn't even pay for overnight express." She snorted. "Economy two-day!" The memo floated to the floor as Berlina tossed it away. "It'll take us weeks to get rid of the smell around here, and we probably won't be able to find out much from the tissue, either."

Scully swallowed, hoping to deflate the other woman's tirade. "If I submit a sample using proper procedures, may I request a favor?"

Berlina Lu Kwok fixed her with a glare from narrowed almond eyes. Finally she laughed with a sound like a storm breaking. "Sorry, Agent Scully. Of course. Is this for your DOE exec murder? We've been told to give you high priority."

Scully nodded and handed over the sample,

along with a note Mulder had written expressing his suspicions as to the identity of the substance. Lu Kwok scanned the words. "Interesting," she said. "We can check out Agent Mulder's speculations fairly quickly—but if it doesn't match, we could be weeks identifying the substance."

"Do what you can," Scully said. "And thanks. Meanwhile, I've got two autopsies to perform."

"Lucky you," the Asian woman said, scrutinizing the powdery sample. Still muttering to herself about the stench in her lab, she turned and walked back toward her equipment.

It was a messy and exhausting afternoon.

Scully completed the autopsy on Nancy Scheck, as well as the old rancher, Oscar McCarron, who had been packaged and shipped to her lab—following proper procedures, she hoped—thanks to the helpful people at the White Sands Missile Range. Scully suspected they simply wanted to wash their hands of the matter and let her deal with the questions.

But now that she had studied three victims who had apparently died by the same impossible method, she still had no guess as to what the lethal weapon could have been.

It was easy enough to list the cause of death as "sudden and violent exposure to extreme levels of heat and radiation," but that still didn't explain the source of the exposure. Was it a new kind of death beam, or a pint-sized nuclear warhead?

From her own undergrad classes, Scully knew the physics of nuclear explosions well enough to understand that a warhead could not fit inside, say, a small package bomb or a hand grenade. Critical mass and initiators and shielding required a certain amount of bulk—and such things left debris, none of which had been found at any of the three death scenes. The only piece of trace evidence she had in her possession was the vial of strange black ash Mulder had fished out of Nancy Scheck's swimming pool.

Letting other FBI staffers clean up the autopsy arena and take care of the two burned bodies, Scully moved to her smaller lab, analyzing another portion of the ash. In a sterile metal tray she carefully used a long, narrow-bladed scalpel to spread the greasy, powdery residue flat so she could inspect it. Using a magnifying glass, Scully studied the substance, probing delicately to inspect its material properties.

She took out her tape recorder, inserted a new microcassette, and pushed the RECORD button, letting the voice-activated microphone deal with the long pauses in her narration. She stated the case number, the evidence sample number, and then began her off-the-cuff report.

"The black substance found in the Scheck swimming pool appears to be fine and flaky, partially granular, composed of two distinct components. The bulk of the material is soft, ashen, and appears to be composed of some sort of organic residue. The powder is mostly dry now, although I believe it may have been contaminated by 'chlorine and other chemicals from the pool. We may have to compensate for those impurities in our final analysis.

"The second component in the mixture is grainy and . . . " She isolated a couple of the grains with the point of her scalpel and pressed down on one, hearing it pop and skitter to the side of the metal pan. "And it's hard and crystalline, like some sort of rock or . . . sand. Yes, it reminds me of dark sand."

Scully scooped a small amount of the black substance onto her scalpel blade, spread it on a clean microscope slide, and then slid it under her stere-omicroscope. She hunched over the eyepieces and adjusted the focusing knob, studying the substance under low and then higher powers of magnification, using a polarizing filter, prodding with the tip of her scalpel to distribute the tiny pieces more evenly.

"Yes, it does seem to be sand," she said out of the corner of her mouth, hoping the microcassette recorder would pick up her words. She frowned. "One possibility could be that the ash was scraped up from a beach somewhere, and the sand was inadvertently combined with the primary material. This is strictly conjecture, however." She would have to await the results of Berlina Lu Kwok's chemical tests on both components.

On a hunch, but already dreading the answer, Scully went to an equipment cabinet and retrieved a rarely used device she had requested for the autopsies that afternoon—a small alpha counter, a delicate radiation meter that could pick up residual radioactivity beyond the usual background counts.

Scully pointed the sensitive end of the alpha counter, playing the silvery rectangular foil cells over the smear of black ash and sand she had placed in the metal tray. With the detector's output linked to her own computer and running obscure alpha-counting software, she was able to trace a nuclear spectrum. Considering the circumstances of the overall case, she was not surprised to find residual radioactivity in the sample. Fortunately, the specimen was small enough that the dose could not harm her. Its spectrum was slanted to the high end, enough that it was obviously something of unusual origin, something resulting from a high-energy burst.

The software did most of the work for her,

comparing the nuclear spectrum with thousands of others it kept in its database, searching for a match it could offset.

Scully heard a knock on the door, and Berlina Lu Kwok came in, holding a folder full of papers. "Here are your results—special delivery for you, Agent Scully."

"Already?" Scully said, surprised.

"What, you wanted me to pack it in dry ice and send it UPS?" Lu Kwok laughed. "I just wanted to get a breath of fresh air from my lab." Scully gratefully took the folder, but before she could say anything else, the Asian woman spun about and marched back down the hall.

Scully looked at the folder, then sat down next to her computer to wait for results from the radiation scan. To her surprise she discovered that during the brief interruption, the computer had already found a match. Before she opened up Berlina Lu Kwok's Biological Analysis report, Scully studied the nuclear spectrum results.

The error bars were large, but due to the unique half-life properties and the unusual nuclear cross section of the sample, its best guess was that this black residue had been exposed to high levels of ionizing radiation between forty and fifty years earlier.

Scully swallowed, deeply troubled. Reluctantly, she flipped open the Biological Analysis folder, already suspecting the answer. The only way Lu Kwok could have identified the substance so quickly was if Mulder's lead had indeed proven accurate.

She scanned through the analysis summary, paging to the end, interested only in the final result for now. Her stomach sank.

The black powdery sample was indeed *human ash*, almost completely incinerated—exposed to high radiation something like forty years ago, mixed with a black grainy sand.

Radioactive human ash four decades old, found at the death site of a victim who had been obliterated by a similar atomic flash.

Sand.

Ash.

Radiation.

Scully sat back in her seat and tapped her fingernails on the folder. Then she picked up the phone. She couldn't put it off any longer.

Mulder was going to love this.

TWENTY-ONE

 When Miriel Bremen went into the upper floors of the Honolulu high-rise business complex, she felt intimidated. Outside, traffic streamed by in the sunshine, flowing along the seaside, while Diamond Head reared its blocky spire like a sentinel over the waves and the sunbathers. Inside the Kamida Imports office building, Miriel felt as if she had stepped into another world.

She had no interest in the balmy climate, the lovely ocean, the beaches crowded with fishbelly-white American vacationers or swarms of Japanese tourists who stayed up shopping all hours of the night. Her message to Kamida was far too grim to worry about vacation trivialities.

Miriel waited for the receptionist to announce her arrival. She paced in the waiting room, too distracted to read any of the colorful but banal magazines spread out on the low tables.

GROUND ZERO

Miriel had known Ryan Kamida for a year now. She had met him immediately after the personal epiphany that had turned her against nuclear weapons work and transformed her into a vehement protester. The extravagant funding Kamida donated anonymously from the coffers of his successful imports business had kept Stop Nuclear Madness! free of financial worries during its one-year existence.

From their first meeting, Miriel realized that she and the scarred blind man had so many things in common that it was almost eerie. Even so, his very presence sent a thrill of fear through her. She found it hard to understand Kamida's offhanded acceptance of his tragic fate, but he swept such thoughts away with his strange charisma.

As a respected researcher at the Teller Nuclear Research Facility, Miriel Bremen used to feel comfortable meeting many important people, holding her own in any conversation. After she had learned of Ryan Kamida's power and his generosity—and his personal drive—Miriel had promised herself that she would not return to ask more of her benefactor except in the direst emergency.

Circumstances now warranted such a visit.

For months, Kamida claimed to have been making preparations, forming contingency plans, and speaking of desperate measures, as if he could see the future. She did not relish the thought of taking him at his word again. Now she had no choice.

Ryan Kamida emerged from his back offices, led by the receptionist. He maintained only the slightest touch on her shoulder, simply an acknowledgment that he required her to guide him. His eyes were milky, the color of a half-cooked egg; his face was scarred, like the bust of a very proud man done by a poorly trained sculptor.

Kamida cocked his head to one side, as if he

could detect Miriel's presence from the faint per-
fume in the deodorant soap she had used, or perhaps the sound of her breathing. Miriel wondered if
he had more abilities than he let on.

"Mr. Kamida," she said, standing up. "Ryan, it's
good of you to see me on such short notice."

He came forward, homing in on the sound of her
voice and releasing his grip on the receptionist, who
took his dismissal as a matter of course. She returned
to her station just as the phone began ringing.

"Miriel Bremen, what a pleasant surprise. It's
kind of you to come all the way to the Islands just to
see me. I was about to go to my greenhouse for
lunch. Would you join me?"

"Yes, I would," she said. "We have certain things to
discuss."

"I'm sorry to hear that," he said. "Or am I
pleased?"

"No, you're sorry," she said. "Definitely sorry."

Kamida turned to the receptionist. "Shiela,
please have a nice lunch for two brought into the
greenhouse. Ms. Bremen and I would like to relax
for some private conversation."

An enormous room on the top floor had been
converted into a lush tropical forest. Skylights fun-
neled sunshine through the ceiling, while an entire
wall of plate glass allowed daylight to stream in
from the side. Mist generators kept the air humid
and warm, smelling of damp organic greenery and
compost and plant food. Ferns and flowers grew in a
wild profusion—not potted or ordered in any way,
simply a riot like the dense rainforest one might find
on an isolated Pacific island. Several captive birds
flitted about in the treetops.

Ryan Kamida walked in without guidance,
weaving through plant-bordered aisles. He held
both hands out in front of him like a preacher giving

a benediction, going out of his way to brush against the vegetation. He bent over to smell flowers in bloom, inhaling deeply, closing his eyes.

A mist generator spat a rain of spray near him, and he adjusted his hand to touch it, letting the cool droplets form in a glittering sheen on his rough, blistered skin.

"This is my place, Miriel," he said, "a special place where I can enjoy the sound of growing leaves and inhale the smell of fresh earth and blooming flowers. The experience is quite remarkable, from my humble point of view. I'm almost saddened to think of the profusion of windows that your other senses open for you, so that this full and focused experience is denied you."

Though blind, Kamida led the way to a small table nestled in the midst of the dense foliage. He pulled out an ornate metal chair and waited for her to sit down, then pushed her closer to the round glass table. Its size was perfect for two people to dine in the seclusion of a jungle paradise.

"I'm afraid the news is bad, Ryan," she blurted, before he even took his seat.

He felt his way to the opposite chair and sat in it, pulling it snugly up to the table. Before she could continue, though, an employee of Kamida Imports hurried in, bearing two large salads and a plate of fresh pineapple, papaya, and mango slices. She fell silent, looking at him while waiting for the employee to leave.

Ryan Kamida had used his handicap to great advantage, Miriel thought, as if he were watched over by angels. Blessed in business, he had developed his exotic imports company into a wealthy corporation.

Though she had met him accidentally that first time in Nagasaki, Miriel held the uncertain suspicion that he had set up the entire encounter himself, and that events were even now playing out exactly the way he wished.

Now she shuddered and hunched her shoulders as she bent over her salad.

When she had turned away from her mentor, Emil Gregory, Miriel had looked to Kamida as a new supporter, someone who shared her vehement beliefs. Ryan Kamida knew an enormous amount about nuclear weapons testing, about the entire military industry. He was someone to whom she could divulge the dire designs concocted by unenlightened weapons scientists, the blueprints passed along to her through a few sympathetic workers who remained at the Teller Nuclear Research Facility.

Miriel had told Kamida everything, without qualms about spilling classified information. She had vowed to devote her life to the cause; she now responded to a higher calling, not one decreed by the military industrial complex (who had, after all, caused so many of the problems in the first place). She knew what she was doing was right.

Now the time had come for their work to reach its climax. If they could not stop Bright Anvil soon, then all their efforts were simply smoke blown in the eyes of people who wanted to believe.

Kamida ate his salad, waiting for her to continue. His stiff, grave demeanor, however, led her to suspect that he had already guessed what she was about to say.

"Everything I've tried has failed," Miriel said, picking at the greens on her plate and then spearing a chunk of pineapple with her fork. "The government has a momentum behind what it decides to do—and no one, not me, not you, can stop it once it's started."

"I take it that means that no one has heard our complaints."

"Oh, they've heard them all right," Miriel said. "They just don't pay attention to them, any more than they would bother with a gnat buzzing in their ears."

The blind man sighed, and his scarred face fell. Miriel continued, speaking louder, leaning across the table toward him—though he could hear her perfectly well. "The Bright Anvil test is going ahead, even without Dr. Gregory. Somewhere out in the Marshall Islands, on an abandoned atoll."

Ryan Kamida sat up sharply. "Of course," he said. "Enika Atoll. That's where it will take place."

"How do you know?" she asked.

"How could it not take place there?" he practically shouted. With a sharp gesture Kamida knocked his salad plate sideways, hurling it off the table. It smashed on the floor of the greenhouse. The noise was thunderous, but he paid no attention to it. He turned and fixed his milky gaze on Miriel Bremen.

"Our greatest nightmares are about to unfold," he said.

TWENTY-TWO

A blind man has no need for lights. Alone in his spacious house, Ryan Kamida sat in the darkened living room lit only by outside reflections from the moon shining over the placid ocean and a warm glow from the glassed-in fireplace behind him.

As the evening chill deepened, he had started a fire, carefully stacking small sticks of cedar and pine, aromatic wood that made pleasant-smelling smoke as it burned. Kamida enjoyed the incense of the smoke, the velvet touch of radiating heat. He listened to the snapping and popping as the flames gnawed the wood. It sounded like . . . whispers.

He opened the glass patio door so that the ocean breeze could drift in. In the distance he could hear the gentle pounding of the surf, the steady drone of traffic on the coast highway below. Tourists coming to Oahu from time zones all across the world never slept, but busied themselves constantly, sightseeing, shopping, eating.

Kamida sank back in his chair, scarred hands gripping the rough-textured arms. Waiting. The cushions conformed themselves perfectly to his body. Year after year, the weight of his body had shaped them during this nightly ritual.

The voices would come soon. He both dreaded and anticipated them. This time, though, the dread felt stronger, more ominous. The situation had changed, worsened. He knew it and so did the spirits. A chill swept down his spine, and he turned his head to the left toward the fireplace, feeling the heat spill on his cheek.

Bright Anvil. Enika Atoll.

Kamida was more distressed than Miriel Bremen could ever know. He showed it in a different way. Regardless of the circumstances, though, he could not be with her this evening. He had obligations—to the ghosts.

The spectral voices demanded their share of his time, and he had no choice but to give it. He could not complain. Ryan Kamida was alive, and they were not.

Outside, ocean waves continued to roll in, sounding like pebbles rolling in a steel drum.

On a table next to his chair, close at hand, he kept his collection of tiny soapstone sculptures. He amused himself by picking the small objects up, using the sensitive ends of his fingers to explore the details of their carving. His hands were scarred but his mind was sharp. The intricate yet minuscule figures of dolphins, elephants, dragons, and ancient gods fascinated him.

Heard through the open porch high up on the hillside, the soughing sound of waves became muted. Kamida sensed a static building in the room, a charge in the atmosphere. His hand tightened around the sculpture in his hands, an image of Pele, the female fire god from many Island mythologies.

Then the voices buzzed in his ears, speaking his old, never-forgotten language. The phantoms were clustered all around him.

Kamida had never seen the spectral images directly, though he visualized their distinct shadows in his mind, echoes transmitted by senses other than his fried optic nerves. He knew the spirits bore faces frozen in a shriek at the moment of nuclear conflagration as their every cell became an inferno. He couldn't see the harsh white light that bathed his own face as the spectres swirled in front of him, filling his home with blazing, cold light.

But the apparitions did not harm him. These spirits were not here to destroy. Not tonight. They had another purpose altogether; they had a use for Ryan Kamida, the sole survivor of his people.

The faces separated from the glowing, swirling cloud one by one and floated in front of him, giving him their names, telling of who they had been, describing their lives' triumphs and losses, their stolen dreams.

His people's lives had been cut short, but the phantasms had to relive every moment, force Kamida to witness it all. He *remembered* for them.

Though Enika Atoll had never been heavily populated, the mass of demanding ghosts seemed never-ending as they forced him to think of their lives, their names, one by one . . . as they had done every night for the past forty years.

Ryan Kamida sat in his chair, helpless, gripping the small figurine of Pele. He had no choice but to listen.

TWENTY-THREE

Following a hunch, Mulder went to see Nancy Scheck's "friend," Brigadier General Matthew Bradoukis, in his Pentagon office.

Mulder thought that he might have to talk fast to bluff his way into a brief meeting with the general, now that the man had had additional time to recover from his shock. Mulder frequently found that people avoided him because of his knack for asking constant, uncomfortable questions. This morning he suspected Bradoukis would be in a convenient meeting or otherwise occupied away from his desk.

Surprisingly, though, the general's administrative assistant spoke quickly into the intercom, then motioned for Mulder to make his way back to the large office Matthew Bradoukis called his own.

The brigadier general stood from behind his desk and extended a beefy hand. His wide, swarthy face looked as if it had been drained of self-confidence—a quality few generals lacked. He squeezed his generous lips together as if to squash his nervousness.

"I've been expecting you, Agent Mulder." The general's red-rimmed eyes gave him the appearance of not having slept well in recent nights.

"Frankly, I was afraid you would refuse to see me, General," Mulder said. "Some people don't want me looking into certain aspects of this murder investigation."

"On the contrary." Bradoukis sat back down and folded his hands together, staring at his wooden desktop before raising his eyes to meet Mulder's gaze. "You might not believe this, but I've been looking forward to your arrival—you in particular. I was upset with you yesterday and your embarrassing questions, wondering what the hell an FBI guy was doing at Nancy's house. But then I looked into your background with the Bureau. I've got my sources, and I've learned a bit about your reputation, read summaries of some of the cases you've investigated. I've even met your Assistant Director Skinner. He seems a good enough man. He speaks highly of you, though guardedly."

Mulder was surprised by the information. He and the assistant director had been at odds many times, because of Mulder's insistence on exotic explanations that Skinner didn't want to hear. Mulder couldn't tell which side Skinner was on.

"If you know my reputation, sir, then I'm doubly surprised that you agreed to see me," Mulder said. "I'd have thought my track record would scare you off."

Bradoukis squeezed his hands together as if he wanted to pop all the knuckles simultaneously. His face took on a deeply serious expression. "Agent Mulder, we both know something highly unusual is going on here. I can't say this in any official capacity—but I think your . . . willingness to accept certain things that others might find laughable could be a great advantage in this investigation."

That got Mulder's attention. "Are you aware that there were two other bodies found, apparently killed by identical means? One was a weapons designer at the Teller Nuclear Research Facility. The other was an old rancher down at the White Sands Missile Range near the Trinity Test Site. The bodies were found in a condition very similar to Nancy Scheck's."

The general pulled open a side drawer and removed a folder. He tossed it across the desk to Mulder. "And two more," Bradoukis said, "two you don't even know about. A pair of missileers at Vandenberg Air Force Base on the central coast of California."

Surprised, Mulder opened the file. Glossy photographs revealed the now-familiar details of the hideously burned corpses. Mulder noted the control racks on the walls, the outdated buttons and oscilloscopes, the plastic knobs blackened and folded in on themselves in what appeared to be a cramped room somewhere, a sealed chamber that had contained the deadly blast.

"Where was this taken?" he asked.

"Deep underground in a buried Minuteman III missile control bunker. Those bunkers are the safest possible construction, which is why we place them so far below the surface where they can survive a nuclear attack. The bunker is hardened against a direct strike. Only those two men were down there. For security reasons no one else is allowed. We have complete records. The elevator was not used."

He tapped the gruesome pictures. "But still . . . *something came in and obliterated them.*"

Leaving Mulder to stare at the photos, the general leaned back in his chair. "I know one of your operating theories in this investigation is that some new weapon under development at the Teller Nuclear Research Facility was triggered in Dr. Gregory's lab, and that another such device went off at the White Sands Missile Range.

"Such an explanation, however, fails to take into account these two young officers in the missile control bunker, or—" he stopped and swallowed as his voice caught, "or Nancy at her home."

Mulder thought to himself that Scully could probably come up with some far-fetched but scientifically plausible scenario to convince herself that there was still a rational explanation.

General Bradoukis continued. "Believe me when I tell you this, Agent Mulder. I work at the highest levels of the Defense Department. I manage some of those invisible programs you mentioned yesterday. I can tell you with *utter certainty* that no weapon we are currently considering or have under development can do this."

"So it doesn't have anything to do with Bright Anvil?" Mulder asked, fishing.

"Not in the sense you mean," the general answered, then took a deep breath. "Ah, would you like some coffee, Agent Mulder? I can have some sent right in. Perhaps a pastry?"

But Mulder would not allow himself to be distracted. "What are you saying, 'not in the sense you mean'?" he asked. "How are these events connected with Bright Anvil? Is there a spinoff of the weapons project?"

The general sighed. "Nancy Scheck was in charge of the Department of Energy oversight on the entire Bright Anvil Project, and Dr. Gregory was the lead scientist. The test of the prototype device will be conducted on a small atoll in the Marshall Islands, sometime in the next few days."

Mulder nodded. He had surmised or known all of this information already.

"The Marshall Islands," Bradoukis repeated. "Bear that in mind, because it's important."

"How so?" Mulder asked.

"Immediately before those two missileers were killed," the general said, his voice laden with import, "they had gone through a routine missile-targeting exercise. Since the U.S. and Russia are no longer enemies, we're not allowed to aim our Minutemen toward them, not even for practice." He shrugged. "Diplomatic constraints. For the exercises we choose random coordinates around the world."

"So how does that tie in?" Mulder said.

The general jabbed a finger at him. "For that morning's exercises, their missile was targeted toward a small atoll out in the Marshall Islands—the same atoll where the Bright Anvil test is scheduled."

Mulder stared at the general. "What are you suggesting?"

"I leave that for you, Agent Mulder. You're reputed to have an active imagination. But you may think of some possibilities I couldn't suggest to my superiors because I'd be laughed out of my rank."

Mulder frowned, looking down at the gruesome photos again.

"One other piece of information," Bradoukis said. "The atoll—Enika Atoll—has a bit of history of its own. Another hydrogen bomb test took place there in the fifties—Sawtooth—though you won't find it in any record book. It took place shortly after we went through such enormous efforts to clear those islanders off Bikini Atoll. In this instance, the scientists and the military were in a hurry, and the island wasn't as thoroughly checked as it should have been. There is some evidence that an entire group of indigenous islanders was obliterated."

"My God," Mulder whispered. Sick horror prevented him from saying anything else. The general waited, and finally Mulder said, "And you think this . . . this tragedy on the atoll forty years ago has something to do with these unexplained deaths today?"

Suddenly he remembered the results of Scully's analysis on the residue in the vial found in Scheck's swimming pool. Human ash, four decades old, and grainy sand. Coral sand.

The general unfolded his hands again and stared at his fingernails. "I suggested no such thing, Agent Mulder. You are, of course, free to think what you choose."

Mulder closed the folder and tucked the photographs into his briefcase before the general could take them back. "Why are you telling me all this?" he asked. "Do you want to make sure someone is caught for Nancy Scheck's death?"

Bradoukis looked deeply saddened. "That is part of it," he said, "but also, I fear for my own safety."

"Your safety? Why?"

"Nancy was the DOE liaison for the Bright Anvil Project. *I* am the Department of Defense liaison. I'm afraid I might be next on the list. I'm trying to hide—I've been staying in a different hotel every night. I haven't been home in days. Though I doubt such measures will do any good against a force that can swoop down through bedrock and attack two soldiers in an underground missile control bunker."

"I don't suppose you have any suggestions on how we might stop this . . . thing?" Mulder asked.

The general flushed again. "Bright Anvil itself seems to be the link. Whatever has been awakened, or at least triggered into violent action, came about because of this impending test. There's no telling how long the force has been around, but it became active only recently."

Mulder jumped in. "Then whatever is going to happen, whatever event these killings are building toward, will probably occur out in the Marshall Islands. That's the only place we can be sure of." He plunged ahead without thinking. "General, my partner and I need to be there. I need to be at the site to see what's happening."

"Very well," Bradoukis said, "my feeling is that these attacks could be attempts to prevent the test from occurring, with some of these other murders perhaps being incidental . . . or it might be the force, whatever it is, lashing out at other targets and then returning its focus toward the main goal. Since the Bright Anvil test is already in place, I believe that is where the next strike will occur. But I'm taking no chances that it won't come after me as a loose end."

"If Bright Anvil is such a highly classified test," Mulder said, "how will my partner and I get out there?"

The general stood up. "I'll make a few phone calls. I'll even call Assistant Director Skinner, if need be. Just be ready to get on a plane. We don't have any time to lose."

TWENTY-FOUR

With a suitcase lying open on his bed, Mulder dashed back and forth, packing everything he would need for a vacation in the Pacific islands.

Because of the amount of traveling he did for the Bureau, he kept his toiletries already packed in a small dopp bag in the suitcase; all that remained was to throw in sufficient changes of clothes.

Smiling, he carefully removed three garish Hawaiian floral shirts from his bottom drawer and placed them in the suitcase. "Never thought I'd be called on to wear these for business purposes," he said.

Then he packed a pair of swim trunks; he hadn't had a chance for a long, strenuous swim down at the FBI Headquarters pool for more than two weeks, and he looked forward to the opportunity. Unless he exercised regularly, he couldn't keep his body—or his mind—at peak performance.

GROUND ZERO

He stashed a battered paperback of an old Philip K. Dick novel he had been reading and a fresh bag of sunflower seeds in his luggage as well. It would be a long flight across country to the Alameda Naval Air Station, near San Francisco, where their transport plane would depart for Hawaii; then a smaller plane would take them out to Enika Atoll along with the rest of the Bright Anvil team.

In his living room the television blared loud enough for him to hear. He had seen those old movies a dozen times already, but he simply couldn't pass up the "Monster Madness Marathon" of black-and-white films from the fifties, each showing a giant lizard or insect or prehistoric beast that had somehow been awakened or mutated by ill-considered atomic tests. The movies were morality plays, chastising the hubris of science while celebrating the genius of the human spirit. Right now, giant ants had infested the cement-lined drainage canals of Los Angeles, much to the consternation of James Whitmore and James Arness.

In his kitchenette several small white cartons of carry-out Chinese food sat on the table, flaps open, next to two paper plates. He'd already heaped one of the plates with steamed rice, kung-pao chicken, and dry-fried string beans with pork. As he packed, he shuttled back and forth between his suitcase, the television, and the kitchenette, grabbing a few bites to eat.

With his mouth full of garlicky string beans, Mulder heard a sharp rap on his apartment door. "Mulder, it's me."

He swallowed quickly before rushing to let his partner in. Dressed in professional, though comfortable, traveling clothes, Scully carried a bulging duffel bag. "I'm all packed. I'm even ten minutes early," she said. "That gives you plenty of time to tell me what's going on."

171

He gestured her inside. "I've arranged for two tickets to paradise. You and I are going off to the South Seas."

"Your message told me that much," she said. "But what for?"

"We've got a pair of front row seats at the Bright Anvil test. I asked for season tickets to the New York Knicks, but this was the best they could do."

She blinked her blue eyes in astonishment. "The test? How did you manage that? I thought—"

"Connections in certain high places," he said. "One very frightened brigadier general who was willing to go out on a limb for us. I picked up some Chinese carry-out for a quick dinner before we head to the airport." He indicated the extra paper plate. "I got an order of kung-pao chicken—your favorite."

Scully set her duffel bag on an empty chair and looked at him curiously. "Mulder, I don't recall that we've ever gone out for Chinese food together. How would you know what my favorite meal is?"

He favored her with a reproachful look. "Now what kind of FBI agent would I be if I couldn't find out a simple thing like that?"

She pulled up a chair at the small dining room table and scooped out some of the chicken chunks laden with red Szechuan peppers. Taking an appreciative whiff of the aromatic spices, she snagged the extra pair of disposable chopsticks next to the napkins.

Mulder came out of the bedroom, lugging his packed suitcase. He secured the locks, then placed his briefcase on top of it. "I think I told you once, Scully, that if you stuck with me I'd show you exciting lands and exotic places."

Scully shot him a wry look. "You mean like an island about to be flattened by a secret nuclear weapons test?"

Mulder placed his hands in front of him. "I was thinking more of coral reefs, blue lagoons, the warm Pacific sun."

"I thought it was hurricane season out there," she said. "That's what Bear Dooley and the Bright Anvil scientists kept studying on their weather maps."

Mulder sat across from her to eat his food, luke-warm by now. "I'm trying to be optimistic," he said. "Besides General Bradoukis said something about us going on a 'three-hour tour.'"

Scully finished her meal and checked her watch. She reached inside her jacket to pull out the two air-plane tickets. "I picked these up from the Bureau travel office on my way over, as you requested," she said. "Our plane leaves Dulles in about ninety minutes."

Mulder tossed their plates in the wastepaper basket, looked at the remains of the Chinese food in the white boxes, and without a thought dumped the remnants of all three dishes together into a single container. Scully watched him in astonishment. "It's good for breakfast that way," he said. "Add a few scrambled eggs—delicious." He placed the container in the refrigerator.

Scully picked up her duffel. "Sometimes you really are spooky, Mulder."

After switching off the television—the giant ants had been superseded by a gargantuan tarantula out in the Mojave Desert—he followed her out.

He noticed that the metal "2" of the "42" on his apartment number had fallen off again onto the floor. "Just a second, Scully," he said, picking up the number.

He ran back in to the junk drawer in his kitchen, where he pulled out a screwdriver. "This number keeps coming off. Very suspicious, don't you think?" He checked it for listening devices on the inside, rubbing his finger along the curve of the thin metal. At one time he'd been certain someone was spying on him, so he had removed every detachable thing in his apartment including the numbers on his door. Now the "2" refused to stay where it belonged.

"Mulder, you're paranoid," Scully said with wry amusement.

"Only because everybody's out to get me," he said.

After reassuring himself that the metal number was clean, he used a spare set of screws to attach it tightly to the door. "Okay. Now we can go. I hope you brought your suntan lotion."

She shouldered her duffel. "Yeah, and my lead umbrella for the radioactive fallout."

TWENTY-FIVE

The atoll had recovered remarkably well in forty years. The low, flat island, little more than a massive coral reef with a shallow dusting of topsoil, was once again burgeoning with lush tropical vegetation, breadfruit and coconut palms, vines, ferns, tall grasses, and low taro plants and yams. The reefs and lagoons swarmed with fish; birds and butterflies thronged in the foliage above.

When Captain Robert Ives had left here four decades earlier, he had been a young seaman recruit who had barely learned to shut up and do as he was told. The spectacular Sawtooth nuclear test had been the most awe-inspiring sight his slate-gray eyes had ever witnessed. It had reduced Enika Atoll to a hot, blasted scab, its entire surface sterilized, its coral outcroppings sheared off in the boiling froth of the sea, vegetation crisped, wildlife exterminated.

The intricate network of reefs extended far past

the portion of the atoll that actually rose above the surface, in many places lurking only a few feet beneath the water. With amazing recuperative powers, Nature had reclaimed the territory that humans had so swiftly and violently snatched away. Once again, Enika Atoll looked like an isolated island paradise, pristine and uninhabited.

At least Captain Ives *hoped* it was uninhabited this time.

On the shore of the atoll, sheltered behind the rugged coral rocks that formed the highest point of the island, Bear Dooley and his team of researchers used sailors and Navy engineers to help make preparations for their secret test.

A small landing strip had been cleared along a straight stretch of beach. Bulldozers, off-loaded from the *Dallas*, plowed through the jungle, scratching narrow access roads from the sheltered control bunker to the lagoon on the far side of the atoll, where the Bright Anvil device would be set up and detonated.

Trapped aboard drab gray ships for so much of their tours of duty, the Navy engineers enjoyed the work, riding heavy machinery and knocking down palms and breadfruit trees, leaving naked paths of churned-up coral dirt like raw wounds on the island.

They needed to construct a bunker to house the controls that would run the small warhead detonation. Because the control bunker would be so close to the detonation, it had to be incredibly sturdy. Captain Ives instructed his engineers in an old trick.

After laying down electrical troughs and pathways to a backup generator in a shielded substation next to the blockhouse, the engineers stacked bags of concrete mix and sand around and around a bowed wooden frame in a shrinking circle, creating a structure that looked like an igloo or beehive. Then, with pumps hooked up to clunky ship fire-hoses thrust into the ocean, the engineers sprayed the outside of the structure, soaking the sand and concrete mixture. After a day or two of hardening in the warm Pacific sunshine, the bunker would be virtually indestructible.

NASA engineers had used the same technique at Cape Canaveral to erect protective bunkers for control systems and observers close to the early rocket launchpads. Such bunkers had withstood the explosive stresses inflicted upon them—and in fact had survived so well that the Corps of Engineers had abandoned the old structures in place out in the Florida swamps because they could think of no way to demolish them!

As the sandbags dried against the reinforced parabolic frames that held them in place, Bear Dooley supervised the installation of his test equipment inside. The broad-shouldered deputy project leader helped install the control racks that had been carefully crated and stored down in the Navy destroyer's hold. He was willing to roll up his sleeves and get his hands dirty to speed up the work.

The bearlike man sweated in the tropical heat, but he refused to wear cooler clothes, treating his flannel shirt and denim pants as required dress. Dooley listened in on the shortwave radio to regular weather updates for the Marshall Islands. Every time the announcement tracked the approaching tropical depression, now nearly a full-fledged hurricane, he grew ecstatic.

"It's coming," Dooley had said to Ives the last time he received such news. "And we've got a lot of work to do. Timing is crucial."

Ives let the man have his way. He had his orders, after all.

He didn't think Bear Dooley was even aware of the previous H-bomb test that had taken place in this same area. Dooley didn't seem the type of man who wasted time studying history or worrying where things came from.

For the rest of his life, though, Robert Ives would be haunted by the knowledge that they had made a horrendous, tragic mistake here at Enika Atoll.

By now Ives had seen the Bikini Islanders repatriated, after the government had stripped the topsoil from their blasted island and replaced it with fresh dirt, replanted the jungles, restocked the lagoons.

The mysterious islanders on Enika, though, had not enjoyed such solicitous treatment.

Sawtooth had been one of the first H-bomb tests, kept quiet at the time, just in case the device failed. During those Cold War years the U.S. couldn't afford to let anyone see that its thermonuclear devices didn't function well enough to keep the Commies awake at night.

But Sawtooth had worked—spectacularly well.

It was in the days before spy satellites, and the perimeter of the atoll had been ringed with gunboats, calmly confident that they wouldn't be seen. These waters were infrequently traveled, and the captains of the cutters had instructions to chase off any fishing boats or sightseers. Even so, the anticipated flash of the Sawtooth device was visible for hundreds of miles across the open water, rising like the brief glow of sunrise in the wrong part of the sky at the wrong time of day.

Everyone had been so naive then. They had assumed that the small, barely charted atoll was uninhabited, and so the scientists and sailors had not looked too hard to find any indigenous islanders.

GROUND ZERO

The Navy expected to find no one on Enika, and so no one had ever really searched.

During preparations for the Sawtooth explosion, the engineers and sailors had not bothered to report signs of encampments, tools, nets found washed up on the rough reefs. They dismissed the junk as old artifacts and looked no farther, because they didn't particularly want to find anything else. Such information might cause problems.

The perimeter boats had all pulled back and the main destroyer, the USS *Yorktown*, had moved out to a safe distance beyond the reef line. Those lucky few observers who had been assigned welding glasses stood on deck to see, while the others promised not to open their eyes at the critical point. Still, when the Sawtooth detonation went off, several dozen crewmen suffered from brief flash blindness.

Ives remembered. Some things were impossible to forget. The roar sounded like the world cracking open, and the mushroom cloud rose like Old Faithful geyser in Yellowstone—only about a million times as big—sucking up vaporized coral and sand along with an immense volume of seawater. The incandescent plume towered like an awesome thunderhead heralding Armageddon. The shockwaves slamming through the water caused the *Yorktown* to rock like a toy boat in a bathtub. . . .

Several hours later, after it was all over and the sea had grown calm again, initial inspection teams from the *Yorktown* suited up and took their small cutters back to the atoll to plant radiation counters and to map out the effects of the fallout. A seaplane drifted overhead, taking photographs for before-and-after images to determine how the atoll's topography had changed.

Being one of the most junior seamen, Ives had been "volunteered" to be part of a small group on a perimeter cruise around Enika to study any anomalies in the aftermath. What they found proved even more astonishing than the detonation itself.

Standing out in open water more than two miles from shore was a boy about ten years old. All alone. Just waiting.

At first young Robert Ives had quailed in terror, thinking that some vengeful angel had come to punish them for what they had done to the pristine island. The boy appeared to be standing right on the surface of the water like a marker buoy, aimless and lost. Only later did the rescuers remember that the low reefs stretched in a labyrinth just beneath the surface far from the actual island. The boy had somehow walked on them, following the submerged reefs away from what had once been his island.

They hauled him aboard. He was speechless and shaking, horribly burned, his face puckered, his eyes sunken and sightless from the glare of the blast. Most of his hair had been scalded away, and his skin was an angry red, as if he had been boiled alive. The agony of the boy's burns must have been even greater due to the constant lapping of saltwater that drenched him.

No one expected him to live when they brought him back to the *Yorktown*. In fact, the ship's doctor seemed ambivalent, as if he didn't *want* the boy to survive, because he would be blind and hideously scarred for his entire life . . . and because the very existence of a survivor was an accusing finger, proof that natives had lived on Enika Atoll. An entire tribe had been wiped out in the Sawtooth blast, save for this sole survivor.

But to everyone's surprise the boy had recovered, despite his festering injuries. He remained utterly silent for days, and then finally croaked out words in a strange language that none of the crew could understand.

GROUND ZERO

The data obtained from the Sawtooth test were filed away with the Defense Department, and the Navy placed the entire event under the strictest order of silence.

When the *Yorktown* finally docked again at Pearl Harbor, the horribly burned boy was taken quietly to an orphanage in Honolulu. Official records showed that he was the only survivor of a terrible house fire that had killed the rest of his family. Having no other living relatives, the boy was raised as a ward of the state, although he received a generous (and mysterious) allowance from the Navy.

Ives had never seen or heard of the boy again, and he wondered how the poor victim had managed to fare in life. He had not thought of the boy in some time, but now all those memories had come flooding back with nightmare intensity—ever since Ives received his orders to take the *Dallas* out to the Marshall Islands.

Captain Robert Ives had hoped never to see Enika Atoll again. But now he had returned . . . for yet another secret nuclear test.

TWENTY-SIX

Mulder and Scully arrived in the San Francisco Bay Area, red-eyed and exhausted from the non-stop travel, knowing they had a much longer trip still in front of them.

Mulder rented a car, and they drove toward the Alameda Naval Air Station, then spent the better part of an hour at the gates showing their paperwork, answering questions, and finally arguing with a stoic military policeman who made repeated phone calls to his superiors inside.

"I'm sorry, sir," the MP came back for the third time, "but your story doesn't check out. We have no C-5 transport plane leaving for Hawaii this afternoon. We have no record of you coming, or of your place on board such a plane, if one existed."

Mulder wearily pulled out the paperwork again. "This was signed by Brigadier General Bradoukis, directly from the Pentagon. It's regarding a classified project out in the Marshall Islands. I know you don't have the authorization sitting on the top of your desk, because they wouldn't make it so blatant—but my partner and I are authorized to go on this flight."

"I'm sorry, sir, but there *is* no flight," the MP insisted.

Mulder heaved an angry sigh, and Scully squeezed his arm to calm him. Before he could speak again, Scully broke in, "Why don't you talk to your superior again, Sergeant," she said, "and this time mention two words to him: *Bright Anvil*. We'll wait here until you come back."

The MP retreated to his guard shack wearing a skeptical expression and shaking his head. Mulder turned to Scully in surprise. She smiled at him. "You rarely accomplish anything by getting angry."

Mulder sighed, then forced a chuckle. "Sometimes I wonder if I ever accomplish anything—period."

Within minutes, the MP came back and opened the gate for them. He offered no apologies or any explanations whatsoever. He simply handed them a map of the base and directed them where to go.

"Wasn't your father stationed here at one time?" Mulder asked. He knew how deeply the death of her father had affected her.

"Briefly," Scully said, "around the time I started college at Berkeley."

Mulder looked over at her. "I didn't know you went to Berkeley. As an undergrad?"

"Just for my first year."

"Ah," he said and waited for her to continue. But Scully seemed uncomfortable about the subject, so he didn't press her for details.

Exactly where the guard had directed them, they found the whale-sized C-5 transport. Small hydraulic vehicles hauled cargo, stuffing crates into the swollen, olive-colored belly of the plane.

Forklifts raised pallets filled with the final loads of equipment, while civilian passengers and military personnel climbed aboard, using a set of steps that had been hastily rolled up against the plane.

"See, Scully," he said, "they have no C-5 transport plane here on the base, and nothing whatsoever is scheduled to depart." He opened his hands in a helpless gesture. "But then, a tiny aircraft like this must get misplaced all the time."

Scully, who had long ago accepted the secrecy and the denials surrounding classified projects, made no rejoinder. Carrying his suitcase and briefcase, Mulder bounded up the metal steps that led up to the aircraft passenger compartment. "I hope we can get ourselves a window seat," he said. "Nonsmoking."

"I think I'll try to take a nap on the way," Scully answered.

Inside the no-frills transport plane, Mulder looked around the sharply shadowed interior, which was lit from behind and below by the open cargo doors. Other passengers—naval officers and enlisted men, as well as half a dozen nonmilitary types—milled about, finding places to sit.

Mulder saw no baggage compartment, only webbing stretched across the metal wall panels, where others had already secured their personal baggage. He went back to tuck his suitcase into an empty spot, then returned to take Scully's bag, securing it next to his own. He kept his briefcase with him so that the two of them could look over notes and discuss the case during the long flight to Pearl Harbor; after a brief stopover, they would change to a much smaller plane and head out to the Western Pacific.

When he returned to Scully, she reached inside her purse and handed him a few sticks of chewing gum. "What, is my breath bad?" he asked.

"No, but you'll need it for the flight. I've flown on these Navy planes before with my father. They're not pressurized. Chewing the gum helps equalize the pressure in your ears—trust me, it's my professional medical advice."

Mulder took the sticks skeptically and slipped them into his shirt pocket. "I knew we were getting a bargain ticket, but I at least expected some oxygen."

"Blame it on military budget cuts," Scully said.

Mulder and Scully searched for a comfortable seat, but all the chairs were hard and stiff-backed. They both buckled in. Finally, the cargo doors closed, and muffled shouts from inside announced the plane's readiness for departure. One of the sailors pulled the thick passenger compartment doors shut as the engines began to power up with a loud vibrating hum.

"I guess they don't have a first-class section," Mulder said.

He turned around in his seat and recognized some of the civilians already buckled into their seats, scientists and technicians he had seen at the Teller Nuclear Research Facility. Mulder smiled and waved as a bespectacled redhead blushed and tried to look small. "Hello, Victor! Victor Ogilvy—fancy meeting you here."

Victor stammered, "Uh, hello Mr. Agent . . . I didn't know the FBI was scheduled to watch the test preparations."

"Well, Victor, I told you I was going to make some phone calls," he said feeling like a bully, and somewhat embarrassed at it.

Scully leaned closer to Mulder. "We've got a long flight ahead of us, so let's be friends. We're all here with our country's best interests at heart, right Victor?"

The young redheaded technician nodded vigorously.

"Right, Mulder?" She elbowed him in the ribs.

"Of course, Scully."

The hulking transport plane began to lurch along, lumbering into motion like a behemoth, as aerodynamic as a bumblebee, but orders of magnitude louder. The C-5 accelerated down the runway and gracefully lifted off, hauling its enormous bulk into the air with a roar of jet engines. Before long, the aircraft had gained altitude, circled over the hills east of Oakland, and then headed straight out to sea.

Mulder turned back to look at Victor Ogilvy. "So, Victor, why don't we make this into a regular tropical vacation with sun and surf and sparkling beaches?"

Victor looked surprised. "No such luck, Agent Mulder. Did you both bring along your rain slickers?"

"What for?" Scully asked.

Victor blinked again behind his round eyeglasses. "And I thought you two had done your homework. Maybe you didn't get as many details as you thought.

"The Bright Anvil test—we're heading directly into a hurricane."

TWENTY-SEVEN

Leaving Pearl Harbor behind on a perfect picture-postcard morning, Scully, Mulder, and the entire crew took off in a smaller plane headed out over the monotonously blue, sun-dappled Pacific. While dawn chased them over the horizon, Scully looked out the window, her mind drifting far away.

"So," Mulder said, slouched next to her in a cramped seat, getting comfortable, "did you enjoy our all-expense-paid government trip to Hawaii? A fine day of boredom and waiting, but you can't beat the hospitality."

Scully squirmed in her seat, then pulled down the window shade; she couldn't find a comfortable position as easily as Mulder seemed to. "It was everything I've come to expect from a government-paid vacation."

The plane rattled and hummed as it roared over the ocean. Clouds began to gather in the western skies, and Scully had no doubt that as they proceeded the weather would get worse. Mulder didn't seem the least bit concerned for the safety or integrity of the plane—but then traveling never seemed to bother her partner.

Curious to see how the rest of the passengers were holding up, Scully turned around to look at the small cliques scattered throughout the plane. Victor Ogilvy and some of the other Teller Nuclear Research Facility technicians had gathered in the back and were poring over their notebooks and technical papers.

The Navy troops all sat by themselves, talking loudly, completely relaxed as the plane rattled along. Scully knew from her own background that sailors traveled often on a moment's notice. Thrust together with new groups of seamen, either with plenty in common or few shared interests, they found ways to amuse themselves without difficulty.

Mulder had fixed his attention on two young black men diligently playing a game of Stratego with a travel-sized board that used small magnetic pieces. He watched them for a few moments, then looked away with a troubled expression on his face.

Another group of sailors surrounded a broad-shouldered seaman with close-cropped dark hair and a Hispanic cast to his features; he sat intently reading the latest enormous technothriller by Tom Clancy. The three spectators loudly discussed the merits of Clancy's work and the excitement of being a CIA agent like Jack Ryan. Scully wondered if they had the same view of the exciting life FBI field agents led.

Then the three began discussing the classified information woven through Clancy's work. "Man, if you or I wrote something like that, we'd be thrown in the brig so fast we wouldn't have time to cash our royalty checks!" said one.

"Yeah, but you and I have security clearances—key point. We've signed papers that hold us accountable. Clancy doesn't have any access to that sort of stuff, so who's gonna believe him?"

"Are you telling me he's making it up? He's got a damn fine imagination, if that's the case. Look at all those details."

The critic shrugged. "Doesn't matter. He's just an insurance agent, man. He has no 'implied credibility' like we do, because we work directly with the material."

"I still think somebody should break Clancy's knuckles for letting out classified secrets like that."

"No way," said the third. "He wouldn't be able to write no more books if he had broken knuckles."

"Well, break his kneecaps then."

Paying absolutely no attention to the three spectators hovering over his shoulders and speaking around his ears, the reader casually flipped a page and continued with the chapter.

The aircraft struck heavy turbulence, jouncing the passengers from side to side in their seats. Scully gripped the arms of her chair. Mulder nonchalantly chose that moment to lean forward against the bucking carnival ride and pull out his briefcase. He snapped it open on his lap, ransacking it for papers.

"Let's go over a few things while we have time," he said.

The jostling became so rough that the two sailors playing Stratego finally gave up, brushed their magnetic pieces into the carrying case, and clicked their board shut.

With her teeth rattling together, Scully couldn't imagine how her partner could think clearly—but then she thought Mulder might be doing this to keep her mind off the turbulence. She silently thanked him for it.

"Just what do you expect is going to happen out there on the island, Mulder?" she asked.

"General Bradoukis seems to think that whoever or whatever has been killing people around the country is going to try once more to stop the Bright Anvil test. This is its last chance."

"You keep saying 'it,' Mulder," she pointed out.

He shrugged. "Fill in your own pronoun of choice." He hauled out a map of the Pacific Ocean with the island chains highlighted. He unfolded it on top of the other papers in his briefcase. "If you're still worried about that hurricane, I've got some good news for you."

Scully, still holding tightly to the arms of her seat, looked questioningly at him. The plane continued to rattle. "Right now I'm worried about this plane staying aloft—but if the best you've got is good news about the hurricane, I'd be happy to hear it."

With a mischievous gleam in his eye, Mulder said, "The good part is that we aren't flying into a hurricane after all."

The brief wash of relief surprised Scully, but she knew him better than that. "What do you mean? Have the weather conditions changed? Has it been downgraded to a tropical storm?"

"Not at all," he said, pointing to the map. "Look here, we're heading out to the Western Pacific. Meteorologically speaking, storm systems in this region aren't called hurricanes. They are technically designated *typhoons*. No other real difference, though. Same damage potential."

"What a relief," Scully said. "Aren't semantics wonderful?"

Mulder studied the tiny flyspeck dots out in the

vast blue areas of the map. He circled the specks with his finger. "I wonder why they're going way out here. The Marshall Islands are a U.S. protectorate, so I'm sure that has something to do with it. Could it be just to intercept the storm?"

Scully perked up, glad to have a subject on which she could discourse. She forced herself to ignore the rocking turbulence as she added her knowledge to the discussion. "It probably has more to do with the track record of nuclear testing out here. The Marshall Islands chain is where most of the U.S. bomb blasts took place between 1946 and 1963—hydrogen bombs and cobalt bombs, thermonuclear devices, everything too big to be detonated in Nevada. In fact, between 1947 and 1959, forty-two nuclear devices were set off on these islands alone.

Scully was amazed at how these facts came back to her, as if she were reading from a textbook, or a political diatribe, in her mind. "The entire atoll of Eniwetok was like a hopscotch ground. Test detonations stepped from one clump of islets to another, vaporizing one lump of coral, then the next. The inhabitants were evacuated, promised adequate compensation, but Uncle Sam never really came through for them. In all fairness, nobody knew exactly what they were doing at the time, not even the weapons scientists. They made mistakes—some bombs fizzled, others produced a much higher yield than expected. It still amazes me how they just . . . *played* with all that destructive potential."

Mulder raised his eyebrows. "You're sounding pretty passionate there. Is this a particular interest of yours?"

She looked at him, feeling her walls go up. "Used to be."

"So what happened?" he asked. "With the testing, I mean."

"All atmospheric testing of atomic explosives ceased in 1963 with the Nuclear Test Ban Treaty. But by that time over five hundred nuclear weapons had already been detonated by the United States and various other countries."

"Five hundred!" Mulder said. "*Above*ground? You're kidding, right?"

"Have you ever known me to exaggerate, Mulder?"

"Not you, Scully," he said. "Not you."

The plane suddenly lost altitude for a terrifying two seconds, then caught itself. The sailors in back whooped and cheered, applauding the pilot. Scully hoped the pilot wasn't about to leave the controls to come back and take a bow.

She sucked in a deep breath. Mulder waited for her to continue. "There's even been an off-and-on moratorium of underground testing." she said. "The French and Chinese and others have continued their work, although they deny it. The French recently resumed testing out on some other islands near Tahiti—and sparked a firestorm of public opinion against them. With seismic surveillance and high-resolution spy satellites, however, it's awfully difficult to mask the signature of a nuclear explosion."

"Ten to one this approaching storm isn't just a coincidence then."

"I think that's a safe bet, Mulder."

TWENTY-EIGHT

Enika Atoll, Marshall Islands
Friday, 2:11 P.M.

The weather grew even rougher, tossing and batting the small plane about as they neared the isolated atoll. Scully found herself wishing for the stability of the immense C-5 transport plane they had flown from Alameda to Pearl Harbor.

The plane circled around to attempt a second approach to the small island's crude landing strip. "They haven't told us to assume crash positions yet. That's a good sign," Mulder said.

Wind shear knocked the aircraft sideways, and even the seasoned sailors embarrassed themselves with nervous gasps.

"Mulder, I didn't realize you were such an optimist," Scully said, but he had distracted her just long enough for the plane to make its final run. Through the rain-splattered window, Scully could make out a distressingly short landing strip that had been bulldozed along a flat stretch of beach.

She squeezed her eyes shut. When the plane finally bounced and rattled to a rough halt, the passengers burst into a round of spontaneous applause.

Sailors already on the island rushed forward, heads bent, to put chock blocks behind the plane's wheels. The side door swung downward on reinforced cables, converting into creaking stairs. The cargo section was pried open from below, and a group of Navy men swarmed out of storm shelters, where they had hidden from the freshening wind and the approaching typhoon. In a well-choreographed routine, they began unloading the remaining crates.

Scully walked on rubbery legs to the airplane stairs, but declined Mulder's help getting down. She stepped onto the hard-packed coral gravel of the "runway," holding the side of the staircase for support, and stared around at the flat, foliage-covered island, the reef outcroppings of coral, and the clean sand.

The bowl of sky surrounding them was a muddy gray-green from the approaching hurricane. The air itself held an ominous crackle of ozone mixed with the salty iodine smell of the sea. The wind gusted in short sharp breezes from random directions.

Scully's light auburn hair blew around her face. Mulder stood beside her, his maroon striped tie flapping up and off to the side of his suit jacket. "See, what did I tell you? Two tickets to paradise."

Scully glanced sidelong at him. "You must have gotten the bargain tickets."

In a sheltered bay farther down the rough shoreline, Scully spotted a small enclosed boat, the captain's gig, used to shuttle crew and materials from the Navy destroyer anchored in view farther out beyond the treacherous reef line. Scully recognized the type of ship, a Spruance-class destroyer, a powerful vessel primarily designed for rapid response and antisubmarine warfare.

"The Navy must be taking this test seriously," she said. "That kind of destroyer isn't something to mess with."

A trim young officer came directly toward them. He had short-cropped sandy hair and eyeglasses with Photogray lenses that had managed to turn dark even in the gloomy light of the rising storm. "You must be the FBI agents," he said and stood rigidly in front of them. "I'm Commander Lee Klantze, the *Dallas*'s XO. I'll take you to meet Captain Ives. He's here to supervise the last-minute preparations, though I believe he intends to observe the test from the *Dallas*."

Klantze turned about and then set out along the beach, taking long strides. "We received word from Brigadier General Bradoukis in Washington that you'd be VIP guests, though we're all a bit mystified as to your purpose here. This isn't an FBI matter, as far as I can see."

"It dovetails with a pending investigation," Scully said.

"Oh," Klantze answered.

You could always tell a career military officer, Scully thought with a smile. They *knew* when to stop asking questions.

"We'll take you to the Bright Anvil control blockhouse and let you get on with whatever you need to do. Just try to stay out of the way of the test preparations. Plenty of delicate instruments. Careless hands can cause more damage than the hurricane will . . . and Mr. Dooley tends to over-react in his protectiveness."

"Thank you," Scully said. She and Mulder followed the executive officer as he struck out toward where coral outcroppings formed the edge of a sheltered lagoon. A high-rising bluff shielded a small cluster of buildings from the opposite side of the island, the direction from which the storm approached.

Mulder turned back and pointed to the cargo being unloaded from the plane. "Our suitcases and bags are over there," he said.

Klantze didn't seem worried. "They'll be taken back to the *Dallas*. We've got staterooms for you to sleep in, although everybody is pretty much going to be working round the clock until the blast goes off. The test is set for oh five-fifteen tomorrow."

"That soon?" Mulder said.

"No choice," Klantze answered as he continued briskly along the beach. Sand whipped around them, stinging their faces. "That's when the storm is due to make landfall."

Scully wanted to ask why they were so concerned about making their test coincide with the hurricane, but she decided to save those questions for Bear Dooley or someone else in charge.

The executive officer led them to an unusual, igloo-shaped control bunker, to which all sorts of generators, air-conditioning units, and satellite dishes had been linked.

"Look, it's the Enika Holiday Inn," Mulder said.

Scully could see many figures moving in and out of the blockhouse, checking generators and electrical connections. A man in a white captain's uniform saw them and waved Klantze over.

Upon approaching the captain, Scully automatically took out her ID, and Mulder did the same. The captain dutifully accepted the FBI badges and studied them, genuinely paying attention before handing them back. "Thank you, Agents Scully and Mulder. I'm Captain Robert Ives," he said, "of the USS *Dallas*."

Scully reached out to shake his hand, surprising herself with a sudden rush of memory. "Yes, Captain. I believe I met you once, when I was much younger, at a Naval reception in Norfolk, Virginia. My father was Captain Bill Scully."

"Bill Scully!" Ives looked astonished. "Why, yes, I knew him. He was a good man. How is he these days?"

Scully swallowed. "He passed away recently," she said.

"I'm sorry." Ives stiffened. "When you're at sea so much of the year, a lot of personal news vanishes before you get a chance to pay attention to it. I'm really sorry."

"Thank you," she said.

Ives cleared his throat as if to banish his discomfort. "Now then, I understand that you're here in regards to something unusual about the Bright Anvil test? General Bradoukis was reluctant to give details. Is there something we should know about?"

Scully looked to Mulder, giving him a chance to recount the odd connections and the strange theory he had proposed. But he just looked back at her, apparently not wanting to bring up the possibilities.

"We're here to observe and gather a few details," she said. "As you may already be aware, there have been several unusual deaths of individuals involved with Bright Anvil."

Just then Bear Dooley came blustering out of the low door in the beehive blockhouse, blinking his eyes into the wind that tossed his long hair and white-shot beard into wild disarray around his face. His eyes fixed on the two FBI agents, and his expression gathered a fury equal to the storm brewing around them. He had obviously been stewing about their arrival for some time.

"I don't know how you two got the authorization

to come to this restricted testing site, Agents Mulder and Scully. I can't question it, and I can't send you home right now—unfortunately." He planted his hands on his hips. "But get this straight from the start: stay out of the way. We're busy. We have a test to run and a device to set off early tomorrow morning. I do *not* have time to babysit a couple of feds in suits."

"I haven't needed a babysitter in at least four years," Mulder said dryly.

"Mr. Dooley," Scully said, "we apologize for coming out here in the middle of your preparations. Trust me, I would've preferred to have all our questions answered back in California. But since you and your entire team disappeared without notifying us, we had no other choice."

Mulder said, "And you didn't exactly overwhelm me with information when I did talk to you."

"Whatever," Dooley said in complete dismissal. He turned away from them and extended a flapping sheaf of papers toward Captain Ives. "New weather projection from overhead satellite feeds," he said. "Exactly as expected. The hurricane center is only two hundred miles out, and it's big enough that there's no chance it'll miss us. No chance at all. We're in luck—Enika is going to be whomped tomorrow morning."

"We're in luck?" Mulder repeated.

Ives scanned the satellite projection and nodded. "I concur."

"Wait a minute," Mulder said. "First things first. Where is this nuclear device? Is it in one of the crates we flew out with, or is it already set up here in the control bunker—what?"

Dooley gave a scornful laugh. "Agent Mulder, you're not impressing me with your expertise. The blockhouse is supposed to be *sheltered* from a nuclear blast. Therefore, the device isn't going to be set up anywhere nearby. Logical?"

The chance to explain things seemed to calm the big engineer. "The Bright Anvil device is on the other side of the island in a lagoon. It came out on the *Dallas* from San Diego. Everything is all set up and ready to go, waiting for the storm."

Scully spoke up. "You've gone to a lot of trouble to make all your preparations in secret—and you've taken great pains to select a deserted island that just happens to be directly in the path of a major storm system. Most people with any sense would head *away* from a typhoon. Do you have any idea how much damage a storm like that can cause?"

Dooley narrowed his eyes as if about to scold her for her stupidity, then he let out a gruff laugh. "Of *course* I do, Agent Scully. Think about it. With all the damage the hurricane is going to cause when it strikes this island . . . who's going to notice a little more destruction?"

TWENTY-NINE

The pressure of the approaching storm felt like a psychological vise tightening down on Scully. Standing on the rough beach, she looked up at the blackening clouds at sunset, the eerie color of the storm-sickened sky.

Outside the control blockhouse, Bear Dooley, Mulder, and Captain Ives stood together in a moment of relative quiet. In the shallow lagoon in front of the blockhouse, the captain's gig bobbed, waiting for passengers. Shielded by the hummock of reefs, the water was glassy smooth in contrast to the roiling choppiness farther out to sea. A line of breakers foamed around coral outcroppings submerged just beneath the angry waters.

One of the Bright Anvil technicians came running out of the blockhouse as Scully walked up to them. The technician looked flustered. "Captain Ives, sir, there's an emergency message for you over the secure telephone line!" Ives looked down at the

200

walkie-talkie on his hip, disconcerted that the message hadn't come to him directly. "It's from the *Dallas*, sir," the technician continued. "The communications officer on the bridge wants to speak with you."

Mulder looked directly at Bear Dooley as he spoke. "Oh boy, maybe they're canceling the test."

"Fat chance," Dooley said.

"I'm sure they'd issue you a raincheck."

Dooley just shook his head, as if wondering where Mulder got his sense of humor.

All five of them ducked inside the claustrophobic blockhouse. Scully was glad to get out of the damp wind that made her skin crawl. Captain Ives went to a phone box that had been bolted to a plywood wall inside the armored bunker.

"Ives here," he said, then listened intently. The expression on his face quickly became grim. "What are they doing out in this weather?" He waited for an answer. "Okay, how far away?" He waited again. "And we're the only ones within range?" He scowled. "Hold on."

He put his hand to the headset and looked at Dooley. "We've just received a distress call—a fishing boat out of Hawaii, Japanese registry. They're in trouble from the typhoon, and the *Dallas* is the only ship in the vicinity. It's a general mayday, but they're requesting an urgent rescue. We can't ignore it."

Dooley turned red with annoyance. "I thought you said this area was cleared. Everything around Enika was supposed to be free of shipping traffic!" He fumed. "And what are those idiots doing out in this weather anyway? It's crazy to go out in a hurricane."

"Sure is," Mulder said, under his breath.

Ives seemed to be fighting to keep his cool in

front of Dooley. "Because your people needed to keep this test so *secret*, Mr. Dooley, we weren't allowed to send a fleet of patrol boats out to keep the waters clear. You didn't want anyone to notice the activity. We did our best, but something could easily have slipped through—as this fishing boat apparently has. It's a big ocean, after all."

Dooley heaved a huge sigh and stuffed his big-knuckled hands in his jeans pockets. "I think we should just leave them out there. Those bozos will only get what they deserve for setting out without checking the weather reports."

Ives had had enough of the discussion. "Mr. Dooley, it's the law of the sea to attempt a rescue whenever another vessel signals a distress. It's a law by which I live, and I have spent my entire career on ships. That doesn't change just because of your pet project."

"What are we going to do with the survivors once you take them aboard?" Dooley said. "You can't let them witness the test."

"We'll keep them belowdecks—*if* we succeed in rescuing anybody."

"But what if it's a spy ship?" Dooley said. "We might not be the only people with an idea like Bright Anvil, you know. Another country could have developed the same concept."

Scully tried not to laugh, but the bearlike physicist seemed completely serious in his suspicion.

"Yeah," Mulder said, "if those Japanese fishermen spies see too much of Bright Anvil, they'll start making inexpensive imitations, and you'll be able to buy your own warhead the local electronics store."

Dooley glared at him, but didn't seem to know what to do with his own anger. "Well, Captain, at least find out who they are and what the hell they're doing out here. These aren't good fishing waters."

With a sigh, Captain Ives put the telephone to his mouth again. "What's the name of the ship?" he said. "Find out their registry." As he waited for an answer, suddenly Ives's face turned white. "*Fukuryu Maru*," he said. "The *Lucky Dragon*?"

Scully put a finger on her chin, thinking. "*Lucky Dragon*," she said. "That sounds familiar. . . ."

Ives spoke into the phone. "Acknowledge their transmission—tell them we're coming to help. Prepare the *Dallas* for immediate departure." Ives hung up, then he looked at Scully, since she had been the only one to react to the name.

"You're thinking of another Japanese fishing boat with the same identification—the vessel that wandered too close to the Castle Bravo H-bomb detonation on Bikini in 1954. The crew received a huge dose of radiation—the incident caused quite an international scandal."

Mulder perked up. "And now a ship with the same name is straying close to this nuclear test? That can't be a coincidence."

Scully quickly interrupted his train of thought. "Oh no you don't, Mulder. Don't even suggest that this is some . . . ghost ship of irradiated Japanese fishermen coming back to stop the Bright Anvil test."

Mulder held up his hands helplessly. "I didn't suggest any such thing, Scully. I'd say you've got an overactive imagination." He frowned in feigned contemplation. "Interesting idea, though."

She turned to Ives. "Captain, I'd like to go with you out to that fishing boat." She looked at Mulder, asking with her eyes if he wanted to go along.

"No thanks," he said. "I'll stay on solid ground. I want to keep poking around here." Mulder turned to admonish her as she and Ives headed back out into the freshening wind. "Be sure to wear your life jacket."

Scully tried to stay out of the way on the bridge deck of the Navy destroyer.

Captain Ives directed the helmsman to begin accelerating away from Enika Atoll and into the storm-ragged water. The low coral island dropped away as the battleship left the labyrinth of whitecaps that marked treacherous underwater rocks. The *Dallas* headed out to sea, following their charts to where the hapless fishing boat had gotten itself into trouble.

Scully attempted to start a conversation several times, but couldn't find the words. Ives appeared deeply troubled and preoccupied, his salt-and-pepper eyebrows crinkled together, his lips pursed and pushing up his mustache. Finally, she blurted out, "Captain Ives, you looked shocked when you heard the name of the fishing boat. How much do you know about the *Lucky Dragon*? The original one, I mean."

He glanced over at her, setting his lips in a thin, pale line, then continued staring out the rain-streaked bridge windows of the *Dallas*, watching the rough seas. His Adam's apple bobbed up and down once.

"I was an observer at the Castle Bravo test, Agent Scully. I witnessed a lot of the island detonations during my tour of duty as a young sailor. I was a Navy man through and through, and a lot of us ambitious young recruits sort of 'collected' bomb blasts in those days. We tried to get ourselves assigned to ships that were going out to observe the nukes. We thought it was fun.

"It's an awe-inspiring sight, I can tell you that—but Castle Bravo was something else entirely, a new design, the biggest yield ever measured for a nuclear detonation. The Los Alamos scientists had calculated their cross sections wrong, or so I understand. The yield was supposed to be five megatons . . . instead, it turned out to be nearly fifteen. An explosion equivalent to fifteen million tons of TNT.

"That number doesn't really mean anything to the human imagination, until you try to compare it. The Little Boy bomb dropped on Hiroshima was about the same as twelve point five *kilotons* of TNT. That means the blast from Castle Bravo was *twelve hundred times* as powerful as Hiroshima. Twelve hundred Hiroshima bombs all going off at once!" He shook his head. "You should have seen it. The fireball itself was four miles in diameter."

Scully swallowed. "I'm not sure I would have wanted to. Wasn't it dangerous to be so close?"

Ives gave a far-off smile. "A lot of us got a significant dose. This horrendous whitish substance rained down from the sky—we found out later it was calcium precipitated from the vaporized coral thrown up into the air. Obviously, the danger zone from the blast turned out to be much larger than the safe area we had calculated."

Scully continued for him, "And this Japanese fishing boat happened to be in the wrong place at the wrong time."

"The *Lucky Dragon* wasn't so lucky after all," he said. "With a crew of twenty-three, they were trolling more than eighty nautical miles east of Bikini—a good distance, but unfortunately it was directly downwind from the fallout.

"Two weeks later the fishing boat came into home port with a sick crew. The U.S. offered radiation specialists to help treat the men, but refused to give any specifics about the content in the fallout. Somebody was afraid the Soviets could derive a bomb recipe from it. One of the fishermen died of a secondary infection.

"Lewis Strauss, the chairman of the Atomic Energy Commission, brushed aside all responsibility and said that those fishermen had been well inside the danger zone—which I doubt very much—and that the *Lucky Dragon* was probably a Red spy ship anyway."

"A Red spy ship?" Scully's throat clenched in a combination of disbelief and anger. She could find nothing else to say.

"His exact words." Captain Ives gave her a hard look with his narrowed eyes. "And so I don't intend to let this other unlucky ship wallow out there at the mercy of deadly fallout, even if they manage to survive the typhoon."

"But as I understand it," Scully said, "there isn't supposed to be any fallout from this weapon. Bright Anvil is only a small-yield device, nothing that should extend far out into the ocean."

Ives looked at her skeptically. "Of course. And Castle Bravo was only supposed to be a third as strong as it turned out to be. I've learned *my* lesson, even if Mr. Dooley hasn't. This Bright Anvil device is brand new technology—and no matter how many computer simulations the scientists run, sometimes they plain forget about secondary effects. I don't want to take any chances."

Scully swallowed and finally asked, "You don't . . . you don't think there's anything supernatural about the appearance of this other *Lucky Dragon*, do you? At this specific time?"

Ives smiled faintly. "Supernatural? No, it's just a coincidence. For all I know, it could be a common name for Japanese fishing boats. But I'm still not going to let it happen again."

The skies darkened, and the clouds drew in around them like a noose. Before long, the *Dallas*'s forward sensors detected the fishing boat and headed directly toward it. Scully could make out the dim shape bobbing on the rough seas. She didn't know what she expected to see. Perhaps something like the *Flying Dutchman*, a battered old hulk barely remaining afloat, a few ragged survivors clinging to the deck rails.

But the *Lucky Dragon* looked perfectly intact, not even struggling much against the waves. Nevertheless Captain Ives hove the Navy destroyer close to the fishing boat. Below, two Asian fishermen stood on deck, drenched with rain and spray, waving their arms for help, while another remained in the control house.

"The boat looks sturdy enough," Ives said. "We should be able to tow the vessel back to the atoll with us."

Scully quickly nodded, not knowing if he was asking her opinion or just stating a fact. Ives tossed her a rain slicker and summoned a team of his crewmen. "Come on, let's get those people on board to safety. Give them warm clothes and some soup."

On the fishing boat two other silhouettes appeared, shadowy figures behind the rain-streaked windows of the bridge deck. As the Navy rescuers crossed over to help the stranded fishermen aboard the *Dallas*, the other figures emerged. The first was a scarred, Hawaiian-looking man who moved carefully. Judging by his milky white eyes, Scully was sure he was blind. When the second shadowy figure reached for the wet ladder that hung down from the destroyer, Scully gasped with instant recognition.

Miriel Bremen climbed up into the rain.

THIRTY

Enika Atoll
Friday, 6:05 P.M.

Mulder looked up at the angry skies.
Wistfully, he thought of how beautiful the
Pacific sunset should have been. Instead,
oily-gray clouds that bore an unnatural
yellowish-green tint had spread like gan-
grene through the atmosphere.

He hummed the first few bars of
"Stormy Weather," but didn't try to sing, since he
wasn't sure of the words.

"So I'm stuck with you, Agent Mulder," Bear
Dooley said, coming to stand next to him. "Did you
stay behind because you have a technical interest in
Bright Anvil, or because you're afraid of the storm?"

"Yes," Mulder answered cryptically. "That's
absolutely right."

Dooley found the answer funny and let out a
guffaw that could be heard even through the rising
wind. "You're a pain in the butt, and your investigation is getting in the way of this test—but here you
are, and I can't keep you from seeing with your own

two eyes." He sighed. "And I guess that partial information is more damaging than no information at all. So I may as well fill you in."

Dooley shouted back at the other technicians just inside the bunker. "I'm going to hop on a Jeep and head off to the other side of the island to check on the device one last time." He turned to Mulder. "Come along, and you'll see what this is all about."

Victor Ogilvy came out of the control block-house, wiping a few spatters of light rain from his eyeglasses. "According to the reports, they checked it already, Bear," he said. "The team and I went out there first thing after the plane landed. It's all set."

"Fine," Dooley said, his hair and beard whipping around his face. "But I didn't ask if *you* checked it. I said *I* want to see for myself. I'd like a hands-on inspection, all right?"

"We need you here, Bear," Victor said, as if the storm and the impending test had brought him to the verge of panic.

"No you don't, dammit!" Dooley said. "I've got enough trouble babysitting this FBI agent. Can't I trust my own people to do their jobs?"

Victor looked stung, and Bear softened his voice. "Don't worry, Victor. I won't mess with the diagnostics, and you can handle the control blockhouse just fine by yourself. I'll be back in an hour or so. Agent Mulder and I have to get over there and back before full dark—and that'll be any time now, thanks to the typhoon."

Mulder followed Dooley over to a tarp-covered Jeep sitting in the open, but sheltered from the wind by the tan igloo of the blockhouse. Dooley yanked off the thick tarp and tossed it inside a storage shed. He swung into the driver's seat in a manner that reminded Mulder of a burly cowboy climbing onto a faithful horse.

The bearded engineer looked Mulder over as he settled into the passenger seat. Dooley looked warm and comfortable in his denim jacket and flannel shirt. Mulder would have thought the outfit completely inappropriate for a jungle-covered Pacific atoll, but the angry storm had sent a twisted chill through the air. "That fancy suit jacket of yours is going to get wet when the rain starts coming in hard," Dooley said.

Mulder brushed his hands down the fabric of his jacket and loosened his tie. "I've got some nice Hawaiian shirts in my suitcase on the ship, but I never got a chance to change."

Dooley pushed the starter button on the Jeep and roared off. The vehicle jounced along the rough dirt road through the jungle, rocking and twisting like a carnival ride with every rut and root it struck.

Mulder held on, unable to talk because his teeth clicked together every time he opened his mouth. Dooley gripped the steering wheel and kept driving. Watching the road ahead, Mulder finally shouted over the roar of the Jeep and the loud sigh of the wind.

Before long the jungle opened up, and Mulder could see the sprawling ocean again. Large swells rose and fell, creating a dizzying optical illusion, as if the landscape were on some sort of drunken turntable. In a shallow, semicircular lagoon eaten into the storm side of the atoll, rugged reefs sheltered the water from incoming waves. On a raft in the middle of the shallow pool Mulder saw a strange high-tech construction, like a Rube Goldberg machine, or something out of a Dr. Seuss book.

"There's the Bright Anvil device," Bear Dooley said. "Never been anything like it. Isn't it beautiful?"

It looked to Mulder as if an alien ship had

crash-landed there. He decided that the most tactful thing would be to grunt noncommittally.

"See those supports, where it's suspended on the raft? We could have done the detonation underwater, but this way it's easier to hook up the diagnostics."

Long metal pipes and tubes stretched out like spiderwebs into the jungle alongside the rutted road. Substations sat at intersections of the conduits. Dooley pointed to them. "Those are light pipes, carrying optical fibers for our diagnostics. They'll be vaporized in the first second of the blast, but the data pulse will be about a millisecond ahead of the shockwave, so our information will manage to outrun the destruction. We'll get some good signals before the whole thing disintegrates, then some sexy analysis codes on the computers back in the blockhouse will crunch the numbers until they're meaningful. We've also got cameras mounted all around the jungle. No telling how many of them will survive both the blast and the typhoon, but the photos should be spectacular."

"A real Kodak moment," Mulder said.

"You bet."

Mulder stared at the contraption. "So you think nobody's going to notice your atomic blast because any destruction will be attributed to the storm? As I understand it, some of the H-bomb explosions literally erased small islands."

Dooley gestured with his hand, as if brushing aside Mulder's comment. "Yeah, but those were big mothers. Bright Anvil isn't nearly so large. In fact, its yield is only about the same as the Nagasaki bomb—really dinky, as far as warheads go."

Mulder thought about the two Japanese cities obliterated by the atomic bombs in World War II and silently questioned Bear Dooley's use of the word "dinky."

"Shoot," Dooley said, "today's ICBMs in their silos contain fifty or a hundred Nagasaki bombs in every single missile—multiple warheads that target independently. Sure, Fat Man and Little Boy were hefty for their time, back in the Jurassic Age, but that's nothing compared to what we can do now."

A splatter of warm rain rushed across the windshield. Mulder shielded his eyes to stare out at the rickety-looking structure on the raft. "Is there really a demand for small-yield nuclear weapons. For shoppers on a tight budget?"

Bear Dooley shook his head. "You're missing the point. Bright Anvil is *fallout free*, man! Some weird technology that Dr. Gregory thought of, burns up all the dangerous daughter products in prompt secondary reactions. I have no idea where he came up with the scheme, but it removes the big political stigma of using a nuclear weapon. Bright Anvil finally makes nuclear weapons *usable*, not just bluff cards."

Mulder looked over at him. "And that's a good thing?"

"Look, you don't want to drop a bomb on a city if it's going to take half a century before the radiation dies away. You'll get cancer deaths for decades and decades after the peace treaty is signed, and then what have you got?" He grinned and held up a finger. "With Bright Anvil, though, you can flatten an enemy city, then move in afterward, set up your headquarters, and reclaim territory. You can begin reparations immediately. It's sort of the opposite of the neutron bomb—remember that one? All lethal radiation and little blast damage."

"I thought the neutron bomb got canceled because of the bad PR, that it was strictly designed to slaughter civilians."

Dooley shrugged. "Hey, I try to stay away from

the politics of it all. I just do the physics. That's my
part in it."

Mulder pressed him. "So . . . you created Bright
Anvil, a nuclear weapon that our government can
use during a conflict, without worrying about the
consequences—and you're not concerned with the
politics?"

Dooley didn't answer. He got out of the Jeep,
leaving the engine running as he checked the connections on the light pipes, pushed testing buttons
at the substations to make sure all LEDs on the
instrument panels winked green. He was clearly
not interested in the moral implications, but he
seemed to sense Mulder staring quietly at him.
After he had finished tinkering with the diagnostic
sensors, he stood up, slowly facing into the wind as
he looked back.

"Okay, Agent Mulder, I admit I think about it. I
think about it a lot—but the fact is I'm not responsible. Don't go lecturing me."

"A convenient excuse, don't you think?" Mulder
said. He was provoking the researcher intentionally,
curious to see what Bear Dooley might let slip if he
got riled enough.

Dooley seemed oddly calm, intense but not furi-
ous. "I read the newspapers. I watch CNN. I'm a
reasonably intelligent man—but I don't pretend to
know how other governments are going to react,
how foreign policy might be made in some other
country that's as alien to me as Mars. I'm a physicist
and an engineer—and I'm damn good at it. I understand how to make these devices work. That's what
I do. If somebody decides that's a good thing, they
fund me, and then I do my job. I leave it to foreign
policy *experts* to make the best use of what I make."

"Okay, okay," Mulder said. "So if you've created this new type of warhead, and somebody uses

it to, say, wipe out a city in Bosnia, you wouldn't feel the least bit guilty about all those civilian deaths?"

Dooley scratched the white streak in his beard. "Agent Mulder, is Henry Ford responsible for the deaths caused by automobile accidents? Is a gun manufacturer responsible for the people killed in convenience-store robberies? My team has created a *tool* for our government to use, a *resource* for our foreign policy experts to do their jobs.

"If some nutcase like Saddam Hussein or Moammar Khadaffi wants to lob their own home-made uranium bomb at New Jersey, I want to make sure that our country has the means either to defend itself or to strike back. *They* are the policymakers. It's *their* job to see that the tools get used wisely. I have no more business dictating this country's foreign policy than—than a politician has coming into my laboratory and telling me how to run my experiments. That's ridiculous, don't you think?"

"It's one way to look at it," Mulder said.

"The plain fact is none of us researchers knows enough about it," Dooley continued. "If we went messing with things we don't understand, following our consciences based on sketchy information, we could end up like . . . like Miriel Bremen, a rabid protester who doesn't understand who's pulling the strings and why people make the decisions that they do. And I guarantee you, man, Miriel Bremen isn't any more qualified to run U.S. foreign policy than I am."

Bear Dooley was on a roll, and Mulder listened with fascination, not even needing to prompt him. Dooley looked down at his big hands.

"I used to like her, you know. Miriel's a good researcher. Always came up with innovative solutions when Emil Gregory ran into a problem. But then she thought too much about things that weren't in her job description—and now look at where she is. Bright Anvil has suffered quite a few setbacks, with Miriel leaving the project and Dr. Gregory being killed. I am not about to let Bright Anvil fail now after all this work, all those careers." Dooley pointed a large finger at the device out on its raft. "*That* is my responsibility, out there. I've got to see that it works."

Dooley finished checking the equipment, rubbed his hands hard against his jeans to remove the worst of the dust and grime, and climbed back into the Jeep. "Now, this has been a fine debate, Agent Mulder—but the countdown is ticking even as we speak, and I've got a lot of work to do.

"Bright Anvil is set to go off at 5:15 A.M. tomorrow. Kind of like the Trinity Test, you know? That one was delayed by a storm that whipped up in the middle of the night out in New Mexico. But here we're *counting* on the storm."

He tromped his booted foot down on the accelerator, and the Jeep sprayed a rooster tail of sand as they spun around and accelerated back toward the control blockhouse.

Mulder glanced at his watch. Only ten hours remained.

THIRTY-ONE

USS *Dallas*
Friday, 8:09 P.M.

In the full darkness of early night, the roiling ocean had a greasy cast. No moonlight penetrated the barrier of clouds high above. The wind whistled with a cold metallic tang.

Scully shivered as she held the deck rail of the *Dallas*, gray-painted ropes cross-woven to look like a chain-link fence. She watched the recovery operations on the *Lucky Dragon* as seamen swarmed aboard the rescued fishing boat. A team of strong young sailors, wet with spray and perspiration, assisted the three fishermen, the scarred blind man, and Miriel Bremen as they reached the relative safety aboard the destroyer.

Captain Ives stared in stunned amazement at the blind passenger, unable to tear his gaze from the blistered scars on the man's face, the blank look in the refugee's dead eye sockets as he worked his way up the rattling ladder. The blind man reached the

216

deck, seemingly impervious to the gathering hurricane-force winds. He slowly turned and faced Ives, exactly as if he knew the captain was staring at him. A faint smile rippled across his scarred face.

Scully watched the silent encounter curiously, but then turned her attention to Miriel Bremen as the protester came aboard the *Dallas*. For some odd reason Scully felt betrayed, that Miriel had led her along. Scully's stomach tightened with a sinking feeling, and she wondered just what the other woman might have been up to.

Miriel hadn't noticed her yet, and Scully spoke sharply into the sound of the wind and waves, "You don't expect us to believe this is a complete coincidence, do you, Ms. Bremen?"

Surprised, Miriel Bremen turned toward the voice. Then her long-chinned face compressed with sour anger. "So, Agent Scully—it looks like you knew more about Bright Anvil all along. What a sucker I am. You were playing me for a patsy, seeing how much I would tell you."

Scully was taken aback. "That's not true at all. I—"

Miriel just scowled and pushed her glasses more firmly onto her face as the wind whipped her mousy brown hair. "I should have known better than to believe an FBI agent."

Captain Ives stood next to Scully, looking at Miriel's bedraggled form. "You know this person?"

"Yes, Captain. She's a radical antinuclear protester from Berkeley. She was near the scene of the murder of Dr. Emil Gregory, who was originally in charge of the Bright Anvil project."

Captain Ives narrowed his gaze, his eyebrows clenched together as his forehead furrowed. "You chose a convenient place for a pleasure cruise."

Scully frowned again. "And you can bet they

selected the name of their vessel quite specifically. The *Lucky Dragon*—that was no accident. Even if they couldn't be sure somebody would recognize it, they must have thought it an amusing joke."

Ives gestured for several of the crewmen to come over. "Take them all below to one of the empty staterooms each. Get their names and make sure they're comfortable, but don't let them cause any trouble. Things might not be exactly what they seem."

He turned sideways to glance at the blind stranger again. The other man stood rigid, with that faint, contented smile on his scarred face. "We'll contact Mr. Dooley and ask his opinion on the subject."

"I think he might be surprised to hear he has more visitors," Scully said. "Especially these."

"Probably," Ives said.

The three fishermen seemed delighted and relieved to be aboard the large and stable Navy destroyer, while Miriel and the blind man seemed to consider themselves prisoners of war. Miriel walked proudly between the sailors as they escorted her to shelter belowdecks.

One of the sailors called up from the deck of the *Lucky Dragon*. "Captain Ives? Sir, I think you should come down here. We found some interesting items on board that you may wish to inspect."

"Very well," Ives answered. "Coming down."

"I'd like to go with you, Captain," Scully said.

"By all means," Ives answered. "You seem to know as many scattered details of these circumstances as I do. It just gets weirder and weirder."

"Unfortunately, none of us has the whole picture," Scully said.

They lowered themselves over the side and climbed down the slick metal ladder to the deck of the fishing boat lashed to the *Dallas*. Scully gripped the rungs against unpredictable gusts of wind from the storm.

Below, the *Lucky Dragon* pitched and rocked, though the large destroyer blocked the worst of the waves. From what Scully could tell, the fishing boat did not appear damaged: its equipment seemed intact, its deck and its hull unscarred—but then she didn't know enough about small marine craft to be a good judge of its seaworthiness.

One crewman came forward to meet Captain Ives and Scully; he rapidly began pointing out some of the anomalies they had found on the *Lucky Dragon*. "All systems appear operational, sir," the young sailor said, raising his voice over the roar of the ocean. "No damage that I can see, nothing that should have caused them to send out such an urgent distress call. This ship wasn't in any trouble."

"Maybe they were just spooked by the storm," Ives said.

Scully shook her head quickly. "I don't believe they were in distress at all," she said. "They *wanted* us to go out and pick them up. It was the only way they could be certain of getting to the Bright Anvil test site."

Captain Ives worked his jaw and ran his hand over his mustache, but said nothing.

Another sailor popped his head out from belowdecks. "Very unusual hull construction, sir," he said. "I've never seen a small craft designed like this. She's practically armored. I'll bet there's never been a stronger ship this size built."

"Specially constructed," Scully muttered. "I wonder if they were planning to take it into a hurricane?"

"Typhoon," Captain Ives corrected.

"A big storm," Scully said. "You'd need a special design if that was the purpose of your boat."

"But it's a fishing boat," the seaman standing next to them said.

"It's supposed to *look like* a fishing boat," Scully said.

Ives shook his head. "Look at this equipment, the nets—all brand new. Those nets have never even been dropped into water. They're all props . . . just for show. I think you're right, Agent Scully—something goes deeper here."

Another sailor emerged from the rear cargo compartment. "No fish down here, sir. No cargo at all, just a few supplies and one storage barrel."

"Storage barrel," Ives said. "What's in it?"

"I thought you might want to take the top off yourself, sir. Just in case it turns out to be something important."

He and Scully descended into the shelter under the deck, to where a single drum had been chained to the hull wall. Seeing it, Scully's mind raced, thinking of Miriel Bremen and her radical protest activities, the suspicion of her involvement in Dr. Gregory's death—and her arrival out here, which was almost certainly to sabotage the Bright Anvil test. Miriel would take whatever measures she deemed necessary. . . .

Ives took a screwdriver from the sailor and began prying up the top of the barrel. Scully looked again at the drum and suddenly cried out. "Wait! It might be a bomb!"

But Ives had already popped the lid off. He froze, as if expecting to be blasted. When nothing happened, he raised the metal lid higher.

"Nothing," he said. "Just powdery dirt. Black ash of some kind."

Scully's heart was pounding as she approached the barrel. One of the crewmen gave her a flashlight, which she shone down into the barrel, illuminating the glittering, powdery black residue. The barrel was nearly two-thirds full of it.

"Why would they bring a drum full of cinders all this way? Is it an incinerator can?" the sailor asked.

Scully carefully reached in and touched the ash, bringing out a pinch between her fingertips. She smeared it around, feeling the greasy and grainy texture. It seemed identical to the residue in the small vial found in Nancy Scheck's pool.

"No, it's not from an incinerator," she said. "But I think this provides direct, clear-cut evidence that Miriel Bremen is involved in the murders of Bright Anvil personnel."

Ives replaced the top on the barrel and turned to the sailors. "Make sure this boat is secure. Agent Scully, let's get back on board the *Dallas*. I need to find out from Mr. Dooley if he knows anything about this."

Scully followed him out, but she knew her first priority would be to speak directly with Miriel Bremen, to try and get some answers.

THIRTY-TWO

As Scully looked on, the security officer used a jingling ring of keys to unlock the stateroom in which Miriel Bremen had been isolated. He didn't bother to knock; no doubt Miriel had heard them approach. Footsteps rang out on the metal deckplates, even over the muffled echoes of the hurricane.

Scully waited in the corridor, her eyes burning and itchy from too little sleep and too much thinking in the past few hours. The security officer swung the heavy metal door open and gestured for her to enter. Scully swallowed, raised her head, and stepped inside the small room.

Miriel Bremen sat on a narrow bunk, elbows on her knees, long chin in her hands. She glanced up at Scully. Her red-rimmed eyes flashed with recognition, but not hope. "Did you at least bring me some bread and water here in solitary confinement?" she said.

Startled, Scully looked at the security officer, then back at Miriel. "Would you like something to eat? I think we can get a meal fixed for you."

Miriel shook her head with a sigh, running shaky hands through her mousy brown hair. "No, I'm not hungry anyway. It was just a joke."

A thought flashed through Scully's mind, a realization. Miriel Bremen's entire demeanor had changed since their meeting in Berkeley—and now Scully suddenly thought she had pinpointed the subtle difference. The protester remained as determined as before, *but now she appeared frightened.*

Oddly, though, Miriel's fear did not seem to stem from being held prisoner on board a Navy destroyer. After all, she had not done anything illegal, as far as anyone knew, though her intent to impede the Bright Anvil test seemed obvious. No, Miriel Bremen now looked like someone far from home. From the haggard look on her face, Miriel seemed to be in over her head, pushed too far by her own convictions. With the spectre of the upcoming test detonation, her activism had somehow transformed into outright fanaticism, making her willing to abandon all her work in Berkeley and charge headlong into a typhoon in a small fishing boat.

Scully stood just inside the stateroom and tried to cover an uneasiness that ran through her. Ever since meeting Miriel Bremen and setting foot inside the Stop Nuclear Madness! Headquarters, she had been reliving flashbacks from her first undergrad year, during which she had come very close to joining an activist cause herself. Even allowing for the impetuousness of youth, such activities had been very much against her parents' wishes. Then again, joining the FBI a few years later had also been against their wishes. Scully didn't abandon her convictions that easily . . . but now, looking at what had happened to Miriel Bremen, she saw the fine line that she too could have walked. If things had turned out differently, she might have fallen off a precipice just as sharp.

Scully turned to the guard. "Would you give us a few minutes of privacy, please?"

The security officer seemed uneasy. "Should I wait just outside in the corridor, ma'am?" he asked.

Scully crossed her arms over her chest. "This woman hasn't been charged with any crime," she said. "I don't think she's a threat to my safety." Then Scully glanced back at Miriel. "Besides, I've had combat and self-defense training at the FBI Academy at Quantico. I think I can handle her, if I need to."

The guard looked at Scully with a small measure of dubious respect, then nodded briskly as if barely restraining himself from saluting. He closed the door behind him and marched off down the hall.

"You said it yourself, Agent Scully," Miriel began. "I haven't been charged with any crime. I haven't done anything to you, or to this ship, or to the Bright Anvil test preparations. The only thing I've done is call for assistance out in a storm."

As if hearing her words, the winds outside gusted so loudly that they resonated through the destroyer. Scully could feel the enormous craft rocking in the rough water as they churned back toward Enika Atoll.

"Why am I being held here?" Miriel said, continuing her offensive. "Why was I locked in this stateroom?"

"Because people are nervous," Scully said. "You know about the impending test—don't try to tell me your showing up at this precise location and time was a simple accident. We just haven't figured yet what sort of mischief you might have planned."

"Mischief?" Miriel sat back on her bunk with an

astonished expression on her long face. "A fallout-free nuclear weapons test is about to be detonated, in violation of all international laws and treaties—and you're sitting by, a federal representative, *condoning* it—yet you call whatever I might be up to 'mischief'? What did you think Ryan Kamida and I might do? We have one fishing boat, no weapons on board, no explosives. This isn't a Greenpeace sabotage raid."

Scully said, "You brought a barrel of black ash."

Miriel looked surprised. "So? And what's that supposed to do?"

"Similar black ash was found at the site of Nancy Scheck's murder in Gaithersburg, Maryland."

Miriel stood up from her bunk, brushing down her still-damp blouse. "Commandant Scheck? I didn't even know the witch was dead."

"You expect me to believe that?" Scully said.

"It doesn't really matter to me what you believe," Miriel said, "because you probably *couldn't* believe what's really going to happen, what's really going on around here right under your nose."

"Just prove it to me," Scully said. "Give me some objective evidence, and I'll be happy to believe. But don't expect me to take preposterous explanations at face value. You're a scientist yourself, Miriel. You know what I'm talking about. What do *you* think is going to happen during the Bright Anvil test? It's less than five hours away."

"I've got a better idea," Miriel said, pulling up a chair from the small half desk, as if she preferred the uncomfortable hard chair to the narrow bunk. "Let me tell you about something that's already happened, and you can draw your own conclusions. Did you ever hear of the *Indianapolis*, a U.S. destroyer from World War II?"

Scully pursed her lips. "The name sounds famil-

iar." She hedged for a moment. "That was the battleship that delivered one of the first atomic bomb
cores out to the island of Tinian, wasn't it? In prepa-
ration for the raid on Hiroshima."

Miriel seemed surprised but pleased that Scully
knew the answer. "Yes, the *Indianapolis* delivered the
uranium core of the Little Boy atomic bomb out to
Tinian. The Little Boy bomb was dropped on
Hiroshima, the first strike in our world's first nuclear
war."

"Spare me the propaganda speeches," Scully
said, still annoyed.

A fire grew behind Miriel's eyes as she pulled
the chair closer and looked intently at Scully. "Did
you know that during the outbound voyage of the
Indianapolis, the bomb core was actually welded to
the floor of the captain's stateroom? No one knew
what the thing was, just that it was some ultra-
secret, extremely powerful weapon.

"But word got around. Rumors fly on ships,
especially during wartime. The whole crew on board
the *Indianapolis* believed they were carrying a vital
component for victory against Japan. After an
uneventful voyage, the *Indianapolis* safely delivered
its cargo to Tinian, where it was assembled into the
bomb—"

Scully cut her off impatiently. "Yes, and the
Enola Gay took off and dropped it on Hiroshima,
where seventy thousand people were killed. I know
all this. Why is it relevant now?"

Miriel held up a long finger. "What's relevant is
what happened after the *Indianapolis* completed its
mission. Nobody thinks about the aftermath. They
just sweep it under the rug. But with such destruction there must be some sort of atonement—don't
you understand?"

Scully could only shake her head. Miriel sighed.

"I believe that there is a balance of justice in the world. Such mass murder could not be ignored.

"Three days after the *Indianapolis* unloaded its bomb core, the battleship was torpedoed by a Japanese submarine. A casualty of war, you might call it. But 850 of the 1,196 men aboard survived the sinking of the ship. They got life rafts into the water in time . . . but they weren't rescued by the Japanese sub. The Japanese did not take prisoners out of the water. The survivors were stranded.

"The men floated in shark-infested waters all alone for *five days* before a Navy plane spotted the survivors. Five days isolated in the ocean, watching their comrades being eaten alive one by one as the sharks came from all around, smelling the blood in the water, growing hungrier. . . ." Miriel seemed dazed by her own story. "Do you know why it took so long for the search plane?" she asked rhetorically.

Scully didn't even attempt to answer.

"Through a bureaucratic error, the *Indianapolis* had not even been marked as missing. No one had bothered to search for it. They were found by accident! In the end, despite frantic rescue efforts, only three hundred and eighteen people were pulled from the water. Three-quarters of the original crew—two-thirds of those who had survived the actual sinking of the ship—were lost. It was devastating."

"That's horrifying," Scully said, sickened by the thought. "But it still doesn't imply anything unnatural."

"If you think that's horrible," Miriel said evenly, "you should talk to Ryan Kamida and hear *his* story."

"Wait," Scully said, counting the days in her head. "According to what you said, the *Indianapolis* was torpedoed nine days *before* the Hiroshima bomb was dropped. How could any sort of supernatural revenge be involved for an event that hadn't even taken place yet? Lots of ships were sunk in the Pacific during the war. My father used to tell me the stories. You're picking one that serves to illustrate your own ends—but you're not making your point."

"I'm not sure you're ready to hear my point," Miriel said.

"What?" Scully asked, recalling Mulder's suggestion. "That some sort of atomic bomb ghosts are wreaking havoc among nuclear weapons researchers? That they're using paranormal means to stop this Bright Anvil test? How can you expect me to believe that?"

"I'm not telling you what to believe," Miriel said. She seemed calmer now after having told her story. Her long face wore a hardened, resigned look. "Just go talk to Ryan."

THIRTY-THREE

X Scully had just returned to her own cabin for a brief rest when Captain Ives appeared at the door.

"Wonders never cease," he said, bracing himself against the doorframe as the ship rocked. "I've finally gotten through to Bear Dooley on the atoll. I couldn't tell whether he was outraged or hopping excited to learn that Miriel Bremen and her friends had come out here."

"So what did he suggest we do?"

Ives shook his head in disbelief. "He wants us to escort the whole group to the blockhouse so they can be present during the test."

"Why would he do that?" Scully asked, then answered her own question. "Ah—I suppose he wants to watch the expression on Miriel's face when the Bright Anvil device goes off."

Captain Ives frowned and gave a slight shrug. "I don't believe it's as simple as that," he said. "I'm

229

sure gloating might be part of it, but I get the impression that Mr. Dooley honestly respects Ms. Bremen and the work she did in the past. Maybe he thinks the excitement of the countdown will bring her around again, show her what she's been missing. He'd love to snatch her back from what he considers to be antinuke brainwashing."

"Okay, I can understand that," Scully said, unzipping her duffel to yank out her extra rain slicker. She had changed into comfortable, dry clothes upon reaching her room on the *Dallas*. "But what about the blind man, Ryan Kamida. Why should Dooley want him there?"

Captain Ives gave a slight smile. "Because that's the only way Ms. Bremen would agree to come along."

Scully shook her head. "They do enjoy playing their games, don't they? All right, how are we going to get over there?"

"I'm staying here on the *Dallas*," the captain answered. "The wind wall of the storm is approaching, and the gale is due to hit maximum force within the next three or four hours. I can't leave my ship. I'm not comfortable having my captain's gig there at the atoll, but my exec, Commander Klantze, is going to ferry it back here."

"So we'll have to wait for the return trip?" Scully asked. By now Mulder would be wondering what had happened to her, probably having uncovered many details on his own that he needed to share . . . most likely preposterous explanations of supernatural manipulation or alien interference in nuclear weapons development. She could never tell what he might come up with.

"Actually it's more unorthodox than that," Captain Ives said. He stood tall and straight, his feet oddly close together as if he were a statue.

"Ms. Bremen suggested we take the *Lucky Dragon*. Two of my seamen will pilot her, although the fishermen want to go along as well. It seems everybody is determined to go joyriding through this typhoon." He shook his head.

"I have to concede that the *Lucky Dragon* is seaworthy, and I'm not entirely comfortable having her lashed up against my ship if we get to rocking and rolling even worse, as I expect we will. Banging hulls together could cause significant damage, either to the fishing boat or to us."

Captain Ives brooded, an uncertain expression on his face. He had been strangely reticent ever since taking the *Lucky Dragon* passengers aboard. Scully finally asked him about it. She slung her duffel over her shoulder and followed him out into the narrow corridor. "Something is really bothering you about this test, isn't it?"

He paused in midstride, but did not turn to look at her. "Just a lot of shadows from my past," he said. "Things I'm being forced to remember that I'd prefer to forget. I had thought them all safely tucked away, but unfortunately such memories have a habit of coming back to haunt you."

"Would you care to elaborate on that?" Scully asked.

Ives finally turned to look at her and shook his head. His slate-gray eyes seemed expressionless, as he brushed his mustache with one finger. "No—no, I don't think I would."

Scully recognized the look, but it seemed quite alien on the face of a hardbitten old captain who had spent many years on the sea.

She saw the fluttering dark wings of genuine fear.

✳ ✳ ✳

The *Lucky Dragon* easily rode the swells, pulling away from the *Dallas* and heading directly toward Enika Atoll. The boat handled well, according to the seamen Captain Ives had assigned to shuttle it over.

During the brief ride to the island, Miriel Bremen remained with Ryan Kamida, avoiding Scully. The blind man appeared disoriented and agitated, as if afraid of something or overwhelmed by circumstances. Scully wondered what had caused his blindness, the terrible burn scars. She didn't think he could possibly be a Nagasaki survivor. He looked too young, too exotic . . . too strange.

As the fishing boat rode up to shore and anchored in the sheltered lagoon, Scully spotted Mulder waiting for her under the bright light hung over the door of the control blockhouse. He waved his arms, and his wet suit jacket flapped about in the wild wind. She noticed that he had removed his tie and unfastened the first few buttons of his shirt.

Mulder came to meet her, helping Scully climb off the boat onto the damp sand. She handed him her duffel. "It seems as if I'm spending more time here on the island than aboard the ship, so I thought I might need a few things."

Mulder looked up into the looming storm that looked like a giant fist ready to pound down. "Doesn't appear we'll need the suntan lotion at the moment."

Bear Dooley shuffled out of the blockhouse, haggard and preoccupied with his nonstop preparations. The test was due to go off in less than three hours. He stood with his hands on his waist, staring at Miriel Bremen as she stepped off the boat onto Enika Atoll.

Miriel helped Ryan Kamida step onto the

beach—but the scarred man dropped to his hands and knees, not in collapse, but more like an embrace of the crushed coral and sand. He looked up, and Scully saw tears leaking out of his blind eyes.

Miriel stood next to Kamida, a hand supportively squeezing his shoulder. Finally, she directed her gaze toward Bear Dooley.

"Ah Miriel, glad you could join us," Dooley boomed. "You didn't have to go through so much trouble, though. You could have just asked, and we would have included you among the crew."

"I wasn't sure I want to be part of the crew, Bear—not under the circumstances," Miriel said. Her voice remained quiet, but somehow the words cut sharply through the wind. "I trust you didn't have any trouble setting up the test?" Miriel's voice was uninflected, without barbs; Scully thought she sounded defeated, resigned. The Bright Anvil test would indeed go off, despite the protester's efforts to stop it. Scully wondered just how far she had intended to go.

From belowdecks on the *Lucky Dragon*, the three fishermen scrambled up, hauling the half-full barrel of black ash uneasily between them. They nervously carried the sealed drum onto the deck of the boat.

"What are you doing with that?" Dooley shouted. Two seamen prevented the fishermen from taking the barrel over the side of the *Lucky Dragon* and onto the beach.

"We don't want it on our ship," the fishermen said.

"Well, you've had it on your boat all along," one of the Navy men said.

"Now we can take it ashore," the fishermen insisted.

Dooley took two steps closer to Miriel. "What's in that?" he said, "Anything dangerous?"

"It's just some old ash," Miriel said. "Nothing to worry about."

Dooley shook his shaggy head. "Miriel, I used to be able to understand you—but you've been turned into a pod person or something."

The Japanese fishermen managed to bypass the sailors and took the metal barrel ashore. Dooley gestured toward them. "You're not taking that inside my blockhouse," he said.

"But if we leave it here, it'll wash away in the storm," one said.

"Not my problem," Dooley answered.

Ryan Kamida lifted his head and turned a tear-streaked, burned face toward Miriel and then Bear Dooley. "Let them leave it where it is."

Relieved, the fishermen hurried into the shelter of the blockhouse, ducking out of the slicing rain.

"Miriel, why don't you come inside, and I'll show you around our posh quarters," Dooley said. "I'm sure you'll remember some of the equipment."

"Trying to rub my face in it, Bear?" she said.

He blinked his small eyes. "No, I don't think so," he said. "These engineers don't know what I'm talking about half the time, and you at least understand. For old times' sake, for Emil Gregory, come and look at Bright Anvil."

Reluctantly, she tapped Kamida's shoulder, trying to get him to accompany her, but the blind man shook his head. "Let me stay out here for a while longer," Ryan Kamida said. "I will be fine."

Miriel looked uneasy about leaving him there alone, until Scully stepped forward. "We'll stay with him for a few minutes, Miriel. You wanted me to talk to him, remember?" Understanding came to Miriel's eyes, and she nodded before following Bear Dooley and the seamen into the control blockhouse.

On the beach Kamida dug his scarred fingers

into the sand, smelling the coral and the water and the spray. He tilted his head up to the greenish-black hurricane clouds. He breathed through his mouth and closed his blind eyes as he sat back, clenching his fists and gritting his teeth.

"Mr. Kamida," Scully said, "Miriel said you might have something to tell us . . . a terrible story about yourself? She thought we ought to know."

The blind man turned a scarred face toward her, fixing his unseeing gaze to a point directly between Mulder and Scully. "You hope to find answers," he said.

"Do you have any?" Mulder said. "At the moment, we're not even sure which questions we should be asking."

"You shouldn't be asking questions," Kamida said. "You shouldn't be here at all. You are innocent bystanders who could become casualties of war."

Scully said, "Miriel told me that something happened to you, something terrible. Please tell us the story. Is it about how you were blinded and burned?"

His chin twitched downward just a fraction, as if in an unconscious nod. Sitting on the beach with the waves crashing against the reef line out beyond the lagoon, Ryan Kamida spoke with the voice of a ghost in the wind.

"I was born here on Enika—as were all of my people, a small tribe. We lived here . . . although legends tell us we came from other islands on a long pilgrimage. We found this island and we stayed. It was our place. It was peaceful."

"But Enika Atoll is uninhabited," Scully said.

"Yes," Kamida answered. "Yes, now it is uninhabited—but forty years ago it was our home, when the United States was walking tall, striding across the world, proud in its new status as a superpower. You had atomic weapons in your pocket, and you were still flushed with pride over your victory in World War II.

"But your first atomic bombs weren't big enough, so you had to build fusion bombs, hydrogen bombs, thermonuclear warheads. And in building such bombs you had to test them in places where no one would notice . . . places such as Enika Atoll, the home of my childhood."

Scully said, "I know the islanders on Bikini and Eniwetok were displaced to other homelands when the atolls were evacuated for nuclear tests. Is that what happened to your people?"

Kamida shook his head. "The government did not bother with that. I was only a young boy, probably about ten. I have since learned that the name of the test was Sawtooth.

"I had grown up here 'primitive and uneducated,' some might say, while others would call it 'idyllic,' an existence in paradise with fine weather and a warm climate, with breadfruit, coconuts, taro, and yams growing in abundance, with all the fish and shellfish we could possibly want given to us by the sea.

"I was young—small and wiry and strong. In the reef rocks around my island there were many caves, small outcroppings and hollows that, had they been underwater, would have been the homes of moray eels and octopuses. But aboveground they provided openings for me to worm my body through, to go down into tidepools and mysterious mazes . . . half-submerged treasure houses where I could find mussels and conch shells and abalone.

"My parents would wait above with my older sisters and my uncles as I wriggled down into the reef caves to search for delicacies." Kamida's rough face wore a half-smile. "I remember it so clearly— memories are all I've been able to see for most of my life."

A blast of wind curled around the coral uplift that sheltered the blockhouse, and slapped down at them. Scully rocked back to keep her balance; Mulder grasped her shoulder. Ryan Kamida didn't seem to notice the gust at all.

"We knew the strange Navy ships had been cruising around our island, long metal monstrosities, bristling with spines. The sailors had landed in their white uniforms, but we hid in the jungles, thinking they were invaders from some other island. If they were trying to locate and evacuate the inhabitants of Enika, they did not search very hard. We were afraid of them, but also curious. We didn't know why they had placed strange machines on our island, unusual structures with amazing blinking substations and other devices. It was magic to us. Evil magic."

He picked up a fistful of the wet sand, letting it trickle through his scarred fingers.

"I remember that day. Many of my cousins had gone to inspect the device the soldiers had left behind . . . others watched the destroyers pull away. But I had my day's work to do. My father insisted that the water level was perfect for me to find special treasures in the caves, and so I crawled deep down into the winding passages, carrying only my small knife and a net in which to store the shells that I found.

"I had secured a large abalone, enough for an entire meal, I thought, and a few other shells. When I crawled back out of the cave, my father waited for me, standing out in the sunlight. I could see him towering above the opening of the cave. I held up the net that contained the shells. He bent down to take it from me so that I could climb out of the cave. I looked into his eyes. They were cast into shadow as he leaned toward me. . . . "

Kamida paused. His voice caught.

"And then the sky turned *white*, a burning white, a blaze of heat, so hot and so fast that it wiped everything clean, blasted every molecule of color from the world. The last thing my eyes ever saw was my father's silhouette, fuzzy around the edges where I could see right through his skin. For the barest fraction of a second, I could clearly make out the skeleton inside his body as the radiation poured through him—until the rest of the shock-wave blew him to ashes. And then the light engulfed me as well."

Scully stared at him, wide-eyed, her hand to her mouth.

"Somehow, I survived," Kamida continued. "The shockwave was immense, but I tumbled back down into the caves even as the nuclear detonation flattened my island. The water inside the caves boiled and blasted upward like a geyser. My skin was cooked as if I were a roasting pig.

"A long time later I found myself alive and out-side of the caves. Much of the reef overhead had been vaporized. I had been spared, though it was no blessing. No blessing at all.

"I felt my way along the hot steaming rock. I found the lagoon, but it was still boiling hot, scalding my legs . . . which were already too burned to feel any more pain. I walked and waded out to sea, unable to see anything. Still I continued, sloshing farther and farther from the island. . . .

"They say I made it two miles before I was picked up."

"Picked up?" Mulder asked. "Who picked you up?"

"Navy ship," Kamida said. "Sailors, men assigned to observe the Sawtooth test. They didn't know what to do with me. After their immense technological victory, my survival must have been quite an embarrassment to them."

Kamida stared deeply into his memories for a moment, his eyes too blind to see the present.

"After I recovered, they placed me in the care of an orphanage in Honolulu. They changed all the records, and I survived. Oh yes, I survived—and in later years I made a name for myself. I became lucky. I was talented in business. I have become a wealthy man over the past forty years.

"You'll find no record of the Sawtooth nuclear test, or of my people now annihilated, or even of me, the lone survivor of a test the government would prefer to forget."

"But if there's no record and you were such a young boy," Scully said, "how did you get all this information? How can you remember and be sure of the details?"

Kamida directed his blind gaze at her in a way that so unnerved her, she looked away in embarrassment. His hollow voice sent a shudder down her spine. "Because I have been reminded time and again."

Mulder leaned closer. "How were you reminded?"

"They told me," he said. "The spirits of my people. They come and speak to me. They tell me not to forget them or my own past."

Scully sighed and looked at Mulder, but he ignored her. "In other words, your people were annihilated in this secret atomic bomb test, and because you're the only survivor, you can speak to their spirits?"

Scully stood up, ready to leave the man to his delusions. "Come on. We should get inside the shelter."

"Agent Mulder," Kamida said, though Scully couldn't remember ever having introduced him. "The atomic flash blinded me in an instant, but it also *boosted* me somehow. My eyes no longer function, but I can see and hear other things. I am linked to the brooding ghosts that remain with me, like afterimages from that blast."

Mulder's eyebrows shot up, and Scully looked at him, amazed to see her partner believing this tale.

"Think of it, my friend," Kamida said to Mulder—the blind man seemed to know intuitively who was most likely to swallow his story. "For four decades, they have been gathering energy. Their screams have finally reached a peak—to deafen those who brought this upon them, and those who would willingly do it again."

"Wait a minute," Mulder said, intrigued, "are you suggesting that the sheer suddenness and high energy of an atomic blast somehow added power to the souls of those people destroyed in it? Made them different from your ordinary, run-of-the-mill ghosts?"

"I am no scientist," Kamida said. "Perhaps the spirits of an entire annihilated people have greater powers than those killed in a more common fashion. Absolute atomic genocide. They do seem to have a greater awareness. They can sense connections, they know who is involved in the development of such weapons—and they also understand that this Bright Anvil test is a very frightening step down a treacherous path for the entire world." He smiled to himself. "Perhaps the spirits of my people are protectors of the human race."

Scully caught the meaning of his words. "Do

you mean to say that these ghosts have been killing nuclear weapons researchers and other people who had a connection to the atomic bomb?"

"Agent Scully," Kamida said, "I will confess that I bear some responsibility for the death of Dr. Emil Gregory. I had hoped that removing him would bring this test to a halt. But I was wrong. It was too simplistic. Out of spite I also directed the annihilation of an old man in New Mexico who was in some way linked to the first Trinity Test that unleashed nuclear weapons upon the world. So many of the others are already dead from time and illness. His was the first name I could find.

"I was also responsible for the death of a Department of Energy executive, a woman behind the funding for the Bright Anvil project. Without her support, this test could not have taken place.

"But I waited too long. I have held the ghosts in check for too many months, too many years . . . and now they're growing restless, striking even at those I have not designated—those they believe are in some way a threat to our island."

Scully thought of the radiation-burned missileers in their underground control bunker, the photos Mulder had showed her.

"Their attention expands. They grow very restless. But in a few hours they will fulfill their destiny and protect this island again."

"Why are you telling us all this?" Mulder asked. "Confessing to murder isn't something people do lightly."

The storm's growl grew to a persistent roar. Scully touched Kamida's elbow, raising him to his feet. "It's not safe to be out here. We need to get inside—all of us."

"Safe!" Kamida laughed. "Safety is a luxury none of us can afford now. I'm telling you this,

Agent Mulder, just so you have the answers because you are a curious man—but none of us will get out of this alive." He cocked his head to stare up into the storm, as if calling to something.

He spoke in a mystical whisper. "At last the wave of fire will reach the shore of death."

THIRTY-FOUR

Enika Atoll
Saturday, 4:11 A.M.

As howling darkness engulfed the island, Scully and the others huddled inside the shelter of the supposedly indestructible concrete-sandbag walls of the blockhouse.

Bear Dooley paced the control chamber that smelled of dust, new solder and lubricants, chalky concrete, and fresh-sawed wood. Jury-rigged lightbulbs hung from the support beams overhead, shedding uneven light. Dooley triple-checked every diagnostic system on the equipment racks, then went through the entire routine again.

He flashed repeated suspicious glances at Ryan Kamida and the three Japanese fishermen, who sat at an analysis table that had been cleared of all papers and reports. Dooley pointed his thick finger at the fidgeting fishermen. "Don't touch anything," he said. "Just stay there and keep your hands to yourselves."

He looked sourly at Miriel Bremen, as if accusing her of poor judgment for insisting that a blind man and three fishermen accompany her to the blockhouse rather than just staying aboard the *Dallas*. Miriel ignored him. She stood rigid, scanning the instrument racks and diagnostic panels, as if reluctant to move forward for a closer inspection.

Dooley studied the big round dial of the watch strapped to his wrist. "It's 4:15," he announced. "Only one hour to go."

Victor Ogilvy nervously hung up the portable phone set at his station. "Hey, Bear—I just got a communication from Captain Ives. He says the storm surges are already at their maximum projected levels. Wind-wall velocity just topped a hundred miles an hour, and the storm isn't due to peak for another fifty minutes."

"Good," Dooley said. Outside, the typhoon boomed like a series of muffled explosions.

"Good?" Miriel said, shaking her head. "Doesn't it bother you, Bear, that regardless of all the moral and ethical considerations you dismiss so easily, this test goes blatantly against international law? Aboveground nuclear explosions have been banned for more than thirty years."

Dooley looked at her, and his broad shoulders sagged. "Miriel, we had a phrase in my high school class. I think it even showed up in the yearbook as our class motto. 'Everything's legal until you get caught.' And we're not going to get caught. This hurricane will mask the test signature. It'll cover all the destruction on the atoll in case anyone's watching with satellites. No problem.

"And because there isn't any fallout from Bright Anvil, weather stations aren't going to report a sudden increase in radioactive daughter products. We've got it all covered." He clasped his big hands in front of him in an unconscious pleading gesture. "Come on, Miriel—you worked on this baby for years. You and Emil solved most of the problems—"

Miriel interrupted him. "I didn't *solve* any of the problems, and neither did Emil. None of us understands the technology behind Bright Anvil, or even where it came from. Doesn't that bother you?"

He shook his head, stonewalling. "I don't understand how my car engine works, either, but I know it starts every time I turn the key . . . well, usually. I don't know how my microwave oven works, but it reheats my coffee just fine." His wide, bearded face held a boyish sense of wonder, a hope behind it.

"Miriel, I'd really like you to be a part of the team again," he said. "Without Emil, this whole project nearly fizzled. When we lost you, we lost our greatest contender. I've been doing my damndest to keep everything working and running on schedule— but that's not what I'm good at. I'm no match for you, but I'm not going to walk away from my responsibilities. I'm going to see that Bright Anvil goes off as planned, because that's my job."

Scully stood next to Mulder, watching the debate between the two scientists. Mulder seemed intrigued, but Scully felt her abdomen tightening in knots to hear Bear Dooley's unbridled enthusiasm.

"I'm disappointed in you, Bear," Miriel said. His face fell, as if that were the worst thing she could have told him. She remained standing, formal and rigid, one step away from the instrument racks.

"I know you want to test this new weapons system in a 'real use' situation, but I wish you'd let it *bother you* a bit to think of just what that 'real use' may be once Bright Anvil is weaponized. The only advantage to the hydrogen bombs and the enormous thermonuclear warheads we've been stockpiling is that they're too destructive for any sane government to consider using."

Miriel became more animated, waving her hands in front of her like captive birds. "But Bright Anvil gives us precise annihilation, *clean* destruction. It terrifies me to think that the United States may have a brand new warhead it won't be afraid to use."

"Miriel," Dooley said sharply, cutting off her lecture, "I wouldn't want anyone but a professional mechanic to try to fix my car. I wouldn't want anyone but a surgeon to do brain surgery on me—and I wouldn't want anyone but a well-versed diplomat to make decisions on nuclear policy. I know *I'm* not a professional diplomat . . . *but neither are you.*"

She frowned at his outburst, but Dooley continued. "It's the government's job to use these weapons responsibly," he said, blinking his eyes rapidly as if grains of sand had gotten in them. "You have to trust the government," he repeated. "They know what's best for us."

Mulder looked at Scully with his eyebrows raised, an expression of amazement on his face.

THIRTY-FIVE

Enika Atoll
Saturday, 4:25 A.M.

Mulder watched Bear Dooley stride over to the countdown clock bolted to the uneven wall. The bearded engineer squinted, peering at it as if he could barely make out the regularly descending numbers.

"Fifty minutes," he said. "Everything still check out? I want a verification on each subsystem." He looked around, scanning the faces of his team. The technicians all agreed, studying their own stations, checking instrument racks.

"Good. Countdown's proceeding without a hitch," Dooley said to no one in particular, rubbing his hands together as he stated the obvious.

Just then the heavy door to the blockhouse ripped open with a siren blast of wind. Howling rain pelted in at a nearly horizontal angle, like bullets of water in a shotgun spray. Two bedraggled and shellshocked sailors staggered in, gasping; they worked together to swing the door shut, bolting it into its jamb. They were sopping wet, their uniforms yanked and disarrayed by the violence of the typhoon. In the incandescent light inside the sheltered bunker, their skin had a pasty, grayish appearance, reflecting their deep fear. Even seasoned seamen rarely saw a storm of such incredible magnitude.

"Okay, everybody's inside," one of them shouted, as if he thought the storm would still drown out his words . . . or perhaps the throbbing gale had partially deafened him.

"Generator's functioning properly," said the other sailor. "It's sheltered from the rain and wind, and it should hold up even if the typhoon gets worse. The center of the wind wall will be here soon."

Dooley nodded, speaking gruffly. "Generator damn well better keep functioning—that power source is running all our diagnostics. If that fails, this whole test will be a bust even if Bright Anvil does go off as planned."

"Don't forget, we've got the secondary generator, Bear," Victor Ogilvy pointed out.

"I'm sure you'll get your data," Miriel Bremen said sourly. "What could possibly go wrong?"

As if to taunt them, the lightbulbs overhead flickered briefly, then came back on with full strength.

"What was that?" Dooley said, looking up at the ceiling. "Check it!"

"Power fluctuation," Victor answered. "The backup UPS modulated it, though. We're fine."

Dooley strutted around like a tiger in a cage. He glanced at the wall clock. "Forty-three more minutes," he said.

While the technicians focused intently on their stations, Mulder watched the scarred blind man who had told them such an unbelievable story only hours earlier.

After adding Ryan Kamida's tale to the details of the mystery as he saw it, Mulder began formulating a hypothesis that fit all the information. It began to make complete, if fantastic, sense to him. He pondered how best to broach the subject with Scully. She would no doubt find the explanation preposterous . . . but then she often did.

Scully considered it her purpose in life to be Mulder's devil's advocate, to convince him of the logical explanations behind the incredible events they had witnessed in their many cases together . . . just as Mulder himself accepted it as his goal to make Scully *believe.*

He leaned closer to his partner, speaking in a low voice near her ear, though the roar of the typhoon whipping around the concrete beehive was enough to drown out the words for any eavesdropper.

"I've been thinking, Scully—and I've got an idea. If what Mr. Kamida says is true, then we could be dealing with some sort of . . . psychic shockwave, a burst of energy that was transformed into something half-sentient during the original H-bomb blast that took place on this island."

Scully looked at him, blinking her blue eyes. "What are you talking about, Mulder?"

"Let's take a look at this, Scully. Imagine the entire population of islanders here, all together, unsuspecting, living out their normal lives—and then suddenly and unexpectedly catapulted across the brink of death by one of the most powerful instantaneous blasts ever recorded on this planet. Isn't it possible that such a blast could have acted as some sort of *boost* to a . . . a higher level of existence, crossing some sort of energetic barrier."

"That's not how I see it, Mulder," Scully said.

"Just think about it," he insisted. "Every single one of Kamida's people, all screaming at once, all of them not just killed, but utterly *annihilated*, practically disintegrated down to their last cells."

"Mulder, if the energy of an atomic blast can somehow turn its victims into—" she searched for words, then shrugged— "into a vengeful collection of radioactive ghosts with superpowers, then how come there aren't a hundred thousand phantom juggernauts running around after the Hiroshima and Nagasaki blasts?"

"I thought of that," Mulder said, "but those were the first atomic weapons. Even though those bombs were powerful, the Fat Man and Little Boy warheads produced just a fraction of the power that was unleashed in the hydrogen bombs that were detonated out here on the Pacific Islands. The test assemblies in the fifties reached ten or fifteen *mega*tons, whereas the Hiroshima blast was only twelve point five *kilo*tons. That's a big difference—a factor of a thousand.

"Maybe the Hiroshima and Nagasaki blasts weren't quite enough to cross that threshold. And, as far as I know, nobody else was killed directly in any of the other H-bomb blasts."

Scully looked at him seriously. "And you think that this collection of ghosts is hunting down people originally involved in the development of nuclear weapons, as well as individuals in charge of the Bright Anvil test, and . . . assassinating them out of revenge?"

"Maybe revenge," Mulder said, "or maybe they're just trying to prevent the tests from continuing. Everything points toward stopping the Bright Anvil test, which could well be the start of a whole new series of aboveground blasts, not to mention falloutfree warheads that might be readily used in combat. What if these ghosts are trying to prevent what happened to them from ever happening again?"

Scully shuddered. Mulder supposed that if he had made the same proposal in the light of day in the cool shelter of their offices at FBI Headquarters—or anyplace else that seemed safe—she might have scoffed at his reasoning. But here, in the darkest hour before dawn, surrounded by brooding hurricane-force winds out on a deserted Pacific island, any sort of creepy story had a greater ring of truth.

Mulder suddenly had another thought. "The ashes!" He spun around to see that Ryan Kamida sat placidly at the analysis table, his scarred hands folded atop the smooth Formica surface. His ravaged face was directed toward them. His lips were quirked in a mysterious smile, as if amused at Mulder's explanation; he looked as if he had heard every word.

Mulder hurried over to him. "The ashes—what were the ashes all about, Mr. Kamida?"

The blind man nodded in deference. "I think you know the answer, Agent Mulder."

"Those were the ashes of the victims from your island, weren't they? You're using them as . . . as signal flags, or magnets to draw the attention of the ghosts."

Kamida turned his face down toward his folded hands. "When I grew older and accustomed to my blindness, after I had developed connections and earned plenty of money, I came back here to Enika Atoll. The spirits of my people had told me their story, told me my life, told me over and over again what had happened here until I was mad with the repetition. I had to come home, for my own sanity."

He quieted and raised his blind gaze to both Mulder and Scully. "Some entrepreneurs will do strange things for eccentric people without asking questions, so long as the money is sufficient.

"I spent many days here on the reefs, crawling

over this abandoned atoll that had grown its jungle back again. I was blind, but I knew where to go, I knew where to look, because the voices guided me. With a knife and a trowel and a barrel, I spent days in the hot Pacific sun, working, scraping a few bits at a time. I found the scant ashes of my people who had been incinerated in a flash and burned into mere shadows on the rock.

"Much time had passed, and one might have expected the stains to have been weathered away, returned to the coral and the sand, to be eaten away by rainstorms and the surf. But they were still there waiting for me, like shadows in human form out-lined against the sheltered reefs. I collected them one at a time as the spirits guided me.

"I gathered as much of the ash as I could. It seemed a pitifully small amount, all that remained of an entire island population. But it was enough for my purposes . . . and theirs. When I was ready, I sent samples of the ash, like calling cards, to those people who needed to receive them."

"You sent a vial to Nancy Scheck?" Scully asked.

Ryan Kamida nodded. "And a packet to Emil Gregory. And to Oscar McCarron in New Mexico. The spirits didn't really *need* the ash. Left to them-selves, they could find their own targets. But it helped . . . and it helped me to direct them."

Mulder felt sick with horror. "Nancy Scheck and the others each received only a tiny sample of that ash—but you brought an *entire barrel* with you here to this island."

He suddenly recalled the three fishermen, terri-fied, unloading their ominous cargo and setting it on the beach, where it now sat unprotected, because Bear Dooley wouldn't allow it inside the blockhouse.

"It is everything I have left," Kamida said. "It will bring them here. All of them. Finally."

GROUND ZERO

Just then the phone rang. Victor Ogilvy grabbed it. His eyes widened as he pressed the phone headset tight against his head, as if he had difficulty making out distinct words from the transmission.

"Bear!" Victor said, clinging to the telephone, staring at it with his mouth partially open. "Bear, that was a communication from Captain Ives. He said their radar systems aboard the *Dallas* just picked up something big and powerful approaching the atoll. Not a storm. He doesn't know what it is— like nothing he's ever seen before!"

Victor swallowed, waving the phone headset. "And then his transmission cut off entirely. I can't raise him."

"What the hell's going on here?" Dooley bellowed. "We've only got thirty-five minutes until detonation. We can't afford screwups now!"

Then all of the power went out in the blockhouse, plunging them entirely into blackness.

THIRTY-SIX

USS *Dallas*
Saturday, 4:30 A.M.

Captain Robert Ives didn't know how he could possibly remain standing in the turmoil—but a captain wasn't supposed to fall on his butt on the bridge of his own ship, not even at the height of a typhoon. With his muscular legs planted widely apart and feet braced firmly on the deck, he rode the churning roller-coaster of waves. Loose objects on the bridge deck, from pencils to notepads to crates, slid back and forth.

Fists of rain pummeled the bridge windows, and the sickly sky was filled with an unnatural greenish light. Ives checked his wristwatch, knowing it couldn't possibly be dawn—not yet. The eerie glow made his skin crawl. He had seen hurricanes before, and they always seemed otherworldly, but none more so than this one.

"Wind wall levels reaching one hundred fifteen miles per hour, sir," Lee Klantze shouted from his exec officer station. A three-ring binder that listed international signals and codes popped off its shelf and crashed to the deck, making Klantze jump. "That's well beyond the maximum expected levels for this storm. Something's pumping it."

"How far away is the eye?" Ives asked.

"We don't expect it to come through for another half hour, and then we'll get a little coffee break. For the time being, we just have to hold on."

Ives gripped the rail at the captain's station with white knuckles. The tendons in his neck stood out like steel cords. "Brace yourselves. I expect it'll get much worse."

Klantze looked at him, amazed. "Worse than these levels?" He glanced down at his weather read-outs again, then grabbed for balance as the deck lurched. "On what do you base that, sir?"

"On the sense of unrelenting dread building in my gut, Mr. Klantze. Run a check," Ives said crisply. "Make sure every station is secure. Get all nonessential crew belowdecks."

"Already done, sir," Klantze said.

"Do it again!" Ives snapped, and the young executive officer staggered on rubbery legs across the bucking deck to carry out his captain's orders.

"How much longer until Bright Anvil goes off?" Ives said without taking his gaze from the writhing whitecaps in front of the *Dallas*. Though he could look at the chronometer himself, he knew he needed to keep his crew busy doing routine tasks they could understand; otherwise they would spend too much time fearing the damage the typhoon might inflict upon them.

"About half an hour sir," answered one of the tactical crewmen.

"Thirty-eight minutes," said another simultaneously.

"Thank you," he answered. Ives left unspoken his thoughts of how insane these weapons designers must be even to consider conducting a delicate test shot under such circumstances.

A foamy wall of water slammed into the side of the *Dallas*, making the entire hull ring like a struck gong. The destroyer listed to starboard, then slowly righted herself, like a killer whale regaining its balance. Captain Ives held on, riding the motion. He was glad the *Lucky Dragon* was no longer tied to their hull.

Executive Officer Klantze staggered back up to the front of the bridge, leaving behind the intercom station from which he had spoken to various parts of the destroyer. "All stations have checked in secure, Captain," he said. "We're lashed down and ready to withstand anything."

Ives looked at him, forehead furrowed above his salt-and-pepper eyebrows. "Anything, Mr. Klantze? You're an optimist."

"I'm in the Navy, sir." Klantze must have thought his ridiculous answer would impress Ives.

"Captain!" the tactical officer shouted. "I'm picking up something on forward radar. There's— my God, I can't believe it! It's so big."

"What is it?" Ives said swiveling around and nearly losing his balance as another large wave slammed into the side of the destroyer. "Give me details."

The tactical officer remained at his station, peering down at the flickering screen. His eyes were wide and disbelieving. "The thing is huge—and it has extremely high energy. It's heading this way. Other sensors are picking it up as well—even sonar shows a great turmoil in the surface layers of the water, far exceeding the storm disturbance. I don't understand these readings, sir. An electrical storm? A power surge?"

"Contact the Bright Anvil team on shore," Ives said, with a deep foreboding. "Let them know." He lowered his voice so that no one else heard his words. "Maybe it'll give them time to prepare."

"Could it be a glitch in the instruments?" Klantze asked, making his way over to the tactical officer's station.

"Not likely," the officer said. "It's consistent . . . and the speed—the thing is getting closer and closer, just like we're in a targeting cross."

Ives whirled to look through the rain-splattered bridge windshield. He saw a sickening, washed-out glow across the waves, like a fire far out on the water. It reminded him of a high-intensity miniature sunrise coming out of nowhere.

"There it is," Klantze said, pointing—as if Ives couldn't see it. "What is that thing? It's like an inferno."

As the bridge crew watched, the wall of light grew into an incandescent sphere that rushed toward them, brighter and brighter, even through the murky air of the hurricane.

Ives had seen something very much like this several times at nuclear tests back in the 1950s. The light and the shape of an H-bomb explosion was something he would never forget—and now it came toward him again.

Ives grabbed the ship's intercom at his station and switched it to all decks. "All hands! Brace for impact."

The blaze of radioactive light hurtled toward them, riding the crest of a sharp, boiling wave, a line of angry seawater that churned up and vaporized with the hot blast of a holocaust.

Ives stood at the captain's station staring help-lessly out the window. He had no eye protection, but he knew from the depths of his clenched stomach that nothing would make any difference at the moment. So he stared and kept staring as the force slammed into them.

The last thing his eyes registered before his optic nerves surrendered to the onslaught was the sharp bow of his heavily armored Navy destroyer slumping, melting, as the steel plate vaporized.

Then the wall of light and fire swallowed the *Dallas* whole.

THIRTY-SEVEN

Enika Atoll
Saturday, 4:40 A.M.

 In the sudden black chaos following the power outage in the blockhouse, Mulder grabbed one of the emergency flashlights mounted on the wall. He switched on the beam, shining it around the control bunker like a bright spear, hoping that its illumination would restore calm and order to the seamen and technicians there.

Instead, he witnessed Bear Dooley and the other Bright Anvil engineers scrambling around, blindly trying to rescue their subsystems.

"Somebody get that generator restarted!" Dooley roared. "We'll lose all our data if it's not up in half an hour."

Mulder shone the flashlight in a slow circle over the rest of the panicked bustle. He saw no apparent damage to the blockhouse itself. Scully stood beside him, holding on to his arm to keep them from being forced apart in the confusion.

"But we just checked the generator," one of the bedraggled sailors said. "It was working fine."

"Well it's not working fine now, and we don't have much time to fix it before Bright Anvil goes off. Get outside and check it out."

"Excuse me, Bear," Victor Ogilvy said, his thin voice quavering with anxiety. "I don't think it's just the generator."

Mulder shone the flashlight over toward him, and the bespectacled engineer held up the phone. "This phone is on the backup source, and it had a full charge—but I can't raise the *Dallas*. I can't even get a whisper of static. It's dead. Everything's dead. All the control panels, all power, even our secondary systems."

Mulder pulled his satellite-uplink cellular phone from his pocket, wondering if he could possibly get anything on that system. But the phone was a silent lump of plastic against his ear; he should have at least heard a hiss or the beep of an improper connection.

Dooley stood with his fists balled at his hips, suddenly overwhelmed. Mulder knew the big man had been just barely holding onto his composure.

"But what could drown everything out like that?" Dooley asked. "What sort of accident did this typhoon cause?"

"No accident," Miriel Bremen said in a calm, strong voice. "Bear, you know what can cause those effects."

"The *Dallas* reported something huge on its radar," Victor said. "With a high-energy signature."

Dooley swung his face toward Miriel, his expression open and lips trembling as uncertainty set in. "I don't know what you're talking about."

She looked squarely at him. The light from Mulder's flashlight reflected in the sheen of perspiration on her face. "Electromagnetic pulse," Miriel said.

"An EMP? But how? That would require a—" He suddenly looked at the protester in horror. "An air burst—a nuclear air burst! What if somebody *else* is using this hurricane as cover for another test? My God, I can't believe it. Somebody else detonated a device—that's what Captain Ives picked up on his radar. Somebody else is stealing our show!"

He spun around frantically, looking for something to grab, someone to tell. Victor Ogilvy cringed, as if afraid that Dooley would grasp him by the collar. "But who would do such a thing? The Russians? The Japanese? Who would have set off an air burst here? *Here* of all places. I can't believe it!"

"There may not be such a facile explanation," Miriel Bremen said coldly. The heartless conviction in her voice sent a shudder down Mulder's spine. Outside, the wind hissed past the cement-bag walls like water in a boiling cauldron. "It may not be something you can understand at all, Bear," she whispered.

"Don't try to spook me," Dooley shouted back at her. "I don't have time for it right now."

With Scully still grasping his arm, Mulder thought again of the story Ryan Kamida had told. Mulder himself had cobbled together an unlikely explanation from the unfolding tale and the bits of evidence he and Scully had collected.

"Hand me that flashlight, Agent Mulder," Dooley de-manded. "I've got work to do. This is no time for a *kaffeeklatsch*," Mulder quickly handed over the light.

Behind him, Mulder heard the *clank* of a dead-bolt being thrown, the click of the latch raising. Then the heavy armored door to the blockhouse blasted inward and the storm exploded into the confined chamber. Papers spiraled into the air on a whirl-wind.

In the eerie light of the storm outside, Mulder saw a silhouetted form in the doorway, braced against the gale, pushing himself outside into the jaws of the typhoon.

Ryan Kamida had let himself out.

"It is time," he shouted back at them. "They're coming!" Then, as if drawn by an invisible chain, the blind man plunged away from the blockhouse into the ravening storm.

"Ryan, no!" Miriel Bremen screamed.

Kamida turned back toward her for just a moment before the winds and the darkness swallowed him up.

THIRTY-EIGHT

"Don't just stand there," Bear Dooley squawked. "Get that damn door shut."

"Shouldn't we try to get that guy back in here?" one of the sailors yelled.

"You can't just leave Kamida out in the hurricane!" Scully cried, looking helplessly around her. "He'll be killed for certain."

The other team members appeared nervous, but Dooley only scowled. "He shouldn't have run out there in the first place," the big man answered petulantly. "We can't send out search teams now to save an idiot from his own stupidity. Our power is out. The Bright Anvil countdown is still going—and we don't get a second chance! Where are your priorities?"

Mulder watched as two Navy engineers wrestled with the heavy door, pressing their shoulders to it and shoving against the battering ram of wind. Silence fell like a stone in the darkened control blockhouse.

Miriel Bremen stared stricken at the doorway through which Kamida had just vanished. Mulder was surprised to see her standing rigid, holding on to one of the control racks for support. He thought she'd have argued to rescue her friend—but the protester said nothing, apparently resigned to his fate and terrified of her own. "It's what he wanted," she muttered.

The light from a new flashlight made a weird bobbing glow inside the blockhouse. Technicians scrambled to restore their equipment, to get the backup generator jump-started.

"How do we know the equipment out at the device is functioning?" Victor Ogilvy asked, blinking owlishly in the shadows and harsh light. "What if the countdown is frozen because of another dead battery? The EMP could have wiped out everything over there, too."

"We have no proof of any electromagnetic pulse," Scully said.

Dooley tugged at his hair in a comical gesture. "The device itself has a completely different power source, hardened against all accidents, rough weather—and even handling by Navy personnel," he said. "Bright Anvil is one robust sucker." He frowned at Victor. "If you don't believe me, how would you like to take a hike over there and check it out?"

"Uh, no thanks, Bear." The young redhead quickly found something else to do. But from the queasy expression on Dooley's face, Mulder knew that Victor had raised a question the bearded engineer would rather not have considered.

Distraught, Bear Dooley rounded on Miriel, seeking a target for his frustration. He put his face close to hers and yelled so vociferously that in the flickering light from the bobbing flashlight beams

Mulder could see spittle flying from his lips. She flinched, but did not back away from him.

"This is your fault, Miriel," he said. "You came to Enika of your own free will, and I welcomed you—but you performed some kind of sabotage, didn't you? What did you do to the generators? How did you shut down all the power? You've been trying to stop this test since the very beginning.

"I thought you were at least honorable enough to be here and witness it with me for old time's sake—but now you've destroyed Bright Anvil, ruined everything. What did you do? Did you do something to Emil Gregory, too?"

"I did nothing," Miriel said. "Or maybe I didn't do enough. But we'll see. The Bright Anvil test will not take place—not this morning, not ever. It's out of my hands."

"See? You admit it," Dooley said, stabbing his finger at her. "What did you do? We have to get these diagnostics switched back on."

"Talk to Agent Mulder," Miriel said, her mouth a grim line above her long chin. "He's figured it out."

Mulder was surprised to hear her—a former weapons physicist—actually agreeing with his bizarre explanation for the events.

"So you're saying *he's* in it, too? He's not smart enough." Dooley's face crumpled into an expression of disgust, and he stormed away from her. "I want nothing more to do with you, Miriel. That's it. Emil would have been ashamed of you."

Miriel looked stung by the last comment, and her posture sagged, but still she held the edge of the control rack. "We're all going to be obliterated," she muttered. "The wave is coming, a flashfire, a wall of cleansing rage from the Enika ghosts. It's already hit the *Dallas*, and it'll be here next."

Mulder went to her side. "You knew about this? You knew it was going to happen?"

She nodded. "Ryan told me it would . . . but I have to admit—" She gave a short bitter laugh. "A good part of me never actually accepted it. Ryan can be very charismatic, though, and so I went along just to see what I could do to fight with more practical means. But now it's . . . it's just the way he said it would be."

She drew a heaving breath. "At least Bright Anvil's going to be stopped, one way or another. All the test material will be wiped out here, along with the project people. In the wake of this disaster, I doubt such a weapon will ever be developed again."

Miriel closed her eyes, and a strong tremor ran through her body like a seizure that quickly passed. "I suppose I always knew there would come a time when I'd have to test my convictions," she said. "It's easy to decide to volunteer and hand out leaflets or carry signs. It's harder to say that you're willing to get arrested during a protest: that's a line some people aren't willing to cross." She glanced sharply at Scully, who looked away. "But there are other lines farther down the path, more difficult still—and I think I just crossed another one."

Her eyes wide, Scully looked at Mulder and then at Miriel. "I can't believe what you're saying. You honestly think a cloud of atomic ghosts is going to come and stomp on the Bright Anvil test because they won't condone another nuclear explosion here?"

Miriel just looked at her without answering, and Scully let out a long sigh of disbelief. She turned to Mulder in exasperation.

"I think that's exactly what's going to happen, Scully," he said, surprising her. "I believe it. We're sitting ducks if we don't get away from here."

The three fishermen from the *Lucky Dragon*

stood up, looking extremely agitated. "We don't want to stay here any longer," their leader said, waving his hands in front of him as if trying to recapture a spare portion of courage that flitted just out of reach. "This place is a deathtrap. It is a target. We're fools to stay here."

A second fisherman pleaded with Mulder, as if the FBI agent were in charge. "We want to take our chances, get back to our boat."

Scully said, "You can't go out in a boat in the middle of a hurricane. It's safer to stay here."

All three of the fishermen shook their heads vehemently. "No, it is not safer. This place is death."

Mulder said, "You told me yourself, Scully, that their boat's been heavily reinforced, designed to withstand travel through a heavy storm."

Miriel Bremen nodded. "Yes, Ryan wanted to make sure we could make it out here. But I don't know if he had any intention of going back. I don't think he did."

Bear Dooley stormed around, still looking for something to break. "Go on out in the storm—all of you—see if I care. Get away from me. We've got work to do. There's still a chance we can bring this test off. The device is on the other side of the island, and the countdown is going to proceed, whether or not we get these diagnostics up."

Mulder looked at Scully, and in his heart he felt an absolute certainty of what was going to happen— he realized it must be the same confidence that Miriel Bremen and some of the other protesters felt about their personal convictions. The fishermen went to the blockhouse door and worked the bolt to open it.

Dooley stood ranting at them. "You're all insane." Mulder knew that Scully probably agreed with him.

"Come on, Scully," Mulder gestured as he ran to the door. "You've got to go with us."

"Mulder, no!" she shouted, looking torn.

"Then at least help us rescue Mr. Kamida," he said. Her expression changed to one of sudden uncertainty.

The door finally blew open and the storm roared in—though the winds had already blown loose everything that it possibly could. Now, though, the voice of the whirlwind had a different quality, almost like human speech: wailing screams, whispering accusatory voices that lurked behind the gale, growing louder, coming closer.

Mulder's skin began to crawl, and he could see that Scully also felt the violent strangeness, though she probably wouldn't admit it.

With the fishermen beside him, Mulder stood at the threshold, nearly blown back by the storm's force. He looked out at the awesome clouds that hung like sledgehammers ready to pound the island. He could see that, far beyond the brooding presence of the typhoon, something terrible . . . truly terrible, was coming their way.

"By the pricking of my thumbs . . ." Mulder murmured.

Scully still resisted, but Mulder finally dragged her close enough to the door so that she could look out. She protested again until she stared into the night and looked up at the sky.

Then all her objections evaporated on her lips.

THIRTY-NINE

Enika Atoll
Saturday, 4:54 A.M.

The storm spoke to him in its power—
dreadful voices against those others,
welcoming whispers for him. At last.

Ryan Kamida was part of them, a
member of their spectral group, yet he
was the misfit. Not because he was blind
or scarred, but because he was *alive*.

He staggered away from the control bunker,
bumping into winds that punched him with the
force of a catapult, driving him back—but still he
ran. His feet slipped on the rough rock and sand that
the gale flung up around him like shrapnel.

Kamida stumbled, fell to his hands and knees,
felt his numb fingers digging into the cold, wet
beach. He wanted to let it suck him down, to draw
him into the sand to become one with the ashes of
his people, a part of the scarred atoll.

"I'm here!" he shouted.

The typhoon howled, and the voices of the
ghosts grew louder, urging him on. He got up and

ran again. A blast of rain-sodden wind with battering-ram strength snatched up his body, yanking his feet off the ground. He flailed his arms and legs in the air, floating like a ghost himself—but it was too soon. It was not completely finished yet.

Kamida fought the chains of the hurricane until his lungs were about to burst. His heart wanted to stop beating from sheer exhaustion, but he plunged ahead, seeking release to join his family, his people—those unseen companions who had appeared to him for decades.

Kamida called out to them wordlessly, trying to make his mouth form words in the tongue he had known as a child but had not spoken aloud in forty years. It didn't matter how well he formed the language, because the spirits would understand him. They knew.

They were coming.

High up on the beach, Kamida tripped over the barrel left there by the fishermen. Instinctively, unerringly, he had found his way to the metal drum filled with the ashes of his tribe, those bits of charred flesh he had painstakingly separated from the coral and the sand of the atoll.

He embraced the barrel, holding it tightly, pressing his cheek against the curved, rain-slick metal that felt cool even against his insensitive scarred skin. He held onto it as if it were an anchor, sobbing, as the hurricane roared around him.

The eerie whispers and screams behind the wind grew louder and louder, drowning out even the storm in the congealing mass of clouds overhead. Ryan Kamida could feel the power growing in the accusing eye of the hurricane—a static electricity, a surge of energy.

Kamida raised his face up to feel the rain evaporating, the bright heat caressing his skin.

GROUND ZERO

Though he was blind, he somehow knew that in the clouds around the island a searing light was building to a white-hot intensity—growing brighter as the countdown for Bright Anvil continued to zero.

FORTY

Facing into the storm, it was Mulder's turn to keep hold of Scully's arm, to be sure they wouldn't lose each other. They staggered through the blinding rain and clawing winds that threatened to tear their small group apart.

The three fishermen led the way, pushing forward one step at a time, heads down, making their way toward the sheltered lagoon. The high coral outcropping behind the beehive bunker absorbed the brunt of the violence from across the island. Still, the wind was so heavy that it pelted them mercilessly with stinging sand and rocks.

Mulder could not see Ryan Kamida anywhere.

"Mulder, this is crazy!" Scully shouted.

"I know!" he said, but kept going.

As they worked their way along, his own doubts asserted themselves: it was absurd and illogical to go out into such a storm. "Suicidal" was more likely the term Scully would have used—but given the situation, logical alternatives were in short supply, and she must have trusted Mulder enough to follow him. She could see with her own eyes the incomprehensible disaster about to strike. He hoped he wouldn't let her down.

Miriel Bremen plodded beside them, stunned, yet willing to escape—not so ready after all to die for her cause that she would give up this last chance to get away.

"No matter what else you believe, Mulder," Scully had to yell in his ear just to be heard, "the Bright Anvil device is going to go off in a few minutes! If we don't get far enough away, we'll be caught in that shockwave."

"I know, Scully—I know!" But his words were whisked away by the storm, and he didn't think she heard him. He turned to look at the craggy outline of the black uplift behind the blockhouse. The Bright Anvil device was out of sight in its shallow cove on the far side of the island.

The fishermen began shouting, their calls barely discernible in the ripping gale. Beyond the winds, the eerie voicelike chorus echoed, rising to a bone-jarring crescendo within the fabric of the air itself.

The rain and the gloom and the stinging sand made it difficult to see anything. Mulder couldn't locate the reinforced fishing boat where they had left it anchored. For a moment he was terrified that their only chance at escape had been swept away from the lagoon, that they were all stranded and doomed on Enika Atoll without even the uncertain protection of Bear Dooley's control blockhouse.

But a moment later he realized why the fishermen were shouting. Two of them waded out into the churning lagoon to where the winds had dragged the *Lucky Dragon* into deeper water.

The lead fisherman swung himself aboard,

grabbing handholds and climbing the wet rocking hull to reach the deck. He helped his companions get aboard, and they gestured for the others to wade out to them.

Scully hesitated at the shore. "Mulder—"

"Come on in, the water's fine," he yelled and pulled her forward into the lagoon without a thought to their waterlogged shoes. "Don't be afraid to get wet! Remember, this is our vacation!"

The rain had already drenched them to the skin, and there was no sense in delaying now. Whether or not Scully believed in the supernatural danger of ghosts from the Sawtooth blast, the Bright Anvil warhead was due to detonate on the far side of the atoll. They certainly didn't have much time.

Miriel, still silent, waded beside them until they all reached the fishing boat. She scrambled onto the deck of the *Lucky Dragon* ahead of them, like a cat climbing a tree.

One fisherman ran to the deckhouse and started the engines; Mulder felt the vibrations through the boat's hull, more than he actually heard the sound. While the second fisherman ran to disengage the anchor and free the *Lucky Dragon* from its perilous mooring, the third man helped haul Mulder and Scully to safety aboard.

Before Mulder could make sure that his partner had gotten her balance, the fishing boat's powerful engines spun it about, churning up a waterspout of spray as the *Lucky Dragon* headed directly into the heart of the hurricane. Mulder grabbed the deck rail next to Scully and Miriel and held on for dear life.

Turning back to look toward the island, Mulder shouted, "Up there, Scully!" He gestured toward the crackling sky. "That's no ordinary storm!"

The clouds glowed and hissed and boiled with weird energy that made all the hairs on his arms and neck stand up. He glanced at his watch. Any moment now for Bright Anvil. Any moment now—and it would all be over, one way or another.

The boat crashed away from the atoll, threading through the rabid whitecaps that foamed around the treacherous reefs near the surface. The fisherman at the controls guided the vessel, swerving from side to side, searching for a safe passage.

Finally, the waters opened up, deeper and bluer even in the storm's gloom. The engine roared with renewed power, and the *Lucky Dragon* lurched ahead.

Mulder looked out to sea, but could find no trace of the huge Navy destroyer, the *Dallas*. He saw only a roiling froth that could have been a secondary maelstrom caused by the hurricane itself . . . or it might have been the sinking remnants of a massive shipwreck.

Then, with a searing flash, a small sun came up on the far side of the island. It rose hot and yellow, blasting back the hurricane for just a moment. . . .

"It's Bright Anvil," Scully said. "Cover your eyes!"

"So, the thing worked," Miriel Bremen said in a stunned voice, just loud enough to be heard. She didn't bother to avert her gaze.

Strangely, the Bright Anvil blast seemed to act as a catalyst for that other force lurking within the hurricane clouds. With the test detonation, the eerie brightness increased a thousandfold, dropping out of the mass of thunderheads.

A brilliant ball of supernova fire plunged like a spectral blast, knotting itself into the chillingly familiar yet horrifying shape of a mushroom cloud. But the image was distorted and surreal, a seething soup of skulls and faces, screaming mouths, burned eye sockets—an unstoppable molten battering ram that swooped down on the rising blaze from Bright Anvil.

A smothering blanket of caustic fire engulfed the far-smaller test blast, crushed it, subsuming the new light in its blinding supernatural fire . . . and *drew* on the power. It became stronger, more animated.

"Look," Scully said, pointing toward the rapidly receding Enika shore. Terrified, the fishermen increased the power of their engines, roaring through the high whitecaps, away from the vengeful atomic ghosts . . . and into the typhoon.

Even from that distance, Mulder could make out the small form of a lone figure high up on the beach.

"That's Ryan," Miriel said in dismay.

The blind man was standing on top of a metal drum—the barrel of ashes that had been removed from the *Lucky Dragon*—waving his hands toward the skies in a summoning gesture. Mulder had seen similar movements before—they reminded him of a traffic controller.

Ryan Kamida was guiding the blinding apparition.

Like a living thing with a purpose, the crackling, blazing swarm of atomic victims swept over the surface of Enika Atoll. The radioactive backwash incinerated the jungle that had regrown in forty years and vaulted the high coral mound that had shielded the control blockhouse.

"Do you see it, Scully?" Mulder said in absolute awe and astonishment. "*Do you see it?*"

Growing brighter in the blaze of a chain reaction of unleashed nuclear fire, the echo mushroom cloud rushed across the island, plunging down on the sheltered side with enough force to make Mulder shield his eyes and back away. The fury increased, vaporizing coral, turning rock into lava. . . .

As the *Lucky Dragon* continued its race into the

hurricane, the vengeful blaze on the atoll reached a fever pitch—and the bone-chilling screams became more distinct in the wind. The skeletal, phantom faces blurred, swirled together, a mixture of light and shadow. Then another voice joined theirs.

Mulder thought he could recognize the voice of Ryan Kamida, his own triumphant shout joining with those of his family and his people, bound together in one primal, coalescent force—a force whose mission had now been accomplished.

The glow died away on Enika Atoll, leaving it sterile and barren, simmering with residual heat and scoured clean of all life. The *Lucky Dragon* shot onward into the fury of the storm.

FORTY-ONE

Mulder's watch had stopped, but he suspected it had more to do with the harsh treatment and drenching it had received than with any sort of paranormal phenomena. He couldn't tell what time of the day it was, other than late morning. Already the tropical heat in the typhoon's aftermath felt oppressive, pounding down on the *Lucky Dragon*.

The fishing boat looked as if it had been vandalized by a street gang. Every visible surface was scored or scraped, two front windows were smashed, a few deck rails bent, the hull scarred from scraping debris—but somehow the vessel had survived the pummeling. They had fought against the wall of the typhoon for several hellish hours, struggling farther and farther from the aftermath of Bright Anvil, until they had somehow skirted the edge of the wind wall and escaped into the blessedly clear seas beyond.

GROUND ZERO

The *Lucky Dragon* had taken on a good deal of water, and the three fishermen took turns bailing out the cargo hold, though Mulder thought they worked more out of a need for something to do than because the sturdy boat was actually in danger.

At the rear of the vessel, Miriel Bremen kept to herself, brooding, like a broken doll. She had lost her eyeglasses sometime in the frantic push toward the boat, or during the whipping storm, and she blinked into the sun, unable to focus. She didn't talk much. Scully tried to comfort her, attempting to strike up a conversation, but the protester was obviously in shock, overwhelmed by what she had seen.

Sitting out on the deck in the sun, Mulder wore his rumpled suit jacket as protection against the baking rays, though the heat was nearly intolerable. He wished he had unpacked at least one of his Hawaiian shirts, his swimsuit, or—at the very least—his suntan lotion. Now they were all lost. Water still trickled off the deck and stood in briny pools reflecting the sunshine.

In a morbid moment, he considered the grim possibility that the six of them might never be rescued, that someone would eventually find a ghost ship bearing their skeletons drifting alone in the Pacific, rather like the *Mary Celeste*. The scenario had a certain creepy irony to it. It would be a fitting end to this bizarre adventure.

He pulled out his notebook and a waterlogged pen that managed to produce a trail of spotty ink after he shook it several times and scribbled on a sheet of paper. Concisely, Mulder summarized the things he had seen and outlined his hypothesis. At least would-be rescuers would find that much information, if nothing else.

If they ever managed to get back to Washington, D.C., he would type up his full report, create a detailed X-File—and in all likelihood, no one would believe him. He had gotten used to that. In this instance, however, he had numerous eyewitness accounts, pieces of evidence, radioactive bodies, not to mention a secret nuclear test. Once Brigadier General Bradoukis knew that the vengeful Enika ghosts were no longer a threat, he might be willing to stand up for Mulder's work.

Scully came up beside him in the bow and bent down to see what he was doing. She had tied her hair back, and her skin already showed the pinkish flush of sunburn. "You should keep to the shade, Scully," he said. "That's no way to get a good tan."

She squatted down next to him. "What are you writing?"

"Oh, you know," he said, "I neglected to buy a postcard on Enika for Assistant Director Skinner, and I thought this would be the next-best thing. I wouldn't want him to think we forgot about him on our tropical vacation."

She frowned. "You're still convinced this all was caused by a cluster of spectral phantoms seeking revenge for nuclear tests conducted forty years ago, aren't you?"

He looked at her curiously. "Scully, you saw what I saw."

"Mulder, I saw a bright flash in the sky. You heard Bear Dooley when all the power went out—he said that some other government must be attempting the same thing he was trying to do, only they did an air burst, using the same hurricane for cover."

"Sounds like quite a coincidence, don't you think?" Mulder asked.

"I'll believe in coincidences before I go looking for supernatural answers to every unexplained occurrence."

Mulder just shook his head, wondering why, after all the adventures they'd had together and all the evidence she had seen, Scully couldn't just accept it. But then, she didn't *want* to believe, as he did.

"Any luck with the radio yet?" he said, changing the subject.

"No, it was damaged in the storm. We haven't been able to raise anyone. The batteries are wet."

Mulder pulled out his cellular phone. "I think I'll try nine one one again. The storm must be dissipating by now, wherever it is."

Scully looked at him, shaking her head at his optimism. She extended a sunburned hand to indicate the endless horizon of blue waters stretched out in all directions. "Who do you expect to reach way out here?"

"Oh I don't know," he said, "maybe another atomic ghost, a Russian spy ship . . . maybe even the *Love Boat*. You never can tell." He punched buttons over and over, sending signal after signal. Using all the access codes he carried in his excellent memory, adding a few Scully knew, he tried every general emergency number, federal operator, and military extension they could come up with.

Finally, to his utter surprise, someone answered.

"You have reached the United States Missile Tracking and Testing Station on Kwajalein Island." The voice was gruff and robotic. "This is a restricted number. Please get off the line."

Mulder sat up quickly, almost dropping the phone overboard in his surprise. "Hello, hello?"

"I repeat, this is a restricted number—"

"This is United States Federal Agent Fox Mulder with an emergency distress call out in . . . out in the Western Pacific somewhere. I don't know my exact position. I think we're near the Marshall Islands— well, we *were*, anyway."

"Are you requesting assistance?" the deep voice came back. "You should not be on this channel. Please try the appropriate contact numbers."

In exasperation Mulder said, "Then send someone out here to arrest us for using your number! I'm with the Federal Bureau of Investigation, and yes, we are definitely in need of rescue. Six of us barely survived the typhoon—there may be many people injured or missing at Enika Atoll. A group of scientists as well as a Navy destroyer, the USS *Dallas*, may have sustained severe damage. There's a strong possibility of many deaths. We urgently need assistance. Please respond." He glanced up at Scully. Her eyes were bright. "Can you home in on my signal, Kwajalein?"

"We're a *tracking station*, Agent Mulder. Of course we can find you," came the answer. "We'll send a cutter out as soon as possible."

Mulder grinned broadly as Scully reached out to shake his hand in congratulation. He was already scanning the sun-bathed field of ocean, as if a rescue ship would appear any second.

He looked down at the phone in his hands. "Think I should have made that a collect call?"

FORTY-TWO

The FBI Headquarters building in Washington, D.C., was a concrete-and-glass monstrosity that someone had considered "modern architecture" in decades past. Because it housed the Federal Bureau of Investigation, the unattractive building had been dubbed "the Puzzle Palace."

Scratching at patches of dry skin from her peeling sunburn, Agent Dana Scully sat at her computer terminal in her small cubicle. She was relieved to be back in Washington, D.C.—for a few days, at least. She couldn't count on staying home for any length of time, and so she spent whatever free hours she could scrape together assembling her notes for submittal to the assistant director.

Going through the familiar motions, tidying up the details, usually helped her to resolve the case in her mind, to sift through the questions and line up explanations, putting any remaining uncertainties to rest.

Scully sipped another cup of coffee—cream, no sugar—enjoying the taste of fresh-brewed, the first decent cup she'd had in a good many days. She rummaged through her notes, scanned another sheet of paper, double-checked a press release, and went back to her typing.

> The U.S. Navy has released information that the Spruance-class destroyer, the USS *Dallas*, sank due to the unexpectedly severe force of the typhoon that struck the Marshall Islands early Saturday morning. All hands on board were lost. According to the National Weather Service, this hurricane was one of the most unusual such storms on record, both for its odd and unpredictable motion, and for its unexpected intensity, particularly within the vicinity of Enika Atoll. Meteorologists who have analyzed satellite imagery of the storm system at the time it struck the atoll are still unable to explain its behavior.
>
> Rescue teams arriving at Enika in response to Agent Mulder's distress call found no survivors among the members of the Bright Anvil team. The reinforced control blockhouse had been sheared from its foundations, as the attached photographs show. No bodies were recovered, which the Navy notes is not surprising, considering the incredible force of the storm.

She paused to stare at the glowing screen, shaking her head.

GROUND ZERO

Morale at the Teller Nuclear Research Facility in Pleasanton, California, reportedly has been shaken by this disaster. The loss of so many employees is completely unprecedented. The only comparable incident in the facility's history occurred when a small aircraft crashed en route to the Nevada Test Site in 1978.

Curiously, DOE representative Rosabeth Carrera at the Teller Facility released an official report that the team of scientists on Enika was conducting a "hydrologic survey of ocean currents around the reef." From my personal knowledge of these events, however, it is clear that the statement is blatantly false. I recommend that little credence be given to such explanations. I suspect more accurate details are available in certain classified files.

After another long sip of coffee, Scully reread what she had written and was surprised at her open skepticism over the official story. That wasn't what the oversight committee wanted to hear. But Scully knew about Bright Anvil and the test, no matter who wanted to cover it up. She could not report otherwise in her writeup.

Scully paged through her notes again and continued with her report.

Assistant Director Skinner held open the door of his office. "Come in, Agent Mulder," he said. The lights in the office had been switched off, killing the garish fluorescent glare and letting the bright afternoon sunshine provide all the illumination he needed.

"Thank you, sir," Mulder said and entered the room, setting his briefcase down on the wooden desk. Framed portraits of the president and the attorney general hung on the wall, staring down at him.

This place held unpleasant memories for him. Mulder had been called on the carpet many times before for insisting on explanations the Bureau didn't want to consider, for prying the lid off details that other people wished to keep hidden. Skinner had often found himself in an uncomfortable position in the middle, between a persistent Mulder and the shadowy string-pullers who refused to be identified.

Skinner closed the door behind him. He took off his glasses and polished the lenses on a handkerchief. Beads of sweat speckled his bald head. Mulder noticed that the office was quite warm.

"Air-conditioning's not working again," Skinner said, by way of a cordial opening to the conversation. "You didn't get much of a tan in your travels, Agent Mulder—first to California, then New Mexico, then out to the South Seas."

"I was on duty, sir," Mulder said. "No time for sunbathing. Not during the typhoon, at least."

Skinner looked down at the handwritten notes torn from Mulder's damp notebook. Mulder had promised to type them up later, when he got the chance, but the assistant director held the crumpled sheets of paper with a weary look on his face.

"Don't bother with a more formal report, Agent Mulder," he said. "I can't submit this to my superiors."

"Then I'll write it up for my own use," Mulder answered. "And place it in an X-File."

"That's your choice, of course," Skinner said, "but it's a waste of time."

"How can that be, sir? These are events I witnessed with my own eyes."

Skinner looked hard at him. "You realize you have no corroborating evidence for any of these explanations? Neither the Navy nor the Teller Nuclear Research Facility accepts your scenario. As usual, you've handed me a report filled with wild speculation that is proof of nothing except your superior ability to concoct supernatural explanations for events that have rational causes."

"Maybe there aren't always rational causes," Mulder said.

"Agent Scully usually manages to come up with them."

"Agent Scully has her own opinions," Mulder said, "and while I respect her entirely as my partner and as an FBI field agent, I don't always agree one hundred percent with her conclusions."

Skinner sat down, frustrated and not sure what to do with his recalcitrant agent. "And she doesn't always agree with yours either. But somehow you two manage to work together."

Mulder pushed forward in the hard wooden chair. "You must have contacted General Bradoukis at the Pentagon, sir. He can corroborate many of the events that I've described in these notes. He knows about Bright Anvil. He knows about the ghosts. He sent us out there because he feared for his own life."

Skinner fixed Mulder with a sharp gaze. The sunlit windows reflected off the lenses of his glasses. "General Bradoukis has been reassigned," he said. "He can no longer be reached for comment through the Pentagon, and his current whereabouts are classified. I believe he's participating in a new experimental test program."

"How convenient," Mulder said. "Don't you think that's a little odd, the one person officially involved in this entire business? Didn't General Bradoukis provide details when he contacted you about our assignment to the Marshall Islands?"

Skinner frowned. "I received a phone call from the Pentagon, Agent Mulder—but the man refused to give his name. He did, however, submit the proper authorization code. When the Pentagon requested that I approve your travel, I did so. I don't know any General Bradoukis."

"That's funny—he claimed he knew you," Mulder said.

"I don't know any General Bradoukis," Skinner repeated.

"Of course not, sir," Mulder said.

"And about this entire secret nuclear test, this 'Bright Anvil' you keep mentioning—I don't want to see anything about it in your official report. Aboveground nuclear weapons tests have been banned by treaty since 1963."

"I know that, and you know that," Mulder agreed. "But nobody seems to have mentioned it to the Bright Anvil team."

"I did some digging before I contacted you about our meeting this morning. I spoke directly with Ms. Rosabeth Carrera, enough to learn that there are no records of any project named Bright Anvil. Everyone I've talked to denies even the possibility of a 'fallout-free nuclear weapon' or that one was ever under development. They say it's scientifically impossible." Skinner nodded as if satisfied with this development.

"Yeah, so I've heard. And I suppose you believe that Dr. Emil Gregory, one of this country's preeminent nuclear weapons scientists, was in charge of a project to map ocean currents and temperatures around the reefs in the Marshall Islands? That's what the official story says."

"That's not my business, Agent Mulder."

Mulder stood up from his chair. "What I would like to know, sir, is exactly what happened to Miriel Bremen? We haven't seen her since she was rescued along with us. We were separated on the transport plane that brought us back to the States. Her home phone has been disconnected, and a nurse at the hospital where we were treated claims that she departed under guard with two men in military uniforms. Miriel can corroborate our story."

"Agent Mulder," Skinner said, "Dr. Miriel Bremen has agreed to assist in re-creating some of the work of Dr. Emil Gregory. Since she is the only surviving link to his project, she has decided to cooperate with the Department of Defense so that his developments aren't lost."

Mulder was astonished. "She would never agree to that."

"She already has," Skinner replied.

"Can I speak to her?" Mulder said. "I'd like to hear that from her lips."

"I'm afraid that's impossible, Agent Mulder. She's been taken to a secluded think tank. They're quite anxious to get some of the work back on track, and they don't want her distracted by any unpleasant interruptions."

"In other words, she's being held against her will and coerced to work on something she vowed never to touch again."

"Like studying ocean currents? Agent Mulder, you're being paranoid again."

"Am I?" he said. "I know Miriel was facing numerous felony counts of sabotage, trespass, even suspicion of murder. I'm sure the offer of dropping all those criminal charges could be very persuasive in getting her to cooperate."

"That's not my department, Agent Mulder," Skinner said.

"Don't you even care?" he asked Skinner. He stood up and placed his hands on the edge of the assistant director's desk. He didn't know what he expected for an answer.

Skinner shrugged. "You're the only one who doesn't accept the official explanation, Agent Mulder."

Mulder reached over to retrieve his handwritten notes, knowing they would do no good if he left them there in Skinner's office.

"I guess that's always been my problem," he said, and then left.

After pacing the room and pulling her thoughts together, Scully continued her report. She sat down, stretched her fingers, and began typing again.

The events I witnessed as we departed from Enika Atoll on the fishing boat, the *Lucky Dragon*, can best be explained as the air-burst testing of another nuclear device, undertaken by a government or governments unknown. It must also be remembered that through the darkness of the hurricane, the heavy downpour, and high winds, precise details were difficult to ascertain visually.

From my personal observations, I can attest to the fact that the Bright Anvil test device did detonate at approximately the time scheduled, though I have no way of determining the magnitude of this blast or the efficacy of its supposedly fallout-free design.

However, according to reports from
the rescue team, measurements of residual radioactivity on the island were
listed as well within normal levels.
This information has not been confirmed.

She skipped a few lines. On to the next part, the
hardest part.

As to the bizarre deaths of the two
other victims clearly involved in the
Bright Anvil project—Dr. Emil Gregory
and Department of Energy administrator
Nancy Scheck—the explanation remains
vague. The deaths of Scheck and Gregory
might be attributable to a brief but
intense nuclear accident involving un-
specified equipment developed for the
test program.

Spread out on her desk lay the gruesome black-
and-white photographs of the victims, burned
corpses contorted into black scarecrows. Neatly
typed autopsy reports were tucked away in manila
folders beside the photos.

It remains unclear whether any connection exists to three similar deaths
caused by extreme heat and exposure to
high levels of radiation—Oscar McCarron,
a rancher from Alamogordo, New Mexico,
and Captains Mesta and Louis inside the
Minuteman III missile bunker at
Vandenberg Air Force Base. The similarity of circumstances implies a relationship between these events, but the

specific cause of such a powerful and deadly nuclear accident, the origin and types of any equipment involved, and how it might have been transported to such diverse places remains unexplained.

Unsatisfied, Scully looked at the words on her screen. She read them over and over again, but could think of nothing more to say. She was still not comfortable with her path of logic and her hand-waving explanations, but she decided that enough was enough.

Scully stored the document, then printed out a copy for delivery to her superiors. It was sufficient to close the file, for now.

She switched off her computer and walked out of the office.